FORGET ME NOT

LEAH CUPPS

INKUBATOR
BOOKS

Published by Inkubator Books
www.inkubatorbooks.com

Copyright © 2025 by Leah Cupps

ISBN (eBook): 978-1-83756-673-0
ISBN (Paperback): 978-1-83756-674-7
ISBN (Hardback): 978-1-83756-675-4

Leah Cupps has asserted her right to be identified as the author of this work.

FORGET ME NOT is a work of fiction. People, places, events, and situations are the product of the author's imagination. Any resemblance to actual persons, living or dead is entirely coincidental.

No part of this book may be reproduced, stored in any retrieval system, or transmitted by any means without the prior written permission of the publisher.

PROLOGUE

The copper tang of my own blood slides out of the corner of my mouth and down my cheek. If I had any control over the muscles in my arm, I might reach up and wipe it away.

But I don't. In fact, I can't feel most of my body. The only feeling that's really gripping me at this point is shock ...

Shock that I'm here with my body parts broken against these ancient rocks.

Shock that I have fallen forty feet through the air.

Shock that I'm just minutes away from death.

One moment I was standing at the edge of the overlook, the vast expanse of the desert canyon stretching before me like an ocean. The next, my feet were swept from beneath me, kicking at nothing but air. Time slowed as I plummeted, watching the stratified cliff face rush past in rust-colored bands. It was quiet as I fell, as if the desert itself were holding its breath. The wind whistled past my ears, my clothes flapped wildly, and I had time to think, absurdly, that *I didn't even have time to tell anyone what I discovered.*

Then came the impact. A sickening crunch as my body

collided with the stone dwelling built into the cliff side. Pain exploded through my consciousness like a supernova, then mercifully receded into a dull throb as shock took over. If I had to guess, my back has been broken, which explains why I can't move.

Above me, carved into the sandstone cliff, the dwellings rise in terraced levels like a vertical neighborhood frozen in time. Small square windows punctuate the façades; they are dark empty eyes staring out across the canyon. These structures were built with such precision—sandstone blocks meticulously fitted together, the shape still holding after hundreds of years. Handprints in red ochre decorate one nearby wall, the individual fingers splayed wide—a signature from the distant past.

My blood now mingles with the dust of countless generations who lived and died in these cliff dwellings. As someone who studied history their whole life, I should probably be more comfortable with death. Comfortable with following the rhythms of all the people who have come before me. I'm sure I wasn't much different than the thousands, no, millions of people who preceded me. I was born, tried to live a life that bore something resembling some kind of purpose, fell in love, had my heart broken, and now here I am, at death's door.

So I guess I should feel some kind of camaraderie with the people who built the structure beneath me, but instead I feel nothing but bitterness.

Bitter, just like the taste of my own blood.

Because I didn't die surrounded by the people I love, holding my hand as I drifted on into the next life. And I didn't fall off this ancient cliff either.

I was pushed.

And as I lie here, feeling the life drain out of me, the shadows dancing across crumbling stone walls, the desert growing quiet as day transitions to night, I can't help but wonder ...

Why was this secret worth my life?

PART 1

RILEY

CHAPTER ONE

SIX MONTHS LATER

I stand in the kitchen of my modest home, waiting for the clock to turn from 2:59 to 3:00 p.m. Because that's what my life is now—waiting until three so I can have my first glass of wine of the day. I don't have a real job anymore, so I am free to set my own schedule, however arbitrary that may be.

Sunlight filters through the blissfully full wine bottle, casting elongated rectangles across the floor. I stare at them, transfixed, as I wait.

Patiently, I might add.

Of course, it didn't start out this way. At first, it was just a glass of wine with dinner, then it slipped into waiting until five o'clock, then four, and now here we are at three.

I sigh.

So be it.

The kitchen remains exactly as it was when my fiancé, Brody, was alive, save for some subtle changes. The soft yellow paint we chose together now looks jaundiced in certain lights, chipped near the baseboards where I kicked it in frustration during an argument I can't quite remember.

Above the sink, a fine layer of dust has settled on the decorative plates we bought in Barcelona. I haven't had the heart to clean them. Cleaning would acknowledge that time is passing, that I'm continuing to exist in a world where he doesn't.

The hands of the clock on the wall make their final circle. Twenty-eight seconds to go. I drum my fingers against the cool granite countertop. The house is quiet except for the persistent hum of the air conditioning—a sound that used to be comforting. Now it only reminds me of the hospital machines that kept Brody alive in his final weeks.

Some people might think I'm an alcoholic, but I'm really not. At least that's what I tell myself as I reach for the bottle opener in the drawer where Brody's prescription bottles still rattle. Another item I need to purge.

A year ago, I was a young professor of archaeology at Arizona State University, teaching classes, graduating one successful student after another. I was nearly halfway through my thirties, engaged to a handsome engineer, Brody, who worked nearby at a large architectural firm. For a time, we were the consummate "power couple." Hosting dinner parties and traveling to different countries every few months. Friends would comment on how perfect we seemed, how well we complemented each other—his pragmatic nature balancing my dreamier academic tendencies. We'd exchange knowing glances during these comments, secretly proud of the life we built together.

But that life didn't last.

Just when I thought my life couldn't be any more perfect, just as I was in the throes of planning our wedding, Brody got sick. Years of summers spent outside in southern Georgia had left him with stage four skin cancer. It didn't take long, just a few months from diagnosis until he died. And his death broke something in me.

Something I can't seem to recover from.

Now there are moments—fleeting, disorienting moments that happen when I'm drinking—when I can't quite remember the specific sequence of events. When the timeline of his illness shifts and blurs. Last week, I found myself standing in the oncology ward of Phoenix Memorial, unable to recall how I got there or why I'd come. A nurse recognized me, her pitying smile making my skin crawl. "Dr. Donovan," she said gently, "the support group meets on Thursdays now."

Still, I remember the progression of his illness vividly. First, it was just a strange mole on his shoulder blade that I noticed while we were getting ready for bed. Then it was doctor's appointments, surgeries, treatments that left him nauseated and weak. His golden skin turned ashen; his strong hands became bony and trembling. I watched as cancer consumed him from the outside in, stealing pieces of him day by day until the man I loved was unrecognizable even to himself.

The smell of antiseptic makes me gag. Fluorescent hospital lights haunt my dreams. I can't bear the sound of ice chips in a plastic cup or the beeping of electronics reminding me of monitors tracking his fading vitals. When he died, I was holding his hand. His last words were, "Keep going, Riley. Don't let this be the end of your story." Even at the end, he was encouraging my passion.

And so here I am, one year since Brody died, watching the clock until it's time for me to have my first glass of wine. The clock switches, and I flick my bottle opener and begin removing the foil from a fresh bottle of cabernet. I'm no wine connoisseur, so the twenty-dollar bottle of cab from the local liquor store gets the job done. I'm not so much into the hard stuff—the bourbons, the vodkas. They might make me feel a little bit guilty, but somehow, it's easier to justify a glass of wine every night.

But one glass isn't enough. Two glasses become three, become an empty bottle, become nights I can't fully recall. Become mornings waking up on the bathroom floor, the side of my face pressed against the cold tiles, with no memory of how I got there.

I pour myself a glass and head over to the couch to binge-watch another season of *Empires in the Dust: The Great Civilizations That Shaped Our World*. As an archaeologist with a PhD, I should be appalled by the show's dramatic recreations and oversimplified narratives—the host's breathless chat about "revolutionary discoveries" makes me roll my eyes so hard I might strain something. But I tell myself I'm gathering inspiration for my book ... if there's no drama in your story, no one's going to read it. As my agent told me, "Drama sells. Even in history books."

Regardless of my opinion, binge-watching TV is definitely not what I *should* be doing.

What I should be doing is actually writing my book. After my not-so-graceful exit from ASU, I decided to take a "sabbatical." The university and I ended on fairly good terms, and on paper, I stepped down to focus on my work. But nearly all my former colleagues know the truth: I was fired.

My mind flashes to that faculty meeting—the one where I showed up still drunk from the night before, where I accused the department chair of sabotaging my research grant application. The memory is fragmented, like shards of a broken mirror reflecting distorted versions of myself. I remember standing, my voice rising, my colleagues' shocked faces. I remember security being called. What I don't remember is exactly what I said, or how I got home afterward.

I draw the curtains, shutting out the afternoon light. My home is decorated like any archaeologist's would be. Full of artifacts from my travels—a hand-painted ceramic bowl from Santorini sits on the coffee table, filled with smooth stones collected from beaches across the world. A framed textile from a village near Machu Picchu hangs on the wall. The bookshelf sags under the weight of academic texts, travel guides, and a small collection of ancient pottery replicas. And if I'm being honest, some aren't replicas at all.

I glance at Brody's chair—the leather armchair where he used to sit while reading his architectural journals. It's pristine, untouched. After he died, I couldn't bear to see anyone else sit there. But sometimes at night, after enough wine, I see the indentation of a body in the cushion, as if someone has just risen from it. Sometimes I hear the rustle of pages turning when I'm alone in the house.

Maybe I'm losing my mind.

Maybe I should stop drinking.

Maybe tomorrow.

I settle in on the couch and hit play. The leather cushions shift beneath me as I tuck my feet under a throw, the fabric soft against my skin. On screen, a narrator with a British accent discusses the burial practices of the early Egyptians. The familiar topic brings a small comfort—these ancient peoples also grappled with death, with loss, with finding meaning in a world where loved ones disappear.

A couple of minutes into the show and I'm nearly

halfway through my second glass when my phone buzzes on the coffee table in front of me. I groan. I should have put it on do not disturb.

I flip it over and pick it up. It's from my friend Grace, who has texted me some type of image. I read her message first.

> Riley! You're not gonna believe who's speaking at ASU tonight.

My brow furrows as I swipe the message open. The image loads slowly, pixels gradually clarifying until the face becomes recognizable.

I nearly spit out the wine swirling around in my mouth. I set the glass down on the wooden coffee table and hold up the image for closer inspection.

You've got to be kidding me.

CHAPTER TWO

The flyer fills up my phone screen with the image of a handsome face and a name that brings a new set of memories into focus. The title reads:

HISTORY'S GREATEST MYSTERIES EXPOSED!
Join YouTube Star Corbin Cross on a Journey to Our Forgotten Past
Special Presentation at Arizona State University

He will be speaking at seven o'clock. *Tonight.*

I stare at the image of Corbin, my fingers tracing the edge of my phone case. I haven't seen him since the funeral, not my fiancé Brody's, but at the funeral of my college friend Meredith Chin. The two were engaged, and about six months ago, she died in a terrible accident. She and I had been college roommates, inseparable until life took us in different directions—me to Arizona for a fresh start, her staying behind to pursue teaching. We'd promised to stay in touch, but our calls grew less frequent, visits rarer.

One weekend, I just happened to be in Denver for a conference. Meredith and I met up for dinner, and Corbin joined us for drinks afterward. That was the first time we met. At the time, the two of them were just friends, but Meredith confessed to me she had a major crush on him.

As soon as we shook hands, I understood why—the bright hazel eyes, dark hair, broad shoulders. He had a strong jawline and a slight quirk to his left eyebrow that made him look like he was sharing a private joke. What took me by surprise was a quiet flutter in my own chest—a feeling I hadn't anticipated. The three of us had a ball, talking and laughing until the bar closed.

What I never told Meredith was that Corbin emailed me three days after I got back to Phoenix.

> *Hey, Riley, hope this isn't weird, but Meredith mentioned your expertise on Egyptian artifacts, especially disputed dating methods from the early dynastic period. I was hoping you could help me with a few questions?*

That first email seemed innocent enough—just a guy who'd started a YouTube channel on ancient history asking for some expert advice. I sent him a few article links and some notes from my dissertation. No big deal, *right?*

But then the emails kept coming, each one growing more personal.

> *Your take on those third dynasty pieces is blowing my mind. We should grab coffee sometime and talk more about your theories.*

Before I knew it, we were writing these long, rambling messages to each other. He'd send photos of weird artifacts he was researching, asking what I thought, but then slip in questions about my life in Arizona, my work, what I thought about everything from prehistoric gods to the latest Marvel movie. We were developing this ... connection that scared me a little, especially when Meredith started dropping his name more and more in our calls.

When his email popped up—*I'm headed to Phoenix next month for this conference thing. Any chance I could see you?*—I had just met Brody. The guilt sucker-punched me. What the hell had I been doing all this time, nurturing whatever this "connection" was behind Meredith's back? I never answered that last message.

A week later, Meredith called, all excited, telling me they were officially dating. I shoved any lingering feelings aside and threw myself into things with Brody. We fell out of touch after that, each of us wrapped up in a new relationship.

And then Meredith unexpectedly died ... in an awful accident. I saw Corbin again at her funeral, but avoided him, not sure what I would say. I confess, I may have been a little drunk.

I stare at the glowing image on my phone. Seeing Corbin again isn't just about facing him—it's about facing everything I've been avoiding. Every time I think about him, I see Meredith's face, feel the weight of the funeral program in my hands. And then there's Brody's empty side of the closet, still untouched a year later.

Two losses, barely a heartbeat apart. Corbin is the living, breathing connection to both wounds—the only other person who might understand the exact shape of this grief. My phone vibrates with another incoming message from Grace.

> Isn't this Meredith's fiancé? The guy you had a crush on?

A wave of guilt crashes over me. I confessed the whole story about the emails and my growing feelings to Grace one night over drinks.

I write back. No sense in denying it at this point.

> Yes!

> I knew it. We're totally going!

> No way.

> Yes way. You need to get out of the house. We can grab dinner afterward. I promise it'll be fine.

I chew on my lip, tasting the faint waxy residue of my barely there lip balm. She's right—I do need to get out of the house. I've met up with friends here and there since I left my position at the university, but let's be honest, I don't have much of a social life right now.

I stare at the half-empty glass on the table in front of me, the warm red liquid catching the afternoon light from the TV. I let out a sigh. Looks like my wine-and-documentary evening is going to be put on hold.

Grace and I have only known each other for a few months, but she's quickly become my best friend. She's a pediatrician at a local office here in town. We bumped into each other at a local coffee shop, where I had ventured out on a rare occasion. She immediately started chatting me up and invited me to a yoga class—not taking no for an answer.

Once Grace gets an idea in her mind, she'll do everything in her power to talk me into it.

I type, surrendering to the inevitable.

> OK, OK, fine.

> Great! I'll be at your house at 6.

I let out a long sigh and pick up the wine, draining the last of it. The third glass will have to wait until later. The last thing I need is to show up drunk at another university function.

The memory of my final department meeting rises again, more detailed this time. The concerned faces of my colleagues. The way Professor Spencer escorted me from the room, his hand firm on my arm. "You need help, Riley," he said, his voice pitched low. "This isn't just grief anymore."

I shake the memory away and head to my bedroom to find something suitable to wear. My closet is a time capsule—one half filled with the professional clothes from my teaching days, the other with the sweatpants and oversized T-shirts that have become my uniform in isolation. I push past a garment bag containing my wedding dress, pristine, never worn.

I select a navy button-front dress that still has its tags on. Something I bought in that brief period after Brody's death when I thought I might rejoin the world. I lay it on the bed and head to the shower. Once I'm clean, dressed, and have done the best I can with my hair and makeup, I give myself a once-over in the mirror. My hair falls nearly halfway down my back, and I'm sure I could use a haircut, but my green eyes look brighter than they did last week. Of course, I could lose a few pounds, the glasses of wine and endless nights of carry-out haven't done my figure much good.

Either way, it will have to do. I'm going to see Corbin again, whether I like it or not.

CHAPTER THREE

A few hours later, Grace and I are walking down the hallway of the university building. I tug at the hem of my dress, the fabric smooth beneath my fingertips. I figured it would be appropriate to dress professionally at the event. I might not be a prof anymore, but I am still hoping to be a respected author in the field someday.

The space buzzes with energy—that particular mix of intellectual curiosity, professional networking conversations, and a subtle undertow of competition. The air is cool, almost too cold, with that distinct conference-center smell of industrial carpet and burned coffee.

"You look fantastic, by the way," Grace says, nudging my shoulder with hers.

I smile gratefully. Grace has always been good at boosting my confidence when I need it most.

I see many of my former colleagues in the hallway, wearing their name badges and talking with each other. The sound of academic chatter—most likely about methodologies and new discoveries—creates a familiar soundtrack that I didn't realize I missed. A few of them give me a nod and a smile, but most avert their eyes when they spot me, conversations faltering as I pass. One woman—a visiting professor from Yale whose name I can't recall—actually takes a step back, as if my disgrace might be contagious.

She'll get over it. They all will. None of them have ever had to bury their fiancé just a month before their wedding date.

But as we continue down the corridor, I catch fragments of whispered exchanges that follow in our wake.

"—should have gotten help sooner—"

"—threatened to destroy his research—"

"—had to be escorted out by security—"

My face burns with shame. Is that what they think happened? Thanks to the bottle or more of wine I drank that day, the memory remains frustratingly fragmented, like trying to recall a dream after waking.

"That man over there is trying to get your attention, Riley," Grace says, her voice pitching higher with excitement. "Should we go say hi?"

I peek over her shoulder to see my former boss, Professor Spencer, waving in our direction. I return a weak smile and a small wave before pushing Grace in another direction.

"Let's not," I say, the thought making my stomach tighten. "Come on. Why don't we see if they have a bar."

"Riley …" she says, giving me a warning look, her blue eyes narrowing.

"What? I promise it's just one glass. You can't blame me for being nervous. I haven't seen Corbin since the funeral."

As soon as I utter his name, I catch sight of him standing across the room. The world seems to close in on itself for a moment, ambient noise fading as my focus sharpens on him.

He's got a semicircle of admirers—a mixture of academics and, of course, young women—standing in a devotional half-moon around him as he chats with the crowd. Corbin has always been charismatic, his voice carrying that perfect blend of authority and accessibility that draws people in.

He is smiling and gesturing in that animated way I remember so well. I can tell, too, that he's lost a little weight since I last saw him, and he doesn't have his normal healthy robustness about him, but he's still as handsome as ever. His tailored charcoal sports coat fits him like a dream, making him appear every inch the successful academic celebrity he's become.

I see him look up for a moment and catch my eye across the crowded room. A flash of recognition crosses his face—surprise, perhaps a hint of something else.

"It's time for everyone to take their seats for Mr. Cross's presentation," the PA bellows.

I distract myself with my purse, fumbling with the clasp and refusing to look up as he heads back to the speakers' waiting area. My heart is pounding against my ribs. At the very least, I'm out in public again, something I can proudly tell my therapist at our next meeting.

"Come on, let's go grab a seat," says Grace, tugging at my elbow, either oblivious to or kindly ignoring my momentary discomfort.

We walk inside the auditorium, which is, to my surprise, packed. There are probably a thousand people in the room, their collective presence creating a low, constant murmur that fills the space. I guess I shouldn't be surprised at the turnout. Corbin's YouTube channel has over two million followers.

His career trajectory has always intrigued me. As far as I

know, he has zero formal training in history or archeology. But just a few months before he met Meredith, he launched his channel with theories so original and meticulously researched that I've often wondered how he did it.

His meteoric rise began with what seemed like impossible luck—stumbling upon an intact Inca royal burial chamber in the Peruvian Andes, complete with golden funeral masks and ceremonial artifacts. The discovery footage made international headlines and went viral overnight, transforming him from struggling engineer to archaeological celeb. A Netflix deal followed almost immediately, though their first expedition together turned up nothing but empty caves and deeply disappointed investors.

After the discovery, Corbin switched his focus to theories about a lost civilization. His theories, labeled as "shocking" and "groundbreaking," kept the views on his YouTube channel climbing. Meanwhile, Meredith had a book coming out, which Corbin promoted constantly. And then that book hit the bestsellers list.

They were the success story we all envied. The two of them made the perfect power couple, just like the vibe Brody and I had enjoyed. Before cancer came and ruined our lives.

Grace and I settle into our places, safely eight rows back from the stage. The seats are scratchy and uncomfortable, and for a moment I wish I were back at home. I came here to see Corbin out of curiosity—not to reconnect.

Just as everyone gets settled, the lights go out. The sudden, complete darkness is disorienting, and a momentary panic murmurs through the crowd. Then a single beam cuts through the dark, illuminating a small circle. A few seconds later, Corbin walks into it, his footsteps echoing slightly in the hushed room.

"History is like staring into the dark. It's only through careful research and study that we can truly shine a light on our past ..." I'm reminded of how his voice has that perfect resonance—deep enough to command attention but warm enough to feel inviting.

I feel the corner of my mouth shoot up in a smirk. I'm sure the ladies in the audience are loving this. Just like on his YouTube—*which I may or may not have stalked for a while*—Corbin has a flair for dramatics. I notice several young women in the front rows leaning forward in their seats, completely captivated by his presence.

He continues with his speech on ancient mysteries. His presentation unfolds like a carefully crafted conspiracy thriller—starting with satellite images of the underwater structures he claims are Atlantis, then methodically connecting the architectural "impossibilities" of monuments across Egypt, Peru, and Easter Island as evidence of a single advanced prehistoric civilization. With each slide, he builds toward his grand theory: that a catastrophic global event twelve thousand years ago wiped out an advanced human society, forcing us to rebuild from scratch.

Throughout it all, he expertly weaves legitimate archaeological questions with wild speculation, his charismatic delivery making even his most outlandish claims about government cover-ups and "restricted sites" in Antarctica seem tantalizingly plausible.

Despite my training, I find myself reluctantly impressed. The academic in me wants to stand up and challenge every claim Corbin makes—point out the cherry-picked evidence, the logical leaps, the absence of peer review. Yet there's something irresistibly captivating about the connections he draws between sites I've studied my entire career. When he overlays the astronomical alignments of Göbekli Tepe with those at Angkor Wat, I feel a fleeting sense of wonder—that dangerous "what if" that serious archaeologists are trained to approach with skepticism.

As I lean back in my seat, I can't help but marvel at what Corbin has done—filled an entire room with people genuinely interested in archeology and held them rapt for an hour. And in a field where we often spend decades carefully documenting pottery shards and crumbled columns, his grand narrative of lost civilizations offers something intoxicating: *a shortcut to meaning.*

I glance at Grace, who seems equally as captivated as the rest of the room. As the applause finally dies down, Professor Spencer reappears to announce that Corbin will take questions from the audience. Several people line up on either side of the stage next to the microphone stands to ask him questions. Most of them are young women who are just dying to get a look—or maybe a date—from Corbin himself, given that he's now single. The thought sends an unexpected pang through my chest. I watch as he answers each question thoughtfully, giving each person his full attention, that trademark smile never faltering.

Then one young woman stands up, her voice shaky as it carries through the microphone.

"Can you address the rumors that Meredith Chin's death wasn't an accident?"

The room goes instantly silent. Even the constant hum of the air conditioning seems to fade. I feel my body go rigid in my seat, and beside me, Grace reaches over to squeeze my hand. Onstage, Corbin's smile freezes for a moment, a flash of genuine pain crossing his features.

I hold my breath, waiting for his answer.

CHAPTER FOUR

"I'm sorry, folks," Professor Spencer announces, his voice cutting through the uncomfortable silence that follows the young woman's question. "That's all we have time for this evening. Let's conclude with another round of applause for Corbin Cross."

The audience erupts into applause, the sound echoing off the auditorium walls. Professor Spencer's sudden appearance from behind the stage has rescued Corbin from the woman's question. He gives a slight nod, his movements stiff and mechanical. The demeanor of confidence and charisma is gone, replaced with a hollow look and awkward demeanor. The stage lights catch the sheen of sweat on his forehead as he forces a smile that doesn't reach his eyes.

I feel a mixture of sympathy and indignation. *How can people be so cruel?* This poor man lost his fiancée, and they want to make her accidental death into some sort of public melodrama.

Corbin exits the stage behind a black curtain, his shoulders slumping the moment he thinks he's out of sight. I find myself wondering if he's going to take more questions from his eager audience or try to disappear.

"Well, that was something," says Grace next to me, her voice hushed despite the growing murmur of the crowd around us. She shifts in her seat, the red upholstery creaking beneath her. "What do you think?"

I have trouble forming the right words. Meredith was a friend of mine, and the mention of her onstage has left me momentarily speechless. Granted, we didn't always stay in touch like true friends should, but when we did connect, it was like no time had passed between us.

Of course, there was another side to our friendship, a side I've tried to bury. *Jealousy.* While I struggled to find my confidence, Meredith had that It Girl quality that everyone envies—polish and good looks, the kind of approach to the world that comes from growing up in a well-to-do family. Her father was a diplomat who traveled all over the world, bringing his family along with him. Her mother was a librarian, so Meredith grew up as a bookworm, which morphed into a rounded, perceptive world view. Not something I possessed thanks to the limited privilege of a childhood spent in a small town.

Frankly, Meredith had everything I dreamed of, but her personality was so infectious, it was hard to stay jealous of her. We were nearly inseparable in college, sharing the same classes, confiding in the hallways about how terrible our professors were or how difficult the exams were going to be. The memory of her laugh—bright and unrestrained—echoes in my mind, making my chest ache with a complicated mixture of grief and nostalgia.

As the auditorium lights begin to brighten, they reveal the faces of audience members—some confused, others whispering behind their hands, a few dabbing at their eyes. Grace watches me expectantly, waiting for a response.

"I think it was difficult for him to get through the presentation," I finally reply, my voice sounding distant even to my own ears. "But you know, I think he did a great job."

Grace looks at me, a smile spreading across her face. Her blue eyes twinkle with mischief as she leans in closer, the scent of her floral perfume momentarily overpowering the musty smell of the auditorium. "Ohh, I think there's more to it than that. I saw the way you looked at him. Tell me, Riley, do you still have a crush on Corbin Cross?"

I feel heat rise up into my cheeks, but I can't deny what's she implying. Then a brief memory of Brody's smile flashes in my mind, and I push it away before the familiar ache can settle in.

"Come on," I say, looking around. We are among the last people in the room. "I'm starving and in desperate need of a glass of wine."

Grace says nothing, just smiles and stands up from her seat. The chairs around us are mostly empty now, with only maybe a dozen or so people left, scattered in groups around the room. I can almost separate the people into sectors: the academics no doubt discussing the details of the presentation, analyzing everything Corbin said with a doubtful tone in their voices; and the women who are wondering if Corbin is still single and open to dating. The dichotomy between the two causes me to roll my eyes. People can never see past their own agenda.

I follow Grace dutifully through the halls. Our footsteps echo on the polished floor, mixing with the fading sounds of the dispersing crowd. The air becomes fresher as we near the exit, the smell of coffee and perfume giving way to the promise of the outdoors.

We step outside, and the warm Arizona air hits us like a gentle wave. It's still light, although the sun is setting in the distance. Purple and orange streaks are running across the sky, contrasting beautifully with the flat-topped mountains in the distance. The fading sunlight bathes everything in a golden glow, softening the edges of the world. The scent of desert sage and creosote fills my nostrils, that smell that comes after a hot day in the desert begins to cool.

"So, what are you feeling tonight?" asks Grace, her ponytail swaying as she turns to face me. The parking lot is half empty now, car doors slamming as attendees make their way home. "Maybe instead of a glass of wine, you'd be up for margaritas? Mateo's?"

I nod with a smile. "You know I can't say no to Mateo's."

Grace taps me on the shoulder. "Great! My car's over on the other side of the parking lot. I'll see you there!"

She turns and heads off in the opposite direction. I'm left alone, tall lights casting long shadows in front of me as I make a beeline for my car. The whole evening has left me with a tension between my shoulder blades. That margarita can't come soon enough.

"Riley? Is that you?"

The voice sends a jolt of recognition through me. I spin on my heel and come face-to-face with none other than Corbin. He's standing about twenty feet away, his figure silhouetted against the sunset. He's changed from his formal jacket into a more casual blazer, but he still looks every inch the academic celebrity. The golden light catches in his hair, highlighting those flecks of silver at his temples.

"Corbin. Hi." My voice cracks slightly.

"I thought I saw you—"

"Yeah, I heard you were speaking tonight, so ..." I trail off, uncertain how to finish that sentence. The truth is, I came specifically to see him, but I'm not ready to admit that.

Corbin quickly closes the distance between us and wraps me in a hug. I am so shocked by the gesture that I nearly stumble. The warmth of his embrace hits me like an electric current—foreign yet achingly familiar. My body goes rigid for a split second before melting into the contact. It's been months since anyone has held me like this—since before Brody's funeral, when hugs became something I'd dodge with practiced efficiency. A lump forms in my throat, and my eyes prickle with unexpected tears. How pathetic that after so many months of self-imposed isolation, a basic hug could make me crack.

"It's so good to see you," he says.

"Oh, it's good to see you too, Corbin," I manage, pulling back slightly from the hug. The evening air feels cooler against my skin where his warmth was.

"Why didn't you come say hello?"

I tug at a stray piece of hair, feeling a surge of heat creep up my cheeks. "Well ... I ... You looked so busy answering questions, I didn't want to interrupt you."

"Interrupt me? Come on, Riley, we're friends."

Something about the way he says it, so genuine, makes me smile. There is a brief moment of silence before he speaks up again.

"So, what did you think of the presentation?" he asks.

"I loved it," I blurt out.

"You loved it?"

Okay, *love* is a bit strong. I feel my cheeks grow warmer.

"Well, yes, I thought it was great," I say honestly. "And

I'm sorry about the question at the end. That must have been really uncomfortable."

"Yeah, it was weird," he says, his smile faltering. More parking lot lights have started to come on, casting everything in a harsh fluorescent glow that makes the shadows under his eyes more pronounced. "Look, I've been meaning to reach out, but things have been hard since—"

"It's okay," I say, cutting him off, hoping to relieve him of any obligation he has to me. "Grieving is hard."

"Yes, it is. I guess that's something we have in common," he says, his voice sounding very sad. In the fading light, I can see the raw grief in his eyes, so similar to what I see in my own mirror every morning. "Listen, I'd love to catch up sometime," he continues, shifting his weight from one foot to the other. A car engine starts somewhere in the distance. "Would you be okay if I called you, and maybe we could get coffee?"

I open my mouth to respond but can't seem to find the words.

"It's okay. I'm sure you're busy—" he says.

"No, I'm not. I mean, I'm writing a book right now, but —" I sense that my cheeks are a firm red now. "Coffee sounds great. Let me give you my number."

I recite my number, watching as Corbin's fingers move quickly across his phone screen. The blue light illuminates his face in the growing darkness. After confirming the number, he tucks his phone away and takes a step back.

"Great, I'll call you," he says, and there's something in his voice—relief, perhaps—that makes me wonder if he was nervous about asking. "I should go. I've got an early meeting tomorrow. But it was really good to see you, Riley."

With a final smile and a small wave, he heads off to the

other end of the parking lot. I pause for a moment, watching him disappear around the corner. The evening air is quiet, just the hum of traffic from the main road. Suddenly, headlights flare to life, aimed directly at me. I squint and shield my eyes. The car's interior is dark, so I can't make out the driver.

When my vision clears, I realize the car is just a few feet away, barreling past me toward the exit. I feel a whoosh of air as it passes.

"Hey!" I shout, jumping. "Watch where you're going!"

I stumble and drop my phone, immediately reaching down to retrieve it. By the time I stand up again, the car is gone. I shake my head, my earlier excitement of seeing Corbin squashed by irritation. My screen illuminates with a message from Grace.

> Just walked in! First margarita is on me.

I sigh and head toward my own car, telling myself it was probably some college kid texting and driving. But as I turn the key in my ignition, I can't quite shake the feeling that someone was watching us.

CHAPTER FIVE

The next morning, I drag myself out of bed and pad to the kitchen for a cup of coffee. One margarita with Grace turned into three, and after an Uber ride home, I have a bit of a hangover.

The sunlight streaming through the kitchen window is far too bright, forcing me to squint as I measure coffee grounds into the filter. I inhale the aroma deeply, hoping the scent alone might clear the fog from my brain. Still, the hangover could have been worse; after my third margarita, I managed to stop myself.

For that, I feel a small sense of accomplishment. Several months ago, that wouldn't have been the case. I had a few weeks where I drank so much, I blacked out entirely. Waking up on Monday with red wine stains on my shirt and messages from some guy I don't remember meeting. Now I try to keep my drinking safely to the confines of my apartment.

Despite the fog, something about running into Corbin and being there for his presentation has given me a new burst of motivation. We both lost someone we loved, yet he's out there building something—even if that something is a career based on archaeological theories I don't quite agree with.

Meanwhile, I've been floating through my days, barely making it into the shower, let alone finishing my book. It's embarrassing, really. Seeing him on that stage yesterday, confident and purpose-driven despite everything, held up an uncomfortable mirror.

A year of grieving, and what do I have to show for it? A growing collection of wine bottles and a partially finished manuscript gathering digital dust on my laptop. Even Brody would have been disappointed in me, and he was my biggest cheerleader. The thought makes me wince as I pour water into the coffee maker.

Grief isn't a competition, my therapist would say. But seeing Corbin function—no, thrive—while carrying the same weight as me? It strips away my excuses. If he can channel his pain into productivity, then maybe I can redirect mine into legitimate work again. Not because I'm ready, but because I'm tired of the alternative. Tired of disappointing myself.

I stand in the kitchen, my robe wrapped around me, and stare at my laptop perched on the table. The screen saver—a slideshow of archaeological sites I've visited—cycles through images of Karnak, Dendera and the pyramids. Looking at them reminds me of that "spark" I once had to uncover the secrets of the past. It sounds cheesy, but looking back at myself reminds me of how giddy and excited I was to visit Egypt for the first time.

The publishing deal came before Brody died. Meridian Academic Press offered me a contract for my book, complete with a ten-thousand-dollar advance that helped cushion the blow of my quick exit from the university. The catch, of course, was buried in the fine print: if I don't deliver the completed manuscript within twelve months, I have to pay back every penny I've received so far.

That was over a year ago.

And after twelve months, I have a jumbled outline and exactly fifty pages written.

That's right, *fifty*.

Let's be honest, it's hard to get academic work done when you're having at least three glasses of wine every night. The tannins dull the brain, while the alcohol makes coherent thought nearly impossible. The problem, however, isn't the number of words I've written; it's what I did with the money.

Three months after Brody died, I got spectacularly drunk on a bottle of wine that cost more than my monthly grocery budget and bid on a collection of Late Period Egyptian artifacts at an online auction. Canopic jars, ushabti figures, a limestone relief fragment that probably belonged in a museum—pieces I convinced myself I needed for "research." By morning, I'd spent nearly every last cent of my advance on antiquities that now sit in my spare bedroom like expensive paperweights. Paperweights that would take me months to sell and I'd probably get less than half of what I spent.

So not only am I a year behind on delivering a complete manuscript, but I've also blown any chance of paying back the advance.

The cursor has blinked accusingly at me for months now, a silent rebuke each time I open the document, only to close it again without adding a single word. My notes are scattered all over the kitchen table, along with a smattering of dog-eared books. What's left of my savings barely covers the mortgage each month, and my agent has started texting me daily with increasingly pointed questions about my progress. As if summoned by my spiraling thoughts, my phone lights up with her name. I let it ring through to voicemail, the same way I have for the past week.

But today is different. Today I feel a renewed sense of purpose and am determined to get down to work.

I settle at the table, pulling my chair closer to the laptop. Outside, a desert dove coos from its perch on my patio, its gentle sound a counterpoint to the hum of the air con. I tap my password and open my manuscript file, scrolling through what I've written so far. The words swim before me until they come into focus.

I type a whole paragraph, my fingers moving with a fluidity I haven't felt in so long:

> *When a conqueror dismantles the monuments of their predecessor, they are not merely removing stone and pigment; they are attempting to erase memory itself. In the Third Intermediate Period (1070–664 BCE), we see evidence of such erasure in the temple complexes of the Delta region, where cartouches were chiseled away and statues repurposed. The fragments that remain tell us not just what was preserved, but hint at the magnitude of what was lost.*

The words flow more easily than they have in months. I think of the photographs I took at Karnak, where the faces of deities had been methodically chiseled away by subsequent rulers, leaving eerie, blank visages staring out across the millennia. I'd run my fingers over those defaced carvings, feeling the rough gouges in the stone, wondering about the artisans who had created them and those who had been ordered to destroy them.

Of course, the title of my book, *What Was Lost*, rings especially true for me at this point in my life. *In many ways, I've lost everything.* My parents when I was in my twenties, my fiancé and, most recently, Meredith. The parallel between my personal losses and the historical erasures I study isn't lost on me. Sometimes I wonder if that's why I'm drawn to this area of research—trying to recover and understand what's been taken away, trying to make sense of absence.

The morning slips away as I write, the words coming more and more easily as I focus on my thoughts. By midday, I've added nearly two thousand words to my manuscript—a small miracle, especially compared to what I've been able to muster over the last year. My coffee has gone cold, forgotten beside my laptop. The sunshine has shifted, now falling across the dining room floor in long rectangles. My stomach growls, reminding me I haven't eaten yet today.

As I stand and stretch, feeling the satisfying pop of my spine. My phone chimes from the counter where I left it. I walk over, muscles stiff from sitting too long and check the message.

> Hey Riley, really good seeing you last night. Would you be up for coffee tomorrow? Say 2 at Copper State Coffee on Central?

I stare at the message, my thumb hovering over the screen. Part of me wants to decline, to focus on this newfound productivity, this small spark of my old self that's finally returned. Meeting with Corbin could oh so easily complicate things.

Yet there's something that makes me want to say yes. Perhaps it's our shared experience of loss, or maybe it's something else entirely—something I'm not ready to name.

I hesitate for a long moment, then type:

> Coffee sounds great. See you at 2.

As I hit send, I'm not sure if I've done the right thing. But for the first time in months, I'm making decisions based on something other than grief and wine.

I just hope I'm not making a terrible mistake.

CHAPTER SIX

The next day I walk into the coffee shop, finding myself wishing I'd put a second layer of deodorant on. My heart beats a little faster than normal, and I can feel a sheen of perspiration forming along my hairline. I am dressed casually in jeans and a button-down blouse, my fingers having traced over at least a dozen outfits in my closet before settling on something that wouldn't look like I was trying too hard.

This is the second time I've been fully dressed with my hair and makeup done—twice in one week—for as long as I can remember. My therapist might call that progress.

We'll see.

In the very few therapy sessions that I attended after Brody passed, my therapist told me that getting ready for the day really helps with your mental state. She insisted that the simple act of showering, dressing, and presenting yourself to the world could lift your spirits in ways medication sometimes couldn't. As I catch my reflection in the coffee shop window, I hardly recognize the woman looking back at me—

she's someone who looks put together, professional, almost normal.

And now I understand what the therapist meant.

The shop itself is a few short blocks from the university where I used to work. Memories of coming here and meeting with colleagues fill me with a mixture of positive and negative emotions. It feels strange to be back here, like coming home to find someone else living in your house.

I'm a few minutes late. Through the large front windows, I can see Corbin is already at a corner table—waiting with ... huh? *He's not alone.*

A woman sits across from him, her long black hair shimmering down her back. She's leaning forward, animated, saying something that makes Corbin throw his head back and laugh—a genuine, unguarded laugh. My stomach clenches.

I hesitate at the entrance, my hand frozen on the door handle. Through the window, I watch Corbin reach across the table—not quite touching her hand, but close enough that the gesture feels intimate. The woman notices his glance toward the window first, following his gaze until her eyes land on me. She says something quickly to him, and I see his expression shift, the easy smile faltering.

By the time I make it inside, she's already standing, gathering a designer purse from the back of her chair. Corbin murmurs something to her—too low for me to catch—and she nods, offering me a polite smile as she passes.

"Riley, I—" Corbin says, rising to his feet.

"I can come back another time if you're busy," I interrupt, standing awkwardly next to the table.

"What? No." He waves his hand dismissively. "That was

just Cassie—friend of a friend. No big deal. She was just leaving anyway. I'm so glad you're here."

For a moment, I am frozen, deciding whether to bolt for the door or stay. Corbin steps forward and gives me a hug, and I'm immediately wrapped up in his warmth. The fabric of his jacket is soft against my cheek, and I find myself lingering in the embrace a moment too long.

Looks like I'm staying.

I sit down at the table. Corbin is dressed the same as post-presentation the other night, in a sport coat and jeans, though today the jacket is a deep navy blue that brings out the intensity of his eyes. There is a brief silence as I settle into my seat, and I'm thankful for the ambient noise around the room—students typing furiously on laptops, the rhythmic tapping of spoons against ceramic mugs, the occasional burst of laughter from a group in the corner.

Lined up in front of me are three different cups of coffee, their steam rising in wisps that catch the light.

"I wasn't sure what you'd like—black coffee, an Americano, or a latte—so I ordered all three," he says with a sheepish grin, gesturing to the lineup of cups with a hand that bears a small scar across the knuckles. I wonder briefly where he got it, if there's a story behind it.

I'm touched by his thoughtfulness and reach for the Americano, wrapping my fingers around its warmth. "Thank you," is all I say as a smile tugs at my mouth.

Corbin brushes his fingers through his hair, leaning back into his chair. As I take a sip of my coffee—strong and slightly bitter—I glance around, wondering if the woman from earlier is still here.

I don't see her, but I do see a few people casually looking

at our table. They probably recognize Corbin. In other parts of the country, people might not know who he is, but here—just blocks from the university—he's something of a local legend. His videos on ancient technologies and lost civilizations may not be required coursework, but many of the kids watch them and bring up Corbin's theories in their classrooms.

Much to the chagrin of the faculty.

"So, it's been way too long," he says right away, his fingers tapping a gentle rhythm on the wooden tabletop. "Tell me about this book you've been writing. Do you have a publisher yet?"

I take another sip of coffee before responding, buying myself a moment to organize my thoughts. "Yes, actually. I signed a contract with MAP."

Corbin's eyes light up, crinkling at the corners in a way that's both familiar and new. "Really? That's great, Riley. I'd love to hear more about it."

"Well, it's about the intermediate periods of Egypt—the time sandwiched in between the more 'stable' kingdoms of Egypt. It's a book I've been wanting to write for decades." I launch into the pitch for my book—how I sold it to a publisher, what I've been working on, the challenges of piecing together a deliberately erased history. As I speak, I find myself gesturing more animatedly than I have for months, my usual reserve melting away in the face of Corbin's genuine interest.

"What excites me most," I continue, "is how new technology is revolutionizing what we can discover about these lost periods—revealing text that was deliberately removed by subsequent rulers."

He nods thoughtfully, leaning forward. "So you're essentially creating a forensic analysis of cultural erasure? That's fascinating."

"Exactly! And with the new LiDAR technology—"

"Incredible, right?" he interjects, his excitement matching my own. "The detail it provides is insane. What's the title?"

I smile. "*What Was Lost: The Intermediate Periods of Egypt.*"

Corbin asks just the right questions, and we fall into a comfortable rhythm that I didn't expect. The words flow freely between us. It's like we've never missed a beat, even though we haven't really seen or talked to each other in nearly a decade. Our coffee grows cold as we speak, forgotten in the exchange of ideas. Outside, the light shifts as afternoon edges toward evening, casting longer shadows across our table.

I find myself going on about how new imaging techniques might reveal texts that were erased during political transitions, only to stop abruptly when I realize I've been dominating the conversation.

"I'm sorry, I'm rambling on about what I've been doing. What about you? You're, like, this famous YouTube star now." A heat rises to my cheeks; I'm embarrassed by my enthusiasm.

"Well, it's not something I planned on," Corbin says with a slight laugh, brushing off the question as he leans back in his chair. "I went to the Andes on a hunch after watching a documentary about the Incas." He shrugs. "It's funny—I was just documenting it for fun, but then I made that discovery in the burial chamber, and my channel exploded. I wasn't really happy with my career at the time anyway, so transitioning into videos about historical conspiracies sounded like a lot more fun." He pauses. "I guess the rest is history. It's not exactly the career I had planned, but there are definitely some perks to the job."

"Such as?" I ask, genuinely curious.

"I get to do speaking events, for one." His fingers curl around his forgotten coffee cup. "And of course—I don't know if you've watched any of my videos ..."

I nod, urging him on. In truth, I've watched several of his —okay, maybe *all*—of his videos since he started.

"Well, you can see that I get access to some pretty amazing sites I wouldn't otherwise be able to get near. Like the video I did on Göbekli Tepe. Had I not had the notoriety and the connections, I would never have been able to go there."

"That's amazing," I say, leaning forward a little. "I would have loved to see that."

"Yeah, it was pretty incredible. The stonework there predates Stonehenge by six thousand years. Standing among those megalithic structures, you can almost feel the weight of everything we might call history pressing down on you." His eyes take on a distant look, as if he's mentally transported back to that prehistoric site.

"And how do you capture all those incredible shots? Do you travel with a whole production team?"

He shakes his head. "No, usually just me and one other person. Right now, I'm working with this guy Marcus who specializes in drone footage. He's revolutionized the whole operation—people have no idea how massive these sites actually are until you pull back and show the full scope." His hands gesture expansively, framing an invisible landscape. "The human element gets completely dwarfed by these ancient structures."

I nod, taking a sip of water. There's suddenly an awkward break, and I realize we've been talking for nearly an hour. Many of the people have cleared out of the coffee shop—probably students heading to class and so on. The background noise has dimmed, making our silence more noticeable.

As if on cue, Corbin's phone buzzes on the table between us, the screen lighting up with a notification. I glance down and see a photo of him and Meredith on his lock screen. He must have seen it too, because he makes brief eye contact with me before turning the phone upside down.

"I wanted to ask you, Riley—" he starts, but the phone beeps a second time, and his eyes dart down to it.

"You need to get that?" I ask, trying to keep my tone neutral.

"Yeah, just a second," Corbin says. He picks up the phone and swipes it open. He lets out a long sigh, his shoulders dropping slightly. "I'm sorry, Riley, I forgot. It's my assistant, Kelly. She insists I get back to the office. I've got a conference call at four, and I need to prepare for it."

"Wait, your office is here?"

"Yes, I guess I didn't tell you, I moved to Phoenix about a month ago."

I would be lying if I said I wasn't giddy about the news. *He's so close.* But instead of commenting and giving away my excitement, I lean back in my chair.

Then I start to get up, pulling my purse onto my shoulder. The leather strap feels heavy against my collarbone. "Well, I won't keep you. It was great to see you, Corbin."

"Wait." Corbin gets up as well, his chair scraping against the floor. "Riley, I'd love to see you again."

"Okay ..." I say, not exactly sure what he means. My heartbeat quickens, a sensation I almost forgot.

"I mean—" For a moment, I'm taken aback by how nervous he seems. I'm so used to seeing him on his YouTube videos, where he's this confident, authoritative figure. It's sweet, actually. His fingers fidget with the button on his jacket.

"What I mean to say is, would you like to have dinner with me? Maybe this weekend?" He clears his throat, looking directly at me now.

I feel a flutter, something like butterflies in my stomach, a wild sensation I haven't felt in, well, since Brody and I first started dating. The feeling gives rise to a mixture of emotions, colliding in my chest like opposing weather fronts.

"Sure," I say, my voice softer than I intended. "That would be great."

"Great. I'll message you the details, and we'll work something out, okay?" he says, relief evident in his voice.

"Sounds good."

Before I can say another word, Corbin walks around the table and places a kiss on my cheek. The gesture is something that would be common among friends, yet I feel surprisingly giddy about it. His lips are warm against my skin, and the brief contact sends another little flutter darting around in my chest.

I watch him walk across the room and hold the door for a young woman with a toddler on her hip before he exits onto the street. That went *really* well. Almost too well.

Just as I stare off down the street, considering whether I'm ready to date again, I catch a glimpse through the door of someone who looks like the dark-haired woman, Cassie, from earlier. She's standing outside and seems to be staring directly at me with a less-than-friendly stare. *What is she still doing here?* A bus rolls past, and when I look again, she's gone. My skin prickles.

I shake my head and take the last few sips of my cold coffee, dismissing the image of her from my head. If that's how it turns out, Corbin wouldn't be the first guy I dated who had a crazy ex-girlfriend. But I definitely prefer a guy with a simpler past.

I look down at my empty coffee cup, and I take a moment to focus on the feeling welling up inside me that I haven't felt ... well, since Brody's diagnosis—*hope*. Because I might actually see a future ahead of me.

A future that might actually outrun the complications of our past.

CHAPTER SEVEN

"And now we bring our hands back to our heart's center and thank the universe for the gift of today ... Namaste."

Everyone in the classroom behind me answers "Namaste" in unison, their voices creating a hollow echo against the mirrored walls. The word hangs in the air like incense smoke.

It's curious to me that the practice of yoga and these sacred words are used so casually here, stripped of their deeper meaning. Namaste, I've learned, comes from Sanskrit —literally meaning "I bow to you"—and was traditionally a reverent greeting acknowledging the divine spark in another person. I wonder how the room full of yoga moms would feel if they actually knew this history or understood that yoga itself originated as a sacred spiritual discipline rather than a fitness trend.

Regardless, I'm not sure I can legitimately teach a history lesson. Grace has dragged me along for this class, insisting it would be good for me to get out of the house. I've been hammering away at my book, which has felt productive, but

I'll be honest when I say it's been a couple of days since I've felt sunlight on my skin.

The manuscript pages have become my world—black text on white paper, the steady click of keys, the blue glow of my laptop screen burning my retinas in the predawn hours. Sure, I'm making progress, but not nearly enough. I'm still far behind what was promised to my publisher, and I feel the clock ticking.

Grace stretches luxuriously beside me, her movements fluid and practiced as she wraps her towel around her neck. "Let's grab a smoothie, and then we'll walk out together," she says cheerfully, already moving toward the exit.

"I really should get back …" I say, imagining my afternoon of working growing shorter and shorter.

"Oh, come on, it'll only take a few minutes."

"Fine," I say, though my voice comes out rougher than intended. We make our way to the smoothie bar at the front of the studio, weaving between clusters of chattering women who clutch their designer water bottles like precious, oversized talismans. The blender's aggressive whirring drowns out most conversation as we order a couple of protein smoothies to go.

I admit this is one of the healthier suggestions Grace has made. Most of the time she's trying to lure me into margarita-fueled afternoons or calling round to open a couple of bottles of wine while gossiping about everyone she knows or works with. Or, mostly, some new guy she's dating and stalking online with the dedication of a private investigator.

The smoothie is thick and chalky against my tongue, tasting more like vitamin tablets than fruit despite its intense pink color. We're almost to the glass doors that lead to the parking lot when I realize I have forgotten something.

"Oh no," I say, stopping abruptly. "I left my yoga mat in the studio."

Grace pauses, her hand already reaching for the door handle. "Do you want me to wait?"

"No, it's fine. Just wait outside—I'll be quick." I grip my smoothie, the condensation making my palm slick.

Grace takes the drink. "Don't keep me waiting too long. I might actually combust."

She pushes through the doors, and I watch her disappear into the blazing Arizona afternoon before turning back toward the studio. The main classroom is nearly empty now, just a few stragglers rolling up their mats with post-workout lethargy. The still air hangs thick with the scent of sweat and lavender.

I spot my mat in the back corner where I was practicing, a dark purple rectangle against the light wood floor. As I walk across the room, my footsteps echo strangely in the mostly empty space, and I can't shake the feeling that someone is watching me. The mirrored walls reflect my movement from multiple angles, creating a disorienting kaleidoscope effect.

I'm bending down to roll up my mat when I hear footsteps behind me—deliberate, measured steps that make me straighten and turn slowly. A long black braid catches the harsh fluorescent light. I blink, startled.

It's the woman from the coffee shop.

Her cool blue eyes meet mine with an intensity that makes me want to step backward, but there's nowhere to go —I'm trapped in the corner. It's the same unsettling feeling I got when I saw her in the café with Corbin—like she's looking through me rather than at me, cataloging information I didn't consent to share.

She approaches me with deliberate steps, her smile sharp.

"You're Riley, aren't you?"

How does she know my name? "I ... yes. Do we know each other?"

"Not formally," she says, extending a perfectly manicured hand. Her nails are painted a deep red. "I'm Cassandra. I believe you know Corbin."

The way she says his name—possessive, intimate—makes something cold and sharp twist in my chest. "Yes, I do," I reply carefully, not taking her offered hand. It hangs in the air between us for a moment before she lets it drop, her smile never wavering.

"I thought I should talk to you," she says, her voice softer now, almost conspiratorial. "Woman to woman, you know? I saw you two at the café, and I could tell you were ... interested in him."

The words catch me off guard. So, what, she stayed around to spy on us? *That's just weird.* I force myself to maintain eye contact despite the uncomfortable prickling sensation crawling up my spine. "I'm sorry, what exactly are you getting at?"

Cassandra glances around, as if making sure we won't be overheard. "Look, I don't want to be that girl, but I feel like I should warn you about Corbin. We went out on several dates —really good dates, actually. I thought things were going somewhere." Her voice carries a note of hurt that makes me pause.

My cheeks grow warm, though I'm not sure if it's from embarrassment or the stifling, lingering heat of the studio. "Okay ..."

"And then he just ... disappeared. Completely ghosted

me. No explanation, no text, nothing. He wouldn't return any of my calls." She shakes her head, and for a moment, the polished façade cracks. "That coffee shop was the first time I saw him in three months. Three months of wondering what I'd done wrong."

Her voice cracks with the last words. Despite myself, I feel a flicker of sympathy. The vulnerability in her words seems genuine, and ghosting is something I wouldn't wish on anyone. But the way she's telling me this—the timing, the setting, the intensity of her gaze—feels off.

"I'm sorry that happened to you," I say, shifting my yoga mat to my other arm. "But I'm not sure what you want me to do about it."

"I just thought you should know what you're getting into." Her blue eyes lock onto mine with a fierce gaze that makes the classroom feel smaller. "He's charming, isn't he? Makes you feel like you're the only woman in the world when he's with you. Except, of course, when he's not being pestered by his weird assistant."

The accuracy of her description sends an uncomfortable chill down my spine. That was exactly how Corbin made me feel during our coffee date.

Still, it's really none of her business.

"I have to go," I say, taking a step toward the door. "My friend is waiting for me."

Cassandra nods, but her expression doesn't quite match her understanding tone. "Of course. I just … I hope things work out differently for you than they did for me," she says as she flicks her braid over her shoulder before turning her back to me and heading for the door. Over her shoulder she calls, "Have fun on your date."

The casual mention of my date—information I certainly

never shared with her—sends ice through my veins. *How could she possibly know about that?* My hands begin to tremble as the implications sink in, and the yoga mat threatens to slip from my grip.

I stand frozen for several minutes, trying to process the interaction. It's not until the next yoga class starts shuffling in that I snap out of it and make my way toward the door. When I step outside, Cassandra is nowhere to be seen.

Grace is leaning against the wall in the shade, scrolling through her phone, but she looks up as I approach. She hands me back my smoothie, now warm and unappetizing. "What took so long?" she asks, studying my face with the sharp attention she usually reserves for analyzing potential romantic interests. "You look like you've seen a ghost."

"Just ran into someone," I say, trying and failing to keep my voice light. The words taste bitter in my mouth. "Some girl who apparently has a history with Corbin."

A funny expression crosses Grace's face—surprise mixed with something else I can't quite identify. But she recovers quickly, slipping her phone into her purse. "Oh yeah? Corbin dated her?" She glances over my shoulder toward the studio, where I can feel Cassandra's presence like a weight between my shoulder blades.

I take a sip of my smoothie, letting the Arizona sun beat down on my skin, trying to burn away the chill that Cassandra's words left behind. The drink is too sweet now, cloying and artificial. "Yeah, she seems like a real catch," I say, my voice dripping with sarcasm. "She told me they dated briefly, and then he completely ghosted her."

"Really? Did she say why?"

"She claims she doesn't know ... but honestly? She seemed a little unstable."

"You're being too nice, Riley. Just call it like it is, she was crazy."

I shrug. *I can't say I disagree with her.* "Actually, Corbin asked me out the other day," I say, changing the subject.

"Oh, really?" Grace's voice pitches slightly higher, the way it does when she's processing unexpected information.

"Yeah, we're supposed to go out on Friday. Do you think I should still go?" The question comes out more vulnerable than I intended, and I hate how uncertain I sound.

Grace is quiet for a few seconds, her eyes studying my face with an intensity that makes me uncomfortable. The silence hangs between us, filled only by the mechanical whirr of air-conditioning units working overtime against the heat.

"Of course you should go," she finally says, but there's something forced about her enthusiasm. "Don't listen to some crazy ex he only went out on a few dates with. Besides, you have to get out there at some point, even if the date with Corbin doesn't turn into anything. It'll be good for you to go through the motions. Baby steps, right?"

I can't help but feel grateful for Grace's words, even if her response feels a little off-key. She's right—I do need to get myself out there, regardless of what the outcome will be. Just going through the motions of dating might help me move forward, help me feel like a normal person again instead of a hermit who never leaves the house.

"You're right," I say, though doubt gnaws at the edges of my certainty. "What about you? Do you have any dates coming up?"

"Oh, yes," Grace says, and her excitement seems more genuine now. "I met this guy the other day at the car wash—can you believe that? Who meets someone at a car wash?"

She chatters on excitedly about this man she met, describing his smile and his job and the way he made her laugh while foam covered both their cars.

But I know Grace. I know that after one or two dates, she'll find something inexplicably, irretrievably wrong with him—he'll chew too loudly, or wear the wrong brand of shoes, or text too much or not enough—and he'll be dumped without a second thought. Her dating life is a revolving door of Mr. Almost and Mr. Not Quite.

As we walk toward our cars, the asphalt soft and yielding under our feet from the relentless, blazing sun, I can't shake that strange feeling that I'm being watched. The sensation crawls up my spine, and every instinct I possess is beckoning me to turn around, but I resist.

This Cassandra chick is clearly missing a few marbles and not worth my time. Still, I wonder what kind of history she and Corbin share. The way she spoke about him, the possessive undertone in her voice, gave me a weird feeling.

And that knowledge about our Friday date ... How could she possibly know about that unless she's been watching me? Was she eavesdropping on our conversation at the café? The thought makes my skin prickle. I hope I don't have some unhinged ex-girlfriend to deal with, because despite everything—I find myself actually looking forward to my date with Corbin. It's the first time in months that I've felt anything approaching excitement about the future, and I'll be damned if I'm going to let some woman with boundary issues ruin that for me.

My car engine turns over with a reluctant growl, and I pull out of the parking lot without a backward glance.

CHAPTER EIGHT

I spend far too long getting ready for dinner with Corbin. My closet, normally a wasteland of comfortable outfits I throw on without much thought, has become a battlefield of discarded options. After trying on and tossing away a few dresses that immediately reminded me of dates I'd had with Brody, I finally settle on a deep burgundy wrap dress I haven't worn since before Brody died. The luxurious fabric feels foreign against my skin, like it belongs to someone else's life. When I look in the mirror, I barely recognize myself.

The restaurant Corbin has chosen is one of those upscale places downtown where the lighting is deliberately low and the menu doesn't list prices. He offers multiple times to pick me up, but I decide to take an Uber, just to keep some sense of my own independence. As the driver drops me off at the door, I feel a flutter of nervousness. This is officially a date—my first since Brody. The thought makes me pause with my hand on the car door handle. *Am I ready for this?* Not only that, I can't shake Cassandra's warning, how everything was going great; then he just stopped calling her. I'm not sure I can handle those kinds of mind games and disappointment right now.

But before I can talk myself out of it, I take a deep breath and step out into the cool evening air.

Corbin is already waiting outside the restaurant. He's dressed in a tailored charcoal suit that makes him look like he just stepped out of a fashion magazine. When he sees me, his face breaks into a warm smile that reaches his eyes. He leans in and kisses me on the cheek, sending my heart into a pounding frenzy.

"Riley," he says, his hands on my shoulders as he gazes at me, "you look beautiful."

The compliment sends a shiver through me. I'm not used to being seen that way anymore—as someone who could be beautiful rather than simply broken.

"Thank you," I manage.

He opens the door, and we step inside. The restaurant is a calm oasis of soft lighting and hushed voices—which makes it quiet, almost too quiet. I can't shake the feeling that everyone is staring at us as we walk across the room. Our table is tucked away in a corner, partially hidden by a decorative latticework screen that creates some privacy—and I'm grateful. Corbin holds the chair for me, and I brush my hair back and hang my purse on the chair, trying not to seem nervous.

The waiter appears almost immediately, reciting the evening's specials with precision while I nod too enthusiastically, trying to remember how to act like a normal human being. After we order, there's a moment of silence. I fidget with my napkin, suddenly nervous.

How do you navigate a first-date conversation when

you're both carrying the weight of losing the person you intended to marry?

"So," Corbin says, breaking the silence, "how was the rest of your week? Get much done on your book?"

I'm grateful for the safe topic. "Actually, I've made more progress this week than I have in months. I'm finding the comparison between the modern destruction of artifacts and what happened in ancient Egypt really compelling."

"That's a fascinating angle," he says, leaning forward. "In my Baalbek video, I touched on something similar—how political upheaval leads to cultural erasure."

Everything flows easily from there, moving from archaeological theories to university politics to funny stories to our travels around the world. The wine helps, warming my blood and loosening my tongue. We even manage to share a few memories of Meredith and Brody without completely falling apart. By the time our entrées arrive, I've almost forgotten how nervous I was. I absentmindedly drop a slice of lemon in my water.

"You know Meredith used to have an obsession with having lemon water before bed," Corbin says. "She swore it was the secret to clear skin and good dreams."

The memory makes me smile. "She did the same thing in college. She'd slice those lemons so precisely, like she was performing surgery. And God help you if you used her special lemon knife for anything else."

"I made that mistake once," Corbin says, his laughter fading into a fond smile. "She gave me a twenty-minute lecture on citrus contamination."

"But she was right—her skin was always flawless," I add softly.

Something shifts in Corbin's expression—a shadow

passing across his features. The smile remains, but it's different now, tight around the edges. I realize we've ventured into emotionally dangerous territory.

"How are you doing with everything?" I ask gently. "With losing her, I mean."

Corbin takes a long sip of his wine, his eyes fixed on some point beyond my shoulder. When he sets the glass down, his fingers move along the edge of the stem.

"Some days are better than others," he says finally. His voice has that practiced quality I recognize from my own grief—the rehearsed response that keeps people from probing too deeply. "I throw myself into work. It helps."

I nod, understanding completely. "I did the same thing. Or tried to. The wine helped more, if I'm being honest."

He looks at me then, really looks at me, and I see a flash of raw pain in his eyes before he shutters it away. "I don't really talk about her," he says, his voice dropping. "People expect me to be—I don't know—either completely devastated or to have totally moved on. There's no in between allowed."

"I know exactly what you mean," I say. "After Brody died, everyone had opinions about how I should grieve. How long was appropriate. When I should 'get back out there.'" I make air quotes with my fingers. "As if there's some manual I'm supposed to be following."

A small smile returns to Corbin's face. "If you find that manual, let me know."

"Will do," I promise, returning his smile.

The conversation stalls as our waiter returns to clear our plates. I notice Corbin checking his phone, which he's placed beside his water glass. The screen illuminates briefly with a notification, and his brow furrows.

"Everything okay?" I ask as the waiter retreats.

"Fine," he says, turning the phone facedown. "Just Kelly with some scheduling questions. She can wait."

We order dessert—a chocolate soufflé to share—and as we wait, Corbin reaches across the table and lightly touches my hand. The contact sends a small jolt through me.

"I've felt so alone," he says, his voice barely above a whisper. "This is exactly what I needed, Riley. Someone who understands."

There's something so vulnerable in his expression that it makes my chest ache. I turn my hand over so our palms meet, his fingers warm against mine.

"I understand," I say simply.

The moment is interrupted by a young woman approaching our table, her eyes wide with excitement. She looks painfully young, with a low-cut top that she adjusts as she approaches our table.

"I'm so sorry to bother you," she says, addressing Corbin. "But you're Corbin Cross, right? From the Cross Claims History channel?" She clasps her chest dramatically. "I'm such a huge fan."

I can't help feeling slightly irritated as I take a sip of water. Corbin looks at me first with an expression of "I'm sorry" before turning his attention to her.

"That's me," he says. "Thank you for watching."

He then shifts seamlessly into his public persona—warm, approachable, charming.

"Could I possibly get an autograph?" she asks, holding out a napkin and pen. "My study group watches your videos all the time. Your Göbckli Tepe series literally got me through finals week."

"Of course," Corbin says, accepting the napkin. "What's your name?"

As he signs his name, chatting amiably with the fan, I take a sip of my wine and observe. He's good at this—making people feel special, like they have his full attention. It's the same quality that makes his videos so engaging. I wonder how much of it is genuine and how much is a performance. I can't help but think of Cassandra.

The fan eventually leaves, clutching her signed napkin like a precious artifact. Corbin turns back to me with an apologetic smile.

"Sorry about that," he says. "Happens sometimes."

"No need to apologize," I say. "Must be flattering to be recognized."

"Sometimes," he says.

"Speaking of being recognized, I had something weird happen to me the other day."

"Oh, what's that?"

"Remember when we met at that café, and you were sitting with a woman before I got there?"

He nods, his face expressionless.

"Well, I was at a yoga class, and she approached me. Said you went on a couple of dates, and then you ghosted her? Her words, not mine."

Corbin rolls his eyes. "Oh yes, Cassie. She had some ... issues. I don't want to say anything bad about her, but she became very needy after our first date. Started talking about marriage after our second date, and by the third, she was ready for me to meet her parents. It was all too quick, plus I just wasn't ready. I wasn't sure if she was stable enough for me to break it to her gently ... so I thought it was better if I—"

"Ghosted her?" I say with a teasing grin.

He pulls the edges of his mouth down. "I'm sorry. You must think I'm terrible."

I shake my head. "Oh, no, I get it. She definitely seemed the clingy type."

Crazy is more like it.

Corbin's phone buzzes insistently against the tablecloth. He glances at it and sighs.

"Kelly again?" I ask, unable to keep a hint of irritation from my voice. My memory flashes back to what Cassandra told me in the yoga studio about his "weird assistant."

"She's relentless," he admits, picking up the phone. "Give me one second. I promise this is the last time."

As he types a quick response, I watch his face in the candlelight. Even distracted, he's handsome in a way that makes my stomach flutter. When he puts the phone down, he reaches for my hand again.

"Where were we?"

The dessert arrives, saving me from having to answer. We share the soufflé, our spoons occasionally meeting in the center of the plate. It's a cliché moment from a romantic comedy, but I find myself smiling anyway.

Corbin's phone buzzes twice more before we finish. Each time, he checks it quickly, offers a brief apology, and returns his attention to me. Each interruption grates a little more, but I don't say anything. This must be part of his life now—the constant demands of fame, the people who need pieces of him. I tell myself I shouldn't be annoyed. This is what success looks like, right?

After dinner, Corbin insists on driving me home. The night is clear, stars visible even through the city's light pollution. In his car—an expensive European model with butter-soft leather seats—we sit in comfortable silence, the radio playing soothingly in the background.

"I had a really good time tonight," he says as we pull up to my house.

"Me too," I admit. "It was so nice to talk to someone who gets it."

After parking in front of my house, he jumps out of his seat and charges around to open my door. He walks me to my front porch, his hand resting lightly on the small of my back. The contact feels both foreign and familiar, like returning to a place you've only visited in dreams.

At my doorstep, we pause. The porch light casts shadows across his face, highlighting the angles of his cheekbones. For a moment, we just look at each other, the air between us charged with possibility.

Then Corbin leans in and kisses me. His lips are soft, the pressure gentle and questioning. My eyes close automatically, and I find myself responding, my hand coming up to rest against his chest. The kiss deepens, and for a few seconds, the world narrows to this moment and this moment alone.

When we break apart, I feel dazed, my heart racing in a way it hasn't in over a year.

"Goodnight, Riley," Corbin says, his voice husky. "I'll call you tomorrow."

I watch him walk back to his car, my fingers absently touching my lips. Once inside, I lean against the closed door, trying to process what just happened.

I barely have a moment to consider what it might mean, when my phone starts dinging with a series of text notifications in quick succession. Expecting a goodnight message from Corbin, I pull it from my purse.

Instead, it's Grace.

We need to talk. It's urgent.

Seriously, Riley. ASAP.

I'm not kidding. It's about Corbin.

There's something you need to know. Can I come over?

> I just got home. Can it wait until morning?

I don't think so.

> Okay, I guess. Come on over then.

The warm glow of the evening evaporates, replaced by a cold trickle of unease. What could Grace possibly need to tell me about Corbin that can't wait until morning?

CHAPTER NINE

I've barely had a chance to set down my purse when there's a knock at my door. Three sharp raps that echo through my empty house. I check the peephole to find Grace standing on my porch, arms wrapped around her body despite the mild evening. Her face is drawn, serious in a way that doesn't suit her normally cheerful demeanor.

"That was fast," I say, opening the door. "Shouldn't you be on your own date?"

"It was a bust," she says, brushing past me into the house. Even though she's wearing sweats, I can smell her telltale floral perfume still lingering from her date. "Besides, I figured you'd be home by now."

"Just got in," I confirm, closing the door behind her. I'm still wearing my burgundy dress from dinner, my lips still tingling from Corbin's kiss.

She heads straight for my kitchen, a path she knows by heart after countless wine nights and impromptu therapy sessions. I follow, kicking off my heels at the base of the stairs. The hardwood floor is cool against my bare feet.

"Wine?" I offer, more out of habit than anything else.

"God, yes," she says, sinking into a chair at my kitchen table. "Make it a big one."

I pull a bottle from the refrigerator—a chardonnay I've been saving for no particular occasion—and pour us each a generous glass. The kitchen is illuminated only by the light above the stove, casting everything in a hazy, amber glow. I set Grace's glass in front of her, noticing how she immediately wraps her fingers around the stem, twisting it nervously.

"So," I say, taking the seat across from her, "what's so urgent that it couldn't wait until morning?"

Grace takes a large sip of her wine, then sets the glass down carefully. "How was your date with Corbin?"

The question takes me a little aback. "Fine. Good, actually. But I'm guessing that's not why you're here at—" I glance at the microwave clock "—eleven thirty on a Friday night."

She looks down at her glass, then back up at me, her blue eyes troubled. "Riley, what do you know about what happened to Meredith Chin at Mesa Verde?"

The question sends a chill through me. *Mesa Verde.* The name alone conjures images from news reports, social media posts, gossip-filled whispers. It stands as a haunting monument to an ancient civilization; a sprawling complex of prehistoric cliff dwellings carved into the arid canyons of southwestern Colorado.

It's the place where Meredith fell to her death.

"Not much beyond what was in the news," I admit. "I know she was there researching her next book. There was an accident..."

Grace nods, taking another sip of wine. "An accident,

right at the height of her career. Right when things started to fall into place for her, right when she had a bestselling book."

I remember the book well. It had taken the academic world by storm, then crossed over into mainstream success in a way archaeological texts rarely do. Corbin had leveraged his substantial online following to promote it, featuring it in videos, mentioning it in interviews. The book had shot up the charts, eventually landing on the *New York Times* bestseller list for several weeks.

Where is Grace going with this?

"She even got on a few talk shows," I recall. "I remember seeing her on *Good Morning America*."

"A rising star," Grace agrees. "She was everywhere for a while—magazines, podcasts, speaking engagements. I looked her up after we saw Corbin at the conference."

Of course, I know all of this because I followed her too. It was hard to watch, given my fiancé was going through chemo at the time. I couldn't help but feel a little jealous of them. Now, looking back, I feel a bit guilty about it, given she died just a few months later. It is funny how life can change on a dime.

I take a long sip of my wine, still unsure where this is headed. "Grace, what is this about?"

She sets her glass down and leans forward, her expression deadly serious. "I found out something today. From a friend who works with the National Park Service."

The air in the kitchen suddenly feels too thick. "What?"

"Corbin was investigated after the accident. The police wanted to make sure it was an accident, not a murder."

The words hang suspended between us. I stare at her, waiting for the punchline, but her face remains grave.

"That's ridiculous," I finally say. "It was a tragic accident. They were camping near the cliff. She was sleepwalking. Something I know for a fact she was prone to. Even in college. She walked too close to the cliff's edge. Then she ... fell."

"Did you know they were arguing that morning?" Grace counters. "Multiple witnesses who were questioned at the visitor center heard them having a heated discussion at the cliff dwellings."

I shake my head, unable to accept what she's suggesting. "Couples argue, Grace. That doesn't mean—"

"They were the only two people in that section of the park when it happened, not to mention it was at night," she continues. "No witnesses. Just Corbin's statement that he was sleeping when she left the tent. And when he woke up, she was gone."

A memory surfaces—Corbin's face at the conference when someone asked how he was coping with Meredith's death. That flash of raw pain in his eyes. That wasn't the face of a murderer. It was the face of a man shattered by loss, just like I was.

"What are you saying? That he pushed her?" I roll my eyes dramatically. "That's insane, Grace."

"I'm not saying that. I'm just telling you what I learned. The investigation cleared him—there wasn't enough evidence to suggest foul play. The angle at which she fell ... well, she *could* have been pushed. And I also heard his cell phone was powered down the whole night, almost like he didn't want his whereabouts tracked—"

"Or," I interrupt, giving her a hard look, "he could have turned it off so he could go to sleep."

"Well, there were questions, Riley. Serious ones."

I stand up abruptly. My chair scrapes against the tile

floor, the sound harsh in the quiet kitchen. "There's no way he could have hurt Meredith. They were madly in love; I saw it with my own eyes. Meredith painted him as a saint. And when I met him, he seemed genuine and kind."

"People can hide who they are, Riley," she says gently. "No one's a saint, for starters. And you don't know what their relationship was really like."

I pace the kitchen, my mind racing. The Corbin I know—the one who kissed me goodnight with such tenderness less than an hour ago—couldn't be capable of such a thing. The thought is absurd, offensive even.

"Why are you telling me this?" I demand, turning to face her. "Are you jealous?"

Grace looks hurt by the accusation. "Jealous? No, I'm not jealous. It's just that I care about you, and I'm worried. You've been through so much with losing Brody. I don't want to see you get hurt again. I think you should be careful, that's all."

I see the earnest look of concern on her face. My anger deflates, replaced by a churn of guilt. It's just that she's killing that small glimmer of hope I felt after my date with Corbin. I sink back into my chair and rub my temples.

"Sorry, Grace, I shouldn't have said that. But trust me, Corbin is not a killer."

Grace continues, undeterred. "Look, I'm not saying don't see him. I'm just saying ... be aware. Ask questions. Don't rush into anything."

I nod, not trusting myself to speak. My phone chimes with a notification, and I glance down to see a message from Corbin:

> Had an amazing time tonight. Dinner at my place tomorrow? I'll cook.

Despite everything Grace has just told me, I feel a flutter of excitement at his words. I set the phone on the table and look at Grace. Her eyes are wide, staring at me expectantly.

She's always had a love of drama—whether it's the latest *Housewives* series or office gossip, Grace keeps her finger on the pulse of everything that's happening around her, and she's eager to share every detail. She's also told me countless times how very much she loves murder documentaries.

Getting carried away isn't unlike her.

"You just watch too much crime TV. Not every death is a murder," I say, looking directly at her.

She sighs, resigned. "You might be right. Just promise me you'll be careful, okay? That's all I'm asking."

"I promise," I say, though I'm not sure what being careful even means in this situation. How do you cautiously date someone you've just been told might have murdered his fiancée?

"Now, tell me about this date of yours that got cut short. I need details ..."

Grace spends the next thirty minutes regaling me with the tale of her horrible date with the guy from the car wash, causing me to laugh so hard I'm in tears. After she leaves, I stand in my kitchen for a long time, staring at my phone.

The death at Mesa Verde was ruled an accident. The police carried out their investigation, and given that knowledge, and the time I've spent with Corbin, I have no reason to think otherwise. Still, Grace has planted a small, insidious seed of doubt in my head.

I stare at Corbin's message. Part of me hesitates. Maybe I

should keep my distance until I know more. But another part—the part that felt alive again for the first time in a year when Corbin kissed me—wants to believe in his innocence, in the connection we shared.

I pick up the phone and type a response:

> Dinner sounds perfect. What time?

CHAPTER TEN

It was a thirty-minute drive to Corbin's place, which gave me plenty of time to grow increasingly nervous about our date. While I live in a quaint little house in the suburbs of Phoenix, he lives nestled among the high-rises of the downtown area; his condo appears to be in a newer collection of upscale buildings. Once I arrive, I carefully park in one of the open spots near the main entrance of his building.

And for at least ten minutes, I just sit there.

Our last date went so incredibly well that I should be excited, riding the high of finally moving beyond my grief. Instead, I'm sequestered in my car, questioning whether the man who made me feel alive for the first time in a year might be capable of murder.

This is ridiculous, I tell myself, gripping the steering wheel tighter than necessary even though I've finished navigating the downtown traffic. *Grace watches too much crime TV. She sees conspiracy where there's only tragedy.* But even as I think it, I can't shake the image of Meredith at that conference—radiant, successful, so full of life. And now she's gone, fallen from a cliff in the middle of the night with only Corbin as a witness.

Regardless, I'm here, and if I sit in my car any longer, people are going to start wondering what I'm doing. I open the door and step outside. The building's glass and steel structure gleams in the early evening light, reflecting the sunset in shades of orange and pink that make the building itself seem to glow. I press Corbin's number on the panel, and after a brief moment, his voice comes through—slightly distorted but unmistakably warm: "Riley? Come on up." The door buzzes, and I push through into a marble-floored lobby with modern art installations and soft, recessed lighting, much fancier than anything I'm used to.

Once I step into the elevator, I realize he's on the top floor. Given his success, it's probably some type of penthouse situation. The elevator is mirrored, allowing me a final chance to check my appearance—my hair falling in loose waves, my makeup subtle but flattering. Despite my barely contained anxiety, I look more like my normal self than I have for far too long. I take several deep breaths and let them out slowly.

When I finally reach the top floor, the elevator doors open directly into Corbin's condo. He's standing there waiting, dressed in dark jeans and a charcoal button-down shirt with the sleeves rolled up to reveal his forearms. The subtle scent of his cologne—woody and expensive—mingles with the aroma of garlic and herbs coming from his kitchen.

"Hey," he says, a smile crinkling the corners of his eyes. "You look great."

I grip the bottle of wine in my hands, pressing it against my new dress like a shield. I was out of outfits that didn't remind me of Brody, so I actually went shopping for once, for the first time in a year. The dress I chose is casual but hugs in all the right places—something that I see Corbin is taking in with an appreciative glance.

"I brought a bottle of wine for you," I say, finally pulling it away from my body.

He takes it from me, his fingers brushing mine, and says, "Come on in."

Corbin's apartment is open, spacious, and artfully decorated. The walls are a mixture of navy and deep green with dark trim and adorned with a collection of art that I am naturally envious of. Floor-to-ceiling windows offer a panoramic view of downtown Phoenix. It's clear that Corbin has traveled the world—everything from African masks to Mexican textiles are displayed around the walls, each piece lit by carefully positioned accent lighting.

"Wow," I say, walking in behind him, padding down the polished hardwood floor of the hallway. "This place is really ..." My words trail off as I spot something that makes my breath catch in my throat.

There, on a floating shelf near the kitchen, is a framed photograph. Corbin and Meredith, both grinning at the camera, mountain peaks rising behind them. They're wearing hiking gear, their faces flushed and happy, arms wrapped around each other. Meredith's dark hair is pulled back in a messy ponytail, and she's wearing that bright smile I remember so well from college.

The image hits me like a ton of bricks. Suddenly, I can almost feel Meredith's presence in the room, as if she's watching me from that frozen moment of happiness.

"... really cool," I finish weakly, forcing myself to look away from the photo.

"Thanks," Corbin says, apparently not noticing my reaction as he sets the bottle down on the kitchen countertop. "But I can't take any of the credit. I hired an interior designer when I moved in here, and she put everything together for me."

"Even the stela from Mexico?" I run my hands across a large stone slab that's hanging on the wall, trying to avoid another glance at Meredith's photo. The stone is cool to the touch, its surface worn smooth in places by countless hands over centuries.

"No, that was all me. It's a replica of the stela of Pakal the Great. Have you been to Chiapas or any of the sites in Mexico?"

"No, I haven't. But I'd love to see them. You know, I'm more of an Egyptian girl."

"Of course," he says with a smile, uncorking the wine with practiced ease. The gentle pop echoes in the high-ceilinged space.

I settle in at his kitchen island, which has a large slab of granite and a sink in the middle, but I can't shake the feeling that Meredith is still watching me from that photograph. Every time I glance in that direction, a chill makes me shiver. What happened to her on that cliff? Was it really just an accident, or …?

Stop it, Riley; you're being paranoid.

I try to focus on the present moment. Everything here is new, polished, clean, and most likely expensive. The appliances gleam under the pendant lights hanging from above, not a single watermark or stain to be seen. Clearly, the YouTube channel has been paying Corbin well.

"So, what's for dinner?" I ask. "It smells amazing." The aroma of garlic, basil, and simmering tomatoes fills the air, making my stomach rumble quietly.

"Pasta," he says, stirring something on the stove as it bubbles invitingly. "It's a recipe that my grandmother showed me how to make when I was a kid."

"Wow, I'm honored," I say, accepting the glass of ruby-red wine he offers me. "So, you made the pasta from scratch?"

He laughs, and the sound is genuine and relaxed. "No. I'm good, but not that good. There's a local market nearby that sells the most amazing fresh pasta." He takes a sip of his own wine, closing his eyes briefly to savor it.

"What do you think of the wine?" I ask, hoping that the liquor store clerk knew what he was talking about when he recommended it to me.

"It's delicious," he says without hesitation.

The two of us continue chatting as Corbin moves effortlessly around his kitchen, draining pasta, tossing in sauce, garnishing with fresh herbs from a small pot on the windowsill. He tells me about some of the places he's visited in Italy, and I share some of my own travel stories, though I find myself stealing glances at that photograph whenever I think he's not looking.

I want to ask him about Meredith. I want to ask about the accident, about what really happened that night. But how do you bring up your date's dead girlfriend, who also just happened to be your friend? *Hey, Corbin, Grace thinks you might have murdered Meredith—care to comment?*

The thought is so inappropriate, it makes my cheeks burn with shame. I take another sip of wine, hoping it will wash away the terrible words forming in my mind.

"So both your parents were professors too?" I ask, swirling the wine in my glass.

Corbin nods, adding another pinch of fresh herbs to the

sauce. "Dad taught engineering at Arizona State. Mom was in anthropology at the University of New Mexico. Made for some interesting dinner conversations."

"We have that in common, then. My parents were always bringing their work home too. Dad with his old texts and Mom with her pottery fragments spread across the dining table."

"They're still teaching?" he asks.

I feel that familiar hollow ache in my chest. "No, they ... they passed away. Car accident, about eight years ago."

Corbin's face softens. "I'm sorry, Riley. I didn't know."

"It's okay," I say, forcing a smile. "What about yours?"

"Dad's still around. Retired now, but constantly sending me articles about LiDAR applications he thinks I should cover." Corbin chuckles; then his voice softens. "Mom passed when I was in high school. Cancer."

"I'm sorry," I say, recognizing the familiar shadow that crosses his face.

"You know what helped?" Corbin says, his expression brightening. "My grandmother in Italy. Spent a summer with her after Mom died. That woman could make the most incredible pasta sauce you've ever tasted." He gestures dramatically with a wooden spoon. "She'd wake up at five in the morning just to start the sauce. Said the secret was letting it simmer all day."

I laugh, grateful for the shift in mood. "Is that what you're doing here?"

"Trying my best." He grins. "Though Nonna would probably say I'm doing it all wrong."

Corbin picks up two plates of pasta, and I follow him as we walk into the dining room, which he has set with candles, fine china, crystal glasses—the whole nine yards. The table sits before these enormous windows, the city spread out below us like a tapestry of lights.

It's hard to compare anyone to Brody, given that he was the love of my life, but let's face it, I did most of the cooking in our relationship. Having someone create a dinner for me from scratch is refreshing. In fact, having someone cook a meal for me at all is something I haven't experienced in years, other than, of course, eating out at various restaurants. I can't deny that it's incredibly intoxicating to be with a man who cooks.

We settle into our seats, the candles casting a warm, flickering glow across the table. The lights of the city below provide a spectacular backdrop, and for the first time tonight, I'm not thinking about Meredith or Grace's warnings or Corbin's ex-girlfriends.

"Oh my gosh," I say, after swallowing my first bite of pasta, "this is amazing. What's in it?"

Corbin smiles, a hint of mystery in his eyes. "A secret ingredient I can't tell you about."

"Ah, so you're a man who keeps secrets," I say, raising an eyebrow playfully, though the words feel heavier than I intended. He laughs, but there's something in his expression that shifts—just for a moment—before the easy smile returns.

"Only the good kind of secrets. The kind that makes dinner taste better."

"Mmm-hmm," I say, smiling as I twirl more pasta around my fork.

His phone buzzes in the other room—the familiar chime-ding-chime noise that I've come to associate with interruptions. Corbin's eyes dart to the kitchen as the phone rumbles against the counter.

"Sorry, let me just turn off my phone," he murmurs as he gets up from the table. "It's probably just my assistant—"

"Kelly?" I ask, trying to keep the annoyance from my voice. He glances back at me as he crosses the room, and I can see the pink in his cheeks. He nods.

"I'll be right back."

I take another sip of wine, the familiar sense of aggravation returning—turns out we're not completely alone after all. What is up with this assistant? Why is she always messaging him day and night? I mean, I know he's busy but come on.

As I sit and wait for him, I can't help but wonder, just how many secrets does Corbin keep?

CHAPTER ELEVEN

"I turned my phone off, so it's just you and me for the rest of the night, okay?"

Corbin re-enters the room just as I take another bite, savoring the perfect al dente texture of the pasta. *Finally*, I think, *Kelly can take a break from interrupting our dates.*

I have no idea who this woman is, but the way she seems to have an urgent message for Corbin all day and night makes me wonder if something else is going on. Is she some recent college grad, like the girl from the restaurant the other night, who is shamelessly crushing on her boss? Or some kind of crazy stalker like Cassandra, that girl I ran into after yoga class?

I certainly don't want to come across as a jealous girlfriend, so I keep all these thoughts to myself. At the very least, he's turned off his phone to focus on me, a gesture that gives me a crumb of comfort.

"Thank you," I say quietly. We eat for a few moments in comfortable silence before I turn the topic to his work. "You know, I watched that video you did about the location of Atlantis."

Corbin looks up, a hint of surprise in his eyes. "You did? I didn't realize you'd seen my content."

"Well, after Denver, I was curious," I admit. "That theory about the Richat Structure being the possible location of Atlantis was brilliant. How did you ever make that connection? It seems so obvious now, but nobody had put it together before."

Corbin shrugs, but I can see he's pleased. "Honestly? I was going down a rabbit hole about the earliest trade routes in North Africa for a video. Then I came across this satellite image of the Richat Structure and thought, 'Huh, that looks familiar.' I started digging deeper and realized the measurements were almost identical to what Plato described."

"That's it?" I lean back in my chair. "You just ... noticed?"

He laughs. "I know it sounds simple. But sometimes the best discoveries are hiding in plain sight, you know? Everyone's so focused on looking underwater for Atlantis that they miss what's right there on land."

I study his face, impressed despite myself. "You have a good eye for patterns. That's not common."

"Maybe," he says, looking almost embarrassed. "Sometimes they lead somewhere interesting. Sometimes they don't." He takes a quick sip of wine. "But enough about my weird brain—how's the pasta?"

I don't press further, but I know Corbin is being modest. His perspective on lost cities has breathed fresh air into the study of ancient history. Before the advent of his channel, only nerdy professors like me and my colleagues worried about the lost city of Atlantis and the implications of the technologies those peoples possessed. Now, thousands of people are talking about it.

Dinner turns into dessert—a delicate tiramisu that Corbin admits he bought at the same bakery where he got the pasta—and I realize we're nearly three glasses of wine in. I have to catch myself, be careful about how much I drink because I don't want to get into a situation where I've had too much. I help him take the dirty plates to the kitchen, and then the two of us end up on the couch, sitting close enough that I can feel the warmth radiating from him.

"I had such a great time at dinner the other night," he says, facing me, "but sometimes when I'm out in public, I get nervous—maybe I even feel guilty when people see me with someone else. Like people are judging me for moving on. But sitting here with you ... it just feels so good to be, I don't know, together."

I nod, staring into my wineglass. "I agree."

"Another one?" he says, his voice low and intimate in the dimly lit room. His eyes reflect the city lights beyond, dark and shining.

"No, not for me. I think I'm feeling pretty good right now." The room has a slight, pleasant spin to it, and I know I'm at my limit.

He pours himself another glass, then settles back onto the couch next to me, his thigh pressing against mine. "You know, I have a secret."

The way he says it catches me off guard. It's almost unsettling, and for a brief moment, Grace's warnings flash through my mind.

"I had a little bit of a crush on you when we met in Denver," he says, his voice softening.

"Really?" The admission surprises me. I think back to

our emails, the months of exchanges before I stopped responding. I chew on my bottom lip, debating what to say next.

"Yes," he continues. "You were so confident and sure of yourself. And funny."

I chuckle. "I don't know if I've ever been called funny."

"Then no one has fully appreciated how great you are," he says.

A blush creeps up my cheeks, and I have to look away for a moment.

"Anyway," he continues, "I'm glad you're here now."

"Me too," I say, building up the nerve to look back at him.

Corbin leans in to kiss me. It feels so good, like water filling up an empty expanse of dry sand. His lips are soft but insistent against mine, his hands warm as they trace the curve of my waist. I can tell he's into it too, his breath quickening, matching my own. I don't know if it was the talk of grief or the wine, but suddenly our glasses are sitting forgotten on the coffee table, and the two of us have our hands all over each other.

Suddenly, I feel the urge to pull his shirt off, my fingers fumbling with the buttons.

Corbin pulls back for a moment and looks at me, his eyes questioning. "Are you sure?"

"Yes," I say, the word barely more than a whisper in the stillness of the room.

The two of us slowly undress each other, the rustle of fabric and our quickened breaths the only sounds. My bra comes undone, and Corbin lays me down on the couch, his body pressing against mine.

Maybe it's too soon, or maybe it's grief making me

hungry for human touch, but I give in to the moment, finding in Corbin's body a brief respite from the loneliness that has defined my life for too long.

THE NEXT MORNING, I wake up in an unfamiliar bed, sunlight streaming through the pale floor-to-ceiling curtains. I can tell I had a few glasses of wine last night, but the hangover is minimal—just a hint of dryness in my mouth and a dull throb behind my eyes. The sheets are crisp and expensive against my bare skin, the mattress firm but comfortable.

It takes me a few moments to realize that I am in Corbin's bed. I bite my lip, thinking over the night before. It was tender, passionate, healing in a way I hadn't expected. I guess I probably should have waited longer to sleep with him, but I just couldn't help myself. He couldn't help himself either, he told me after. And I think we both understood what it meant to be with someone after you've lost somebody.

I find a note on the bedside table, written—curiously—on a hotel notepad. The same one in Cairo that I had stayed at many times during my visits there. That little detail strikes me and reminds me of how much the two of us have in common. The note reads:

> *Good morning, beautiful. Had to leave for a meeting. Will call you later. Last night was amazing. XO, Corbin.*

I grab the note and carry it with me as I pull my clothes

off the floor and get dressed. The morning light is unforgiving, but I do my best to smooth my rumpled dress and finger-comb my hair. It feels a little strange to be in his apartment without him here, so I sort of hurry through getting dressed and head out the door.

Unlike Corbin, I don't have any meetings. All I have is an overdue book waiting for me to write it.

Still, the night was, as he wrote, amazing.

What does this mean? What is happening between us?

It's so unexpected and refreshing at the same time. I think about it the whole cab ride home, watching the downtown buildings give way to suburban streets, reliving moments from the night before.

When I arrive at my house, I see a car in the driveway, a car that I instantly recognize. A silver Lexus. All the joy from the night before evaporates.

Because I know who's waiting for me inside.

CHAPTER TWELVE

I stand on my own front porch for several long seconds, keys clutched in my hand, staring at the silver Lexus in my driveway. My body still carries the pleasant ache of last night's intimacy with Corbin, but now a different kind of tension spreads through my shoulders and neck.

Brody's mother, Miranda, has an uncanny ability to show up at the most inconvenient times. Today, with my hair disheveled and wearing yesterday's clothes, ranks high on that list.

I take a deep breath and unlock the door. The familiar scent of my home—old books, faint traces of the jasmine candle I occasionally remember to light—is now layered with the aroma of fresh coffee. Miranda must have made herself at home, as usual.

"Riley?" her voice calls from the kitchen. "Is that you?"

"Yes, it's me," I reply, setting my purse down on the entry table. I catch a glimpse of myself in the mirror hanging above it—my makeup smudged, my hair a mess, the collar of my dress askew. I make a futile attempt to smooth my appearance before heading toward the kitchen.

Miranda sits at my kitchen table, a mug of coffee cradled between her slender hands. At fifty-eight, she still looks remarkably youthful—her blonde hair artfully highlighted to hide the gray, her skin smooth and tanned from weekends on the golf course. She's wearing one of her typical outfits: crisp white linen pants and a navy blouse.

"I used the spare key," she says, answering the question I haven't asked. Her eyes scan my appearance, taking in every detail with the precision of a security camera. "I've been calling you since yesterday evening."

I pull my phone from my purse and see five missed calls. I'd silenced it before my date with Corbin and never thought to check it afterward.

"Sorry about that," I say, heading for the coffee pot. I need caffeine to face whatever intervention Miranda has planned. "I was out."

"So I gathered." There's no judgment in her voice, just observation. That's Miranda's way—she doesn't need to criticize outright when a carefully placed observation will do the work for her.

I pour myself a cup of coffee, the hot liquid scalding my tongue as I take a hasty sip. "What brings you by, Miranda?"

"You missed our lunch on Tuesday," she says. "When you didn't call to reschedule, I got worried."

Lunch. It comes back to me now—a standing monthly commitment I made to Miranda after Brody died. A promise I've kept faithfully until now. Guilt washes over me.

"I'm so sorry," I say, sinking into the chair across from her. "I completely forgot."

"That's been happening a lot lately, hasn't it? The forgetting?"

I stare down at my coffee, watching the steam rise in lazy spirals. She's not wrong. There have been gaps in my memory over the past year—nights when I drank too much and lost hours, sometimes entire evenings. Days that blurred together in a haze of grief and wine.

"I've been better lately," I say, but the words sound hollow even to my own ears.

"Have you?" Miranda sets her mug down with a gentle click against the wooden table. "Riley, I care about you. Brody loved you, which means you're still family to me. That's why I worry."

I feel a tightness in my throat at the mention of Brody's name. Even after a year, hearing it spoken aloud—especially by his mother, who shares his blue eyes and easy smile—feels like pressing down hard on a bruise.

"I'm fine," I insist. It's my standard response, my shield against concern.

"Are you still drinking?" she asks directly.

The question hangs in the air between us. I consider lying, but Miranda has always had an uncanny ability to see through my deceptions.

"Yes," I admit. "But not as much as before."

"And the therapy?" she presses. "Have you gone back?"

"No." I wrap my hands around my coffee mug. "I told you, it wasn't helping."

Miranda sighs, a sound so reminiscent of Brody that my heart clenches. "Three sessions isn't exactly giving it a chance, Riley. Dr. Patel is one of the best grief counselors in Phoenix. She could help you process everything—the loss, the memory issues, the drinking."

"I don't need help processing," I say, an edge creeping into my voice. "I need time."

"It's been over a year," Miranda says gently.

"Grief doesn't have a timeline." The words come out sharper than I intended.

Miranda reaches across the table and places her hand over mine. Her skin is cool and dry, her manicure immaculate. "I know that, honey. Better than most."

The reminder of her own losses—her only son and her husband, who died of a heart attack six years ago—deflates my defensiveness. We sit in silence for a moment, connected by our shared grief for the man we both loved.

"We need to talk about the book, Riley. My boss has been breathing down my neck, wanting answers. How are things coming?"

Did I mention Miranda also happens to be my book agent?

It's how Brody and I met. Miranda introduced us, her son reluctant to go on a date his mom set up, but we clicked, and the rest is history. I chew on my lip so hard it tears away a piece of dried skin. Miranda studies me over the rim of her coffee mug.

"Great, actually. I've been more focused than I have been in a long time. I have—"

"How many pages?" Miranda interrupts, her voice cutting straight through my rambling attempt at optimism.

I take a long sip, buying time. "About a hundred."

The silence stretches between us like a taut wire. Miranda sets down her mug with a deliberate clink against the saucer.

"A hundred pages," she repeats slowly. "Riley, you took a

ten-thousand-dollar check a year ago. The entire manuscript was due three months ago."

"I know, I know. But, Miranda, you have to understand—"

"What I understand," she says, leaning forward with that look I remember from Brody's childhood stories, the one that meant he was in serious trouble, "is that the publisher is questioning whether you can deliver. They're talking about asking for the advance back."

My stomach drops. *Ten thousand dollars*. Money I've already spent.

"Can they do that?" I say, though even as the words leave my mouth, I know they can.

"They absolutely can. And they will unless you give me something concrete. A timeline. A plan. Something I can take back to them that shows you're serious about finishing this book."

I stare down at my coffee, watching the foam dissolve into pale brown swirls. "I've been struggling, Miranda. You know that. After Brody ..."

Her expression softens slightly, but her voice remains firm. "I know. And I've given you every extension I could."

I toy with the handle of my mug, not sure what to say. Miranda sighs. "But I'm happy to hear you've been making more progress. I'll do what I can. So, what inspired you to start writing again?"

"I had a date," I say finally, the confession spilling out unexpectedly.

Miranda's eyebrows rise, surprise evident in her expression. "Oh?"

"With an old friend. His name is Corbin." I don't mention that I spent the night at his apartment, though I suspect Miranda has already deduced as much from my rumpled appearance.

"That's ..." She pauses, searching for the right word. "That's good, Riley. A step forward."

But I can see the conflict in her eyes—relief that I'm engaging with the world again, mingled with something like betrayal, as if my moving on somehow diminishes her son's memory.

"It was just dinner," I lie, downplaying it for both our sakes. "Nothing serious."

Miranda nods, withdrawing her hand from mine. "Well, I'm glad to hear you're getting out." She stands abruptly, smoothing her already perfect pants. "I don't need to stay, after all. I just came to check on you. And that manuscript of yours."

I rise to my feet as well, surprised by her sudden departure. "You don't have to go. We could have lunch now instead."

"No, no," she says, gathering her purse and car keys from the counter. "I have a meeting this afternoon. I really should get going."

I walk her to the door, a strange mix of relief and abandonment churning in my stomach. At the threshold, she turns and embraces me, her slender arms stronger than they appear.

"Call me if you need anything," she says against my hair. "Promise me, Riley. Anything at all."

"I do," I say, the lie easy after a year of practice. "And I'm on it with the book, I promise."

I watch from the doorway as she walks to her car. She raises a hand in farewell before sliding into the driver's seat. As the Lexus backs out of my driveway, I feel the familiar emptiness spreading through my chest. Seeing the hurt in Miranda's eyes when I told her about my date ... it felt almost like losing Brody all over again. I know we'll always have a special bond over her son, but I can't be her surrogate daughter-in-law forever. It feels like another door to my past with Brody is starting to close.

And then it all comes barreling down on me. The memories of life before the cancer. How Brody proposed to me on a hike near Camelback Mountain. The ivory and lace wedding dress that still hangs in my closet. Trying to cope with the memories, the pain and the loss leaves me nearly breathless. I drag myself toward the bathroom, turning on the shower and letting it warm up until it's steaming hot. The water nearly singes my skin as I step inside.

I stand there for nearly thirty minutes. Sobbing.

Once I'm finished, I walk back into the kitchen, pick up my now cold coffee and pour it down the sink. I open the pantry, my eyes immediately finding the bottle of merlot I bought last week.

It's barely noon, but Miranda's visit has left me raw, exposed. The weight of Brody's absence, the complicated guilt of my night with Corbin, the gaps in my memory that terrify me when I allow myself to think about them, the unwritten and overdue book—it's all too much.

I take the bottle from the shelf and pour a generous glass. The wine is cool and sweet, sliding seductively down my throat. I tell myself it's just one glass, just to take the edge off.

But one glass becomes two, becomes three. I carry the bottle to the couch, where I curl up beneath the throw blanket that still smells faintly of Brody's cologne. The television plays in the background—some documentary about prehistoric Egypt that I've seen before—but I'm not really watching.

Instead, I'm thinking about Corbin's hands on my skin, about the way Brody used to kiss my forehead before leaving for work, about the worried crease between Miranda's eyebrows as she asked about my drinking. The thoughts swirl together, becoming muddled and indistinct as the bottle empties itself into my glass.

At some point, I reach for my phone, and there's a message from Corbin:

> Last night was incredible. When can I see you again?

I start to type a response, but the words blur on the screen. I'll answer tomorrow, I decide, when I'm more coherent.

The late afternoon sun slants through my living room windows, casting long shadows across the floor. I should eat something, I think distantly. I should call Miranda and apologize for missing our lunch. I should work on my book.

Instead, I pour the last of the wine into my glass and close my eyes. The familiar numbness spreads through my limbs, promising relief from the pain that follows me like a shadow.

CHAPTER THIRTEEN

When I finally wake up and fully face the hangover, I'm not even sure what day it is.

I'm lying on my couch with several empty wine bottles scattered on the coffee table, their labels peeling at the edges, alongside greasy boxes of takeout pizza. The sour smell of stale alcohol and congealed cheese permeates the air. I realize I'm wearing an old ASU hoodie that was Brody's—the fabric soft from years of wear, the once-bright maroon now faded.

Most of his clothes I donated after he was gone, but there were a few pieces I couldn't bear to part with.

I look down at the hoodie, which is covered with dribbles of dried tomato sauce and dark splotches of wine. The fabric reeks of alcohol and day-old sweat. I am positively disgusted with myself. I know that grief like this keeps to no schedule, but it's been a year, and let's face it, it's probably time to get my shit together.

I glance over at my phone, which is lying on the kitchen countertop. I sit up, intent on checking for any messages. Just the thought sends a stab of fear through my chest. *Did I message Corbin while I was drunk? Who else could I have reached out to and embarrassed myself with?* The list is short, but the thought is painful enough.

When I stand up, it hits me—a throbbing headache and a twisted, empty feeling in my stomach that nearly makes me throw up right then and there. I stumble toward the kitchen, feeling a little woozy, getting my bearings. The room spins slightly before settling into place. I have a case of Gatorade in the fridge, and I make my way in that direction, my bare feet sticking tackily to the hardwood floor.

And then the wave of nausea really hits me. I end up throwing up in the sink, the bitter taste of wine and bile burning my throat. Even though no one's here to see it happen, I feel an utter sense of humiliation.

After the nausea passes, I pull open a Gatorade and chug it, then another, feeling the cold, sweet liquid slide down my raw throat. Cold sweats come and go, making my skin prickle with goosebumps one minute and flush with heat the next. I sit down at the kitchen island, my body shaking, and flip over my phone. It's on the charger, but the power is off. I don't know when I turned it off, but hopefully it was before I sent any messages that I might regret.

When the phone comes on, the bright screen making me squint, I see the date. *It's been two days*—two days since Miranda's visit sent me into a spiral.

I am so ashamed of myself.

I open up the messages and see that three people have contacted me. First, Miranda, letting me know she talked to the publisher and she's optimistic. Asking how I'm doing. I message her back right away.

> Doing great. Just been busy the last couple of days. Pages are coming. Thanks for reaching out. It was good to see you.

All lies. I hit send anyway.

Next, Grace. She only sent one message. I remember her saying something last week about covering for one of the partners in her office, that she'd be busy this week. Thankfully, she didn't catch me in the middle of a bender. She would be worried sick if she knew how I was feeling. I shoot her a message back.

> All good, let's get together soon.

Another lie, but I hit send anyway.

Messaging both of them makes me feel marginally better, even though I'm lying through my teeth. I finally land on the messages from Corbin. First, I reread the one he sent the other day, the night after our date at his apartment. Then another.

> Haven't heard from you. Hope the other night didn't scare you away.

I feel an intense sense of guilt that I left him hanging. I know how hard it was for him to put himself out there, and I wonder if I'm the first person he's been with since Meredith died. I doubt he and Cassie ever got that far. My fingers hover over the phone, knowing I should message him back, but I just can't do it.

I can't lie to him.

Then the reality of my situation sinks in. *How can I let anyone into my life right now?* I mean, look at me—I'm covered in stale food and stink of alcohol. I don't even remember what I did yesterday, although there are some foggy memories of binging movies on my couch. But other than that, it's a blur.

Last week, after a couple of dates with Corbin, I thought maybe I was ready. Maybe I could get my life together enough to start moving on. And Corbin, of course, understands how hard it has been for me.

But while he seems to have pulled his life together and landed on his feet, I, on the other hand, can't seem to rejoin the living. So, even though I know I should probably message him back, I just can't do it. I turn my phone back off and let myself sit there for a few more minutes before I begin the process of cleaning up my own mess. I'm far from a neat freak, but the sight of the empty pizza boxes and wine bottles —all of it is almost unbearable.

I spend the next hour or so cleaning up around the house, collecting bottles that clink together as I drop them into the recycling bin, wiping down surfaces sticky with spilled wine, then finally making my sorry way into the bathroom. I turn on the shower, the steam quickly fogging up the mirror. This time I get in and out quickly—no sobbing, no tears, no memories of what happened. The hot water pounds against my skin, washing away the grease and sweat. I order myself a relatively healthy meal from a fast-food place, and at last, I finally start to feel better.

I pull up my phone again and send a message to the therapist Miranda set me up with.

It's time. *Time to get my life together.*

CHAPTER FOURTEEN

Several days later, I am sitting in my kitchen with a steaming cup of coffee next to me, the rich aroma filling the air, when my doorbell rings. My first thought is it's Grace, who's stopped by to check on me. Or maybe Miranda with more demands from my publisher. I set down the coffee, close my laptop with a soft click, and walk to the door. When I open it, I'm surprised to see Corbin standing there.

"Riley," he says, "I'm sorry to barge in on you like this, but I just …" He shifts his weight from side to side, and I can tell he's nervous. I feel the guilt hit me again. I should've messaged him back.

"I just wanted to check on you and make sure you were okay. I know things the other night … it was probably too soon, and—"

"Corbin, it's okay," I say, stopping him in the middle of his speech. "Please come in. I'll pour you a cup of coffee."

"Thanks," he says. He walks into my house and looks around, his eyes widening as he takes in the details. "I love your place," he says. "Hey, is this what I think it is?"

I feel a flush of guilt as I watch him examine a figurine I brought back from Egypt. It's a small servant's statue called a faience, with a blue-green glaze that's still vibrant after thousands of years.

I nod. "An actual faience. While I was at Karnak during my dissertation research, I made a few good friends." I lower my voice slightly, embarrassed. "One of them, a colleague from Cairo, gave it to me as I was leaving, as a farewell gift. Said it was a family heirloom, passed down through generations."

A colleague, I tell myself, though the memory of Ahmed's hands tracing every inch of my body makes my cheeks burn. "I should have refused it, knowing the cultural significance, but I was young and didn't want to offend him. Now I feel terrible keeping it." I take the statue from his hands and place it back on the shelf.

He smiles, his eyes crinkling. "Your secret's safe with me …"

We continue into the kitchen and settle around the island, two cups of coffee in between us. Thankfully, Corbin arrived today and not a few days ago when my house was a complete disaster zone.

"I'm really sorry I didn't message you back. It's just …" I begin.

He places a hand on mine, his palm warm and slightly calloused. "It's just what?"

"It's just I had an amazing time the other night. It was … I don't even know how to say it. Exactly what I needed, what I hoped for."

"I felt the same way," he says, his voice low and sincere.

"But I don't have things quite figured out, not yet. I don't know if you want to be involved in the mess that is my life right now. I—"

He interrupts me. "Riley, you don't have anything to apologize for. My life isn't perfect either, even though it might look like it on the surface. I'm just trying to figure out what's next for me too."

"I know, but I just have a lot of stuff I still need to work on. My book, my career—it just feels like my life is a mess right now ..." I trail off, realizing I'm oversharing.

"You know, I've been thinking about your work lately," he says, his eyes filled with genuine concern. "Your theories about intermediate periods—they're fascinating. The kind of research that could change everything we think we know about the Old Kingdom."

I feel a flutter of pride. It's been so long since someone has praised my ideas.

"What if we worked on things together?" he continues. "I mean, not just our personal lives, but professionally too. I have connections, and your research would be perfect for my YouTube channel. Maybe I could help you promote your book."

My eyes meet his across the table, deep brown with flecks of amber. I can't help but immediately think of Meredith ... who also appeared on his channel. *Would it be too soon?* The thought holds me speechless.

"Think about it, Riley," he continues. "You could come on as a guest expert, maybe even become a regular contributor. Your discoveries, your insights—they could reach a wider audience."

The idea is actually very appealing. *But Meredith also ...*

"I don't know ..." I say slowly. But the truth is, I do. It's not just our shared past with Meredith ... I would never say this to Corbin, but working on his channel? It would kill my credibility in the industry. I can only imagine what my former colleagues at ASU would say.

He nods thoughtfully. "I understand your hesitation. But times are changing, Riley. The old gatekeepers are losing their power. Social media, digital platforms—that's where the real influence is now. Your research could reach millions instead of thousands."

The more he talks, the more sense it makes. I think about my empty bank account, about Miranda's words, about the long-past deadline and the long-spent advance. Maybe this could be the lifeline I desperately need.

"You might be right," I admit. "I just never thought of myself as a ... public figure."

"You're a natural storyteller, Riley. The way you talk about ancient civilizations, you make them come alive. That's a gift."

I feel myself warming to the idea despite my reservations. "It would certainly be different."

A ding from his phone sounds. I forgot all about his assistant, Kelly, but of course, she's never far from our conversations.

He places his hand on mine, his fingers wrapping gently around my wrist. "Listen, I have a meeting this afternoon, but can I have dinner with you tomorrow night? There's this little Tex-Mex place downtown. The food is great, and they have live music on Saturdays. We can talk about it all in more detail."

I chew on my lip for a moment, but let's face it, I'm helplessly in thrall to the twinkle of enthusiasm in his eyes. "Sure," I say, feeling genuinely excited.

"Great," he says as he leans in and plants a gentle kiss on

my lips. I walk him to the door, and the two of us kiss again, the smell of his cologne lingering after he pulls away.

As I close the door and turn back into my home, I replay our conversation in my mind. His enthusiasm for my work, his offer to help—it all feels like exactly what I need right now. But as I think about it more, something nags at me. *Do I deserve this?* Someone like Corbin wanting to help with my struggling career, wanting to be with someone like me? After the year I've had, after how badly I've let everyone down—Miranda, the publisher, even Brody's memory—Corbin wanting to be part of my life feels almost too good to be true.

I shake my head, trying to dismiss the negative thoughts. Maybe I'm just not used to good things happening anymore. After losing Brody, after watching my life fall apart piece by piece, it's hard to believe I deserve something beautiful again. Regardless, I have to be open to trying.

Otherwise, I'll be stuck in this exact spot in my life forever.

CHAPTER FIFTEEN

The next day I find myself doing research late into the afternoon. It's going ... slowly. While it's easy to get swept up in the missing periods of Egypt, reading page after page of what's vanished, it's much harder to actually form my own words. The cursor blinks accusingly on the document—still painfully short of what the publisher expects.

Corbin's offer to feature me on his channel keeps circling back through my thoughts, and with it an uncomfortable realization returns—this feels eerily familiar to his relationship with Meredith. Mesa Verde creeps back into my mind like a shadow I can't shake. I've been fighting the urge to go digging, telling myself it's pointless, unhealthy even. But after hitting my word count for the day, my resolve crumbles. Almost without thinking, I open my browser and type "Meredith Chin death Mesa Verde" into the search bar.

Images flood the screen: news headlines, photos of the cliff dwellings, and pictures of Meredith herself—alive and smiling in most, but a few tasteless outlets published shots of emergency responders at the scene. I click quickly away from those.

The official story is consistent across all the articles. Meredith and Corbin were camping near the cliff dwellings. She had a history of sleepwalking. Sometime in the night, she wandered from their tent and fell from the cliff's edge. Corbin reported her missing at dawn when he woke to find her gone. Park rangers found her body several hours later.

But Grace's words keep echoing in my head: *Multiple witnesses heard them arguing that afternoon. The police wanted to make sure it wasn't murder.*

I click over to Instagram and search for Meredith's profile. It's still active, preserved as a memorial of sorts. The last photo she posted was from Mesa Verde itself—a stunning sunset shot of the ancient cliff dwellings, the stone structures glowing amber in the fading light. It's captioned:

> Last night at Mesa Verde. Can't wait to share what we've discovered.

The date stamp shows it was posted the evening before she died.

I scroll through the comments, most of which are now expressions of grief and remembrance. But as I go deeper, I notice a comment from the days immediately after her death that stands out from the rest:

> @LostHistory_Fan: So convenient that she "fell" right after making a new discovery ...

My jaw drops as I read it. *How can people be so awful?* Then it hits me. Right now, I'm not much different. Here I am, hunched over my laptop in the dark, feeding on the same conspiracy theories and cruel speculation as these faceless internet trolls.

I close the laptop, my stomach churning with guilt. Corbin has been nothing but kind, understanding, and patient with me. The connection between us feels real—two people who understand each other's grief. Yet here I am, secretly investigating him like he's a suspect in a mysterious cold case.

Still, I find myself drawn back to my laptop. I reopen it and this time I search for "Corbin Cross Meredith Chin research dispute." I soon find an academic forum thread discussing authorship conflicts. Several posts mention tension at a conference in Chicago three months before Meredith's death. One commenter claims to have witnessed a heated argument where Meredith accused someone—the name carefully avoided, but the implication clear—of taking credit for her work.

I pull up Meredith's Instagram again, studying her photos from the months before her death. In most of them, she's alone or with colleagues I don't recognize. Corbin appears in only a handful, and in the last few, his smile seems strained, his arm around her shoulders stiff and formal. Or am I just imagining things, projecting a dynamic that's not really there?

I pull out a bottle of wine and pour myself a glass. The liquid trembles in the glass as my hand shakes. *What am I doing?* Reading and rereading anonymous social media comments and vague insinuations? I set the glass down hard enough that wine sloshes over the rim, creating a crimson pool on the counter. I stare at the red liquid, reminded vividly of blood on primitive stones.

The thought makes me shudder.

Instead of going back to work on my book, I open my contacts and hover my finger over Grace's name. She's the one who planted these suspicions in the first place. Maybe she knows more. But what would I even say? *Hey, did you find any actual evidence that my new boyfriend might have murdered his fiancée?*

I laugh bitterly.

"You're being ridiculous," I say aloud to my empty house. "People argue. Couples fight about academic credit and their careers. It doesn't mean he pushed her off a cliff."

My phone dings, making me jump. I see Corbin's name flash across the screen.

> Surprise! I finished my meeting and thought I'd see if you wanted to grab an early dinner? Pick you up in fifteen minutes?

I bite my lip, feeling both ashamed and excited to see him. Of course, Corbin has no idea what I've been up to. And I have no intention of confronting him either. I sigh. My search for the "truth" about what happened that night has turned up exactly nothing. I've got to accept that Corbin is telling the truth ... and everything else is just paranoia. I pick up my phone and type a response.

> Make it twenty. See you soon

A SHORT WHILE LATER, we're seated across from each other at a weathered wooden table in the Tex-Mex place down the street from my house. He seems different today—energized, vibrating with excitement. He barely touches his chicken enchiladas, instead talking animatedly about a new project.

"I've been invited to film at Tikal during the upcoming solar eclipse," he explains, his eyes bright. "It's the first total eclipse visible there since 1991—a once-in-a-lifetime event. The perfect time to document some of my theories about astronomical alignments in the Mayan city."

"That's amazing," I say, genuinely impressed despite my conflicted feelings. "When do you leave?"

"In two weeks." He reaches across the table to take my hand. "Riley, I want you to come with me."

The offer catches me completely off guard. "To Guatemala? Corbin, I—"

"Think about it," he urges. "It would be perfect. You're an expert in ancient civilizations. We'll have special access to a viewing area behind the main temple, away from the festival crowds. Your perspective would be invaluable. And we can make a little vacation out of it; the hotel where we're staying is incredible …" He gestures vaguely, perhaps indicating the weight of our respective pasts that hangs over us here.

"I don't know," I hedge. "My book—"

"Needs inspiration, perspective," he finishes. "Plus, you've never experienced how those cultures tracked celestial events like this. Think of the research opportunities—seeing firsthand how the eclipse transforms Tikal, just as it did for the Maya centuries ago."

He's right—the opportunity is an awesome one. Under normal circumstances, I'd jump at the chance. But the comments I found online linger in my mind, sounding quietly but urgently like warning bells.

"I'll think about it," I promise.

After dinner, Corbin suggests we go back to his place for a nightcap. The margaritas have made me bold, or maybe it's the way he looks at me in the soft lighting of the restaurant—like I'm something precious he's afraid might disappear. When he slides his hand around my waist as we walk to his car, I feel that familiar flutter of anticipation.

His condo feels different that night. The floor-to-ceiling windows frame the glittering city lights below, and the space feels intimate rather than imposing. He pours us each a glass of wine, but we barely touch them. The tension that's been building between us all evening finally snaps when he brushes a strand of hair from my face.

"Riley," he whispers, and there's something vulnerable in his voice, something that makes my chest tighten.

When he kisses me, it's different from our other kisses—deeper, more urgent. All my doubts, all my fears about Meredith and Mesa Verde, fade into background noise. This is what I need—to feel alive again, to feel wanted, to feel like myself instead of a grieving fiancée.

We make love slowly, carefully, like we're both afraid of breaking something fragile. Afterward, I lie in his arms, listening to his heartbeat, watching the city lights cast moving shadows across the ceiling. For the first time in over a year, I feel entirely complete.

He falls asleep before I do, and I lie in his bed, feeling the rise and fall of his chest. Feeling the warmth of his skin against mine, I make two decisions with startling clarity:

One, I'm going to Guatemala with him.

Two, I'm letting the whole mystery around Meredith's death go. Sometimes the past needs to stay buried—I just hope it does.

CHAPTER SIXTEEN

The suitcase lies open on my bed like a gaping mouth, waiting to be fed. I fold another blouse carefully, smoothing out the wrinkles with more attention than necessary. Tomorrow morning, Corbin and I will be on a plane to Guatemala. Tomorrow night, we'll be watching the sunset over Lake Atitlán. The thought sends a flutter of excitement through my chest, mixed with something I can't quite name —anticipation maybe, or nervousness.

I hold up a sundress, considering. Will it be too formal for breakfast? Too casual for dinner at the boutique hotel? These are the kinds of decisions that used to come naturally to me. Brody always teased me about overthinking what to pack, but he'd also slip little notes into my suitcase when I wasn't looking. *Miss you already* and *Don't forget to have fun* written in his precise handwriting on hotel stationery or napkins.

The memory hits me unexpectedly, and I have to sit down on the edge of the bed. Brody would have loved Tikal. He was always curious about early civilizations, though he had zero interest in studying them. I can picture him now, his face lighting up as he explained some theory he'd heard about Mayan astronomy, getting half the facts wrong but with such enthusiasm that it didn't matter.

Would he approve of Corbin? The question surfaces before I can push it away. Brody was protective without being possessive, supportive without being overbearing. He would have wanted me to be happy, I know that. Even if the circumstances are less than ideal.

I shake my head, forcing myself to focus on packing. A swimsuit for the lake. My good camera—the one Brody bought me for our anniversary three years ago, still barely used. Sunscreen, bug spray, comfortable hiking boots. The mundane tasks help quiet the churning in my mind.

My phone buzzes on the nightstand. Miranda's name appears on the screen, and my stomach drops. She never calls this late unless something's wrong. I let it go to voicemail, not ready to deal with whatever crisis might be unfolding with my overdue book. I sent some pages over last week, but I'm sure it's not enough.

Tomorrow I'll be filming with Corbin for the first time, appearing on his channel. Maybe that will give Miranda something positive to report to the publisher.

I continue packing, trying to recapture my earlier excitement. This trip could change everything. Not just for my relationship with Corbin, but for my career. Being featured on his channel could introduce my work to thousands of new readers. The publisher would have to see the marketing potential in that.

My phone buzzes again. A text this time.

> Riley, please call me back. We need to talk.

The words make my heart plummet. I type back quickly.

> Getting ready to leave for a trip. Can we talk when I get back?

The response comes almost immediately.

> The publisher called. This is serious.

My hands freeze over the screen. Serious how? I try Miranda's number, but it goes straight to voicemail. Of course—she's probably dealing with West Coast clients now. I send another text.

> How serious?

The three dots appear and disappear several times. Whatever she's typing is taking longer than usual. Finally:

> Riley, they want the advance back. All $10,000. Call me immediately.

The phone slips from my trembling hand and clatters to the hardwood floor. I stare at it lying there, half hidden under the bed, Miranda's words glowing on the screen. *Ten thousand dollars.* Money that's been spent and then some. I sink onto the bed beside my half-packed suitcase. My heart is pounding so hard I can hear it in my ears. This can't be happening. Not now, when things were finally starting to look up.

The phone rings again from its position on the floor. I scramble to answer it, seeing Miranda's name.

"Riley, thank God. I've been trying to reach you for an hour."

"Miranda, what's going on? They can't just demand the money back, can they?"

"I just got off the phone with your editor. They're not threatening anymore—they've officially started the process to reclaim the advance. You have ten days, not two weeks. Ten days to show them something, anything, that proves this book is salvageable."

Ten days. The number echoes in my head like a death sentence. "But I'm supposed to leave for Guatemala tomorrow. This trip was going to be research for the book. And I'm filming with Corbin—"

"Riley, listen to me. The lawyers are involved now. They've been patient, more patient than most publishers would be, but your editor is under serious pressure from above. They need to see significant progress, or they're going to have to recoup their losses."

I look at my suitcase, at the careful arrangement of clothes and supplies for a week in paradise. "What if I cancel the trip? Stay here and write?"

"Honestly? I don't know if that would be enough at this point. The trust is broken. But maybe ..." She pauses, and I can hear her thinking. "You said you're filming with Corbin's channel? How big is his audience?"

"At least two million subscribers. Maybe more."

"That could help. If we can show them you're building a platform, generating buzz ... Tell me about it. What's the angle?"

I explain about the eclipse, about Tikal, about how my

expertise in ancient civilizations fits with Corbin's content. As I talk, I almost convince myself that this is the answer, that this trip could save everything.

"It's not a guarantee," Miranda says when I finish. "But it's something I can take up the chain. The marketing department might see the potential. Still, Riley, once the lawyers are involved, it's hard to turn the ship around. You need to be prepared for the possibility that this book deal is over. And not only that ... they may sue you for breach of contract."

Bile rises in my throat. There's nothing more I can say.

After we hang up, I sit in the silence of my bedroom, staring at the suitcase. Ten days. *Ten thousand dollars I don't have.* A career that's about to be over before I gave it a chance to really take flight. I could try to resell the artifacts I bought at the auction, but that would take months, not to mention I'd likely get less than half of what I paid for them.

Outside, the desert wind rattles the windows. Inside, my life hangs by a thread that feels ready to snap at any moment. I could really use a glass of wine, but I resist. I stand up slowly and smooth out a sundress lying on the floor, then fold it into the suitcase.

Maybe this trip is exactly what I need—not just for the book, but to prove to myself that I'm still capable of moving forward, even when everything feels like it's falling apart.

But as I zip the suitcase shut, I can't shake her words. *There are no guarantees.*

CHAPTER SEVENTEEN

I finger the edges of my passport cover, the leather soft and worn under my skin, the faint smell of old paper wafting up as I flip through the pages. The Phoenix terminal buzzes with activity—announcements echoing over the PA system, the squeak of wheeled luggage against vinyl floors, and the constant hum of conversations in multiple languages. Corbin is next to me, his fingers tapping rapidly against his phone screen as he follows up with emails.

"You doing okay, Riley?" he says, glancing over, his brow furrowed with concern.

"Yes, of course. I'm fine. Why do you ask?" I shift in the uncomfortable plastic chair, feeling the edge dig into my thighs.

"Well, you've been over there fiddling with your passport and crossing and uncrossing your legs for the last five minutes."

I let out a long sigh, the tension in my shoulders releasing slightly. The truth is, I can't stop thinking about Miranda's call last night. *Ten days. Ten thousand dollars.* The words circle in my head like vultures. But I can't tell Corbin—not now, not when we're about to board a plane for what could be the most important week of our relationship. I also can't help but wonder if he'd still want to have me on his show if I didn't have a book deal.

"Okay, fine. I'm ... I'm a little bit nervous. This is the first time I've been out of the country since ..." He waits for me patiently to continue, his warm eyes never leaving my face. "Well, since Brody and I ..."

It's not a *complete* lie.

Instead of being offended by me bringing up Brody, Corbin reaches over and grabs my hand, his palm warm and slightly calloused against mine. And that's been the trend over the last few weeks. I clam up, get nervous, and Corbin is there to reassure me. After he came to my house following my two-day drinking binge, things got a little bit more serious between us. I mean, as serious as you can be when you've only been dating someone for a short while, but the thing is, Corbin and I are both at a point in our lives where things can move more quickly.

The last few weeks we've been regularly spending time together at my place and his. We stay up into the night, having wide-ranging, intimate conversations about the world, politics, and, of course, history. The scent of his cologne has become familiar on my sheets. And the sex? Don't even get me started on the sex. It's been *amazing*. The two of us simply can't keep our hands off each other. It's like I've been holding my breath for the last year and a half, and now all of a sudden, I'm able to breathe again.

Hopefully a potential lawsuit against me doesn't ruin that.

Corbin remembered from our second date that I had

never seen any of the ruins of Central America. He was pretty shocked, actually, since it's only a quick flight from Arizona, and it's a part of the world that contains some of its most astounding archeological sites.

He's booked us a five-star boutique hotel on Lake Atitlán near Tikal. I'll be honest, I've been wanting to see Tikal since I was a little girl—and not because I was reading academic books as a kid. It was more because I'd spotted it in the original *Star Wars* film—those iconic temples served as the Rebel base on Yavin 4. Later on, I discovered the significance of Tikal—arguably the most breathtaking achievement of Maya civilization. What makes it truly special is the sheer scale: over three thousand structures spread across six square miles, with limestone temples that soar above the jungle canopy, some reaching heights of nearly 230 feet.

Let's face it—Tikal even *sounds* cool. Cool enough that I'm willing to stake my entire career on filming there, lawsuit be damned. I catch myself biting my lip as I think about the manuscript glowing on my laptop screen, now buried somewhere in the leather bag crumpled at my feet. I promised myself I'd spend every stolen moment of this trip working on it, fingers flying across keys in cramped airplane seats and hotel lobbies. But right now, focusing on anything beyond this moment feels impossible.

Finally, they call the group in front of us for boarding, the announcement cutting through the ambient noise of the terminal. One more to go and then we're on a plane, and I can put the whole book debacle on the back burner for a few days. I pick up my bags, feeling the weight of my carry-on strain against my shoulder, as the two of us stand together.

"Oh crap, it's Kelly," Corbin says, his phone vibrating in

his hand. "Hold on. I've gotta take this." He steps away, turning his back slightly as he answers.

"Wait, Corbin," I snap, irritation prickling under my skin.

"What?" he says, looking at me with an open expression, his phone still buzzing insistently.

"When am I going to meet this Kelly?" The question comes out sharper than I intended, the words hanging in the air between us.

Something changes in his face, a strange look that passes and then disappears, like a cloud moving across the sun. "Do you want to meet Kelly?"

"Yes, I want to meet Kelly." I cross my arms, feeling the stiff fabric of my jacket bunch at the elbows. "I feel like she's always interrupting us, messaging you all the time. Who calls right as we're about to board a plane?"

His expression hardens, his jaw tensing. "It's just my work, Riley. Trust me. You're the most important woman in my life right now."

Although the sentiment feels good coming from his lips, it still rings a bit hollow. Kelly seems to always be messaging him at inopportune times and interrupting us just when we're getting ready to have a deep conversation or do something—she's always there.

"You say that, but ..." I hesitate, watching as his thumb hovers over the answer button. "Go ahead. Take it."

He gives me a grateful look and steps a few feet away, his voice dropping to a murmur. I can't make out the words, but there's a familiarity in his tone that makes my stomach clench. When he returns, the announcement for boarding is echoing through the terminal.

"We should go," he says, reaching for his bag.

I don't move. "What's the deal with you and Kelly, Corbin?"

He freezes, his hand on the strap of his bag. "What? There's no 'deal.' She's my assistant."

"Is that all she is? Because every time she calls, you get this look on your face. And you're always so secretive about her." My heart is pounding in my chest, the blood rushing in my ears. I hadn't planned to confront him like this, certainly not right before boarding a plane to spend a week together in Guatemala, but the words tumble out before I can stop them.

"Riley, this is ridiculous. Kelly is my employee." His voice has an edge to it now, defensive.

"Then why won't you let me meet her?" I press, feeling vulnerable and hating myself for it. People are streaming past us to board, some giving us curious glances. "Is there something going on between you two?"

Corbin's face darkens. "No. Absolutely not."

"Then what is it?" I lower my voice, aware of how public this confrontation has become. "Should I be jealous? Are you hiding something from me?"

"This is not the time or the place for this conversation," he says, his voice tight. He glances at the boarding gate, where the attendant is looking at us expectantly.

"When is the time, then? Because every time Kelly comes up, you turn all weird and shut down."

He sighs, running a hand through his hair. "Riley, honey, are you all right? Because you're really overreacting right now. Are you nervous about flying?"

"What? No, I just—" The final boarding call interrupts me. He looks toward the last couple of people boarding our flight and looks back at me. I sigh. Maybe I am overreacting.

Miranda's call last night has me all amped up, not to mention this being my first trip out of the country in more than a year. "I'm sorry, you're right. I'm sure it's just my nerves. I'm not a great flyer. I get anxious with the turbulence."

He reaches for my hand, and after a moment's hesitation, I let him take it. "There's nothing between me and Kelly except for work. I promise."

We walk down the jetway hand in hand, an amicable silence falling between us. When we step into the plane's cramped interior, Corbin takes my bag with practiced ease, muscles flexing as he hefts it into the overhead compartment. Without missing a beat, he turns to help an elderly woman wrestling with her oversized carry-on, his movements gentle and patient.

She beams up at him, her face creasing with genuine warmth. "What a nice young man you are," she says, then catches my eye with a conspiratorial wink. *Keep him*, she mouths, and I feel heat bloom across my cheeks.

She's right. Why am I overcomplicating things between us? Corbin has been nothing but wonderful to me. Maybe I'm envious that he has persevered through his grief, and I have pretty much flushed my career down the toilet. Or maybe it's the stress of the book deal coming back to bite me. As we buckle our seatbelts, I decide to let the Kelly situation go. We have a week ahead of us in Guatemala, among the ruins and lush landscapes, and there'll be plenty of time to figure out where we stand.

As the plane rumbles down the tarmac, I realize what a hypocrite I'm being. Maybe Corbin's not telling me everything about Kelly, but I haven't been exactly honest either. He has no idea I'm about to be sued for breach of contract.

His hand finds mine again as we pick up speed, fingers

intertwining. The runway falls away beneath us, and I let myself sink into the moment. *Maybe two people can harbor secrets from each other*, I think, watching the ground shrink below.

As long as those secrets don't hurt the people we care about, right?

CHAPTER EIGHTEEN

The next morning, I pull out my phone for the third time since breakfast and stare at the message I sent Miranda as soon as I woke up.

> Any updates from MAP?

The words hang there unanswered, making my skin prickle with anxiety. Finally, three dots appear, then disappear, then reappear. My heart hammers as I wait.

> They're waiting to see the video footage go live from Tikal. Then they'll make a decision. I don't want to put too much pressure on you, dear, but this video had better be a home run.

I type back a quick thank you, then stare out at the circular driveway in front of our hotel, watching a toucan flit between the palm fronds.

Right, no pressure at all, I think, my stomach clenching.

Corbin and I wait at the hotel's front entrance for our private van to transport us to the ruins at Tikal. The five-star resort sits like a jewel on the rim of a small lake, its crystal-clear water perfectly mirroring the lush jungle canopy above. Everything about this place screams luxury—the scent of frangipani and jasmine hangs heavy in the humid air, and the hand-carved wooden furniture on the veranda gleams with fresh polish.

It's been over a year since I've escaped Phoenix, fled the familiarity of the city and everything that reminds me of Brody. I packed my laptop with every intention of working on the manuscript, but I haven't cracked it open since we left yesterday. My entire future hinges on the publisher's response to my appearance on Corbin's YouTube channel. It's my last card to play—after this, I'm staring down the barrel of bankruptcy.

The thought makes me physically cringe.

Of course, I've still not mentioned any of this to Corbin.

He appears beside me, looking polished and ready for our adventure. He's wearing a crisp button-down short-sleeved shirt and black shorts—the second outfit he chose for today. The first, a khaki shirt and olive-green cargos with a Panama hat, were nearly an exact match for the outfit I'm wearing. We both laughed when I came out of the bathroom, realizing that we looked like a couple dressed up as Indiana Jones for Halloween.

Corbin decided to ditch his hat at the hotel, but I kept mine firmly on. Given my fair skin that freckles at the mere suggestion of sunlight, there's no way I could handle the tropical sun. Ever since Brody died of skin cancer, I don't take sun protection lightly.

My phone buzzes, and I glance down, expecting another

update from Miranda. Instead, Grace's name appears on the screen.

> Girl, where were you? You missed yoga today.

I stare at the message, my stomach dropping. I completely forgot about our Tuesday morning class. In fact, I haven't even seen Grace in ages. I feel a guilty twist in my chest.

> Sorry! I'm actually out of town. Should have told you.

The three dots appear immediately, then disappear, then appear again. I can practically feel Grace's irritation through the phone.

> Out of town? Where? When did this happen?

I hesitate before typing back. Things have been weird between Grace and me ever since I started dating Corbin. She's been making comments, asking pointed questions, suggesting we all hang out together. I've offered multiple times for us to double-date or even just grab coffee, so she can get to know him better, but she always finds an excuse. I assumed it was jealousy—Grace has been single for almost two years now, and maybe seeing me happy with someone new is hard for her. Since then, I've kept my status with Corbin close to my chest, giving her very little detail about our relationship.

> Guatemala. With Corbin.

The response comes quickly.

> Guatemala?? Riley, what the hell? You didn't think to mention you were leaving the country?

I let out a sigh.

"Everything okay?" Corbin asks.

"Just Grace," I say, not wanting to get into it right now. "She's mad I didn't tell her about the trip."

He gives me a half-smile—the kind that says he knows there's more to the story but won't push—and returns to his own phone, likely coordinating today's shoot. I've shared enough stories about Grace over the weeks for him to understand her intensity.

Another message appears.

> This is exactly what I was worried about. You're disappearing into this relationship.

The accusation stings because there's some truth to it. I have been spending every free moment with Corbin, but that's what happens when you meet someone amazing, right? Grace should understand that.

> I'm not disappearing. I'm just happy for the first time in months.

Happy or distracted? Because from where I'm sitting, you're making some questionable choices.

My fingers hover over the keyboard. Questionable choices? What does she mean by that? Before I can respond, she sends another text.

> Look, I care about you. But this whole thing with Corbin feels rushed. You barely know him.

> I know him better than you think. And you would too if you actually spent time with us instead of making excuses.

> I'm not making excuses, Riley. I'm being careful. There's something about him that doesn't sit right with me.

It's the same thing as when we were having drinks at Mateo's a few weeks ago. I want to ask what specifically bothers her about Corbin, but then a van pulls up to the entrance—a comfortable-looking vehicle with tinted windows and air conditioning that beckons us away from the sweltering morning heat.

> I have to go. We'll talk when I get back.

> Be careful, Riley. Please.

I shove my phone into my bag, frustration mixing with guilt in my chest. Grace is supposed to be my best friend, but lately it feels like she's determined to find fault with the first good thing that's happened to me since Brody died.

"Finally," I sigh, though my enthusiasm feels forced now. "This heat is brutal already."

Corbin wraps one arm around my shoulders as a young man approaches the vehicle. He's wearing a faded T-shirt and cargo shorts with multiple pockets, well-worn tennis shoes, and has a professional camera slung around his neck. He walks straight up to Corbin, extending his hand with an easy smile.

"Marcus, so glad you made it," Corbin says, gripping the young man's hand firmly. "This is my girlfriend, Riley."

I blush slightly at the reference. Being called Corbin's girlfriend still feels new and exciting, like putting on an identity I'm not quite used to yet. But Grace's words echo in my head: *rushed ... barely know him ... something doesn't sit right.*

"Riley, great to meet you," Marcus says, extending his hand. "Corbin's told me so much about you."

I look over at Corbin hopefully, my eyebrows raised in question, trying to push Grace's concerns from my mind. "All good, I hope?"

Marcus smiles, his teeth brilliantly white against his tanned face. "All good."

The three of us climb inside, Corbin and I in the middle row of seats, while Marcus sits in the driver's seat. He turns toward us so we can chat during the ride, but I find myself distracted, only half-listening to their conversation while Grace's texts replay in my mind.

"So, when did the two of you start working together?" I ask, forcing myself to engage.

"Marcus has been filming for my channel for nearly a year," Corbin explains, adjusting the air-con vents. "Best videographer I've worked with."

Marcus laughs, pulling the van away from the curb. "Flattery will get you everywhere, boss."

"Tell Riley about your plans for today," Corbin says, leaning back in his seat.

"Right! So, I brought the drone equipment," Marcus says, enthusiasm evident in his voice. "I've been practicing these sweeping aerial shots that are going to look incredible."

"Yeah, when viewers see me standing beside these huge

temples," Corbin adds, "they can really appreciate how massive they are. And once you take in the scale, you can understand how unbelievable it is that they were built thousands of years ago. That's something you just can't capture from ground level."

"The scale does get lost sometimes in traditional photography," I admit, though my mind keeps drifting back to Grace's message. *There's something about him that doesn't sit right with me.* What could she possibly mean?

"Exactly!" Marcus chimes in, gesturing excitedly with one hand while keeping the other on the wheel. "Wait until you see what this drone can do. The footage is going to be spectacular."

I nod and smile, trying to match their excitement, but the tension that Grace's words have created sits like a weight in my chest. Maybe she's just protective. Maybe she's jealous. Or maybe—and this is the thought I keep trying to push away—maybe she sees something I don't want to see.

As the van winds through the jungle roads toward Tikal, I tell myself that Grace is wrong. I'm not disappearing into this relationship. All that's happening is that I'm finally moving forward with my life. But her words linger like the humidity in the tropical air, impossible to shake off completely.

CHAPTER NINETEEN

When we arrive at Tikal's Great Plaza, the magnificent ruins should take my breath away. They really should—this massive pyramid temple soaring into the jungle canopy, stones carved with mysterious hieroglyphs, the whole lost-civilization shebang. But I'm too busy checking my phone to fully appreciate it.

No signal. Not even a single bar.

For the first time in days, I actually exhale. No more frantic texts from Miranda about the publisher's decision. No more guilt-inducing messages from Grace about abandoning our friendship. Just blessed digital silence.

"You okay?" Corbin asks, adjusting his camera equipment.

"Perfect," I lie, wiping sweat from my jawline. The jungle humidity is attacking my carefully applied makeup, and we haven't even started filming yet. I can feel foundation sliding down my cheeks despite the expensive setting spray I splurged on back in Phoenix.

The engineering marvel in front of me—Temple of the

Jaguar, rising 148 feet without the benefit of wheels, metal tools, or even beasts of burden—should have my full attention. As an archaeologist, I know exactly how extraordinary this is. The Maya moved these vast limestone blocks using only wooden rollers, rope, and human strength. The Great Plaza stretching before us could easily accommodate one hundred thousand people during the height of Tikal's power, when this city controlled trade routes stretching from the Gulf of Mexico to the Pacific.

But I'm calculating how many times I can blot my face without looking like a complete disaster on camera. This video has to be perfect—charming, knowledgeable, the kind of content that immediately makes publishers think "bestseller." I need to channel my actual expertise about this 1,200-year-old metropolis, not fumble through half-remembered facts like some smart-ass tourist with a guidebook.

Another person approaches our small group, a woman with streaks of silver in her dark hair, which is pulled back in a practical ponytail. She introduces herself as Dr. Josephine Garcia. Her khaki outfit is similar to mine, but somehow she makes it look professional rather than costume-like. She explains that she is one of the local archaeologists who will be giving us an exclusive tour of Tikal.

I drift behind the three of them, listening to the crunch of gravel beneath our feet and watching small lizards dart across our path. My mind keeps circling back to Grace's texts from this morning. *There's something about him that doesn't sit right with me.*

Dr. Garcia speaks animatedly with Corbin, her hands gesturing expressively as she points out features of the site, while Marcus films the entire exchange, the whirr of his equipment barely audible over the jungle sounds.

"Actually," Marcus says, glancing at his equipment bag, "I need to go back and pick up a battery pack that I left in the car."

"And I need another bottle of water," I say, adjusting the sweat soaked hatband on my forehead. The truth is, I need a moment to touch up my makeup and apply another layer of deodorant before the filming starts. All of which requires the items stowed inside my backpack in the back of the van. "I'll come with you. Is that okay?"

"Of course," Corbin says, giving me a quick smile before continuing his conversation with Dr. Garcia.

As Marcus and I walk side by side through the jungle, the path is narrow enough that leaves brush against our arms. Sweat trickles down my back, and I swat away an insect buzzing near my ear, trying to calm my nerves about the upcoming shoot.

"So, do you do a lot of videos like this? Ancient sites, things like that?" I ask, stepping carefully over a gnarled root, my voice tighter than I'd like.

"Actually, this is my first time visiting Tikal," he says, his eyes scanning the canopy above us. "But Corbin and I have done several videos together. I won't lie; the travel and all the attention the videos attract are pretty fantastic."

"Did you always want to be a content creator?" I ask, pausing to admire a brilliant blue butterfly that lands momentarily on a nearby frond, though I'm barely seeing it through my anxiety.

"Actually, I wanted to be a cinematographer," he replies. "But there's a lot of competition for those types of jobs. So I started doing drone work, and the YouTube stuff just kind of fell into my lap."

"That's really cool," I say, though my voice sounds strained even to my own ears. We walk a bit farther in uncomfortable silence—at least, uncomfortable for me—the jungle alive with sounds around us. A scarlet macaw flies overhead, its magnificent plumage a flash of vivid color against the green canopy. I motion to Marcus, trying to draw his attention toward the bird, but he is frowning at his phone. We continue walking in silence, the van now visible ahead of us through the trees.

Once we arrive, I retreat to the third row of seats and dig out my makeup kit. The damage isn't as bad as I feared, but I work quickly—dabbing foundation over the patches where humidity has won the battle, blotting sweat from my temples, adding a few strategic swipes of mascara. One final glance in my compact mirror confirms what I already know: it's not perfect, but it'll have to do. If anything, my slightly smudged, jungle-melted makeup might actually look appealingly authentic on camera.

"Ready?" Marcus asks.

"Ready as I can be," I say, mustering up a smile. "I'm not sure how long my makeup is going to last, but it's the best I can do."

"You look great. Don't worry so much about it. Come on, let's go."

His words of encouragement spark a small bloom of hope in my chest. We walk together in a more comfortable silence for a few minutes, our footsteps muffled by the thick jungle floor, but my thoughts inevitably drift back to Corbin's mysterious assistant. Unease has been simmering beneath the surface, adding to my mounting stress about everything that could go wrong with this filming.

Since Marcus and I are alone, I decide to seize the opportunity. "So, have you ever met Kelly?" I ask, nervousness making my voice shake slightly.

"Kelly?" Marcus looks at me with confusion, his brow furrowing. "Who's that?"

"Kelly, Corbin's assistant," I clarify, watching his face carefully, my heart rate picking up. "He said she does all of his scheduling, coordinates his shoots, stuff like that."

Marcus shakes his head, adjusting the equipment bag on his shoulder. "No, I've never met a Kelly. I didn't even know Corbin had an assistant."

What? My stomach drops, adding another layer of anxiety to the cocktail of stress churning inside me. Corbin said he'd been working with Marcus for nearly a year, so how would he have not met or spoken with his assistant?

Just as I'm about to press for more information, Corbin and Dr. Garcia appear from around the corner of the temple, their faces animated.

"Ready to go?" Corbin calls out, his excited voice echoing against the stones. "We have special access to the top of the main Grand Temple, the Jaguar Temple. Riley, this is it—time for your debut on the channel."

My mouth goes dry. Even though this has been the plan all along, even though I'm banking on this appearance to save my book and my relationships with my agent and publisher, the reality of it makes my palms sweat even more. Corbin seems to pick up on my nervousness.

"Before we start filming, think about this." He reaches toward me and grabs both of my hands, which I hope he doesn't notice are clammy. "You're writing a book—which I know will be fantastic—and this will get your name out there to the public. Not just the academic community. We're talking millions of viewers from all over the world."

I give him a nervous smile. That's the hope, right? Millions of people see me on camera, get to know me, then buy my book—saving me from a lawsuit and a catastrophic career disaster. It's exactly what I need, but a small part of me still hesitates. What if no one in the academic community respects me after this? Being a YouTuber isn't exactly what I had in mind when I started my dissertation on Egyptian archaeology. Then again, I'm not exactly in a position to turn my nose up at a great opportunity. If I don't want to find myself close to bankruptcy, this is my only option.

"I know," I say, my voice barely steady. "I'm just ... nervous, I guess."

"You'll be great," he says, wrapping his arms around my waist. "And you look beautiful."

I lift my eyes to his, trying to project confidence I don't feel. The weight of everything—the possible lawsuit, the missed deadline, my doubts about Corbin—presses down on me, but I force myself to straighten my shoulders. "Okay. Let's do this."

"Fantastic!" He drops my hands and turns toward Marcus. "Let's get her mic'd up."

As Marcus attaches the mic to my shirt lapel with hands that are steadier than mine, I wipe my palms on my shorts again and remember why I'm doing this.

This has to work. It has to.

CHAPTER TWENTY

The limestone steps of the Temple of the Jaguar stretch before me like a stairway to heaven, each one worn smooth by centuries of pilgrims and, more recently, tourists. I trail behind Corbin and Marcus, my thoughts as heavy as my legs on the steep climb. The sun beats down mercilessly and sweat trickles between my shoulder blades.

Corbin turns back, flashing that irresistible smile that first reeled me in at the conference. "You okay back there? Need a hand?"

"I'm fine," I call up, forcing a smile. "Just taking it all in."

His concern seems genuine—his outstretched hand, the crease of worry between his brows. But then, everything about Corbin has seemed genuine up until now.

"Isn't it incredible?" he says, gesturing to the sprawling jungle canopy surrounding us. "Can you imagine building this without modern technology?"

I smile up at him, trying to focus on the magnificence around me rather than the sick feeling churning in my stomach. The view truly is breathtaking—the emerald expanse of jungle stretching to the horizon, the tops of other temples peeking through the canopy like stone islands in a verdant sea.

But all I can do is loop through my earlier conversation with Marcus. If he's been working with Corbin on a consistent basis, surely he would know his assistant, Kelly, right?

"This is perfect!" Marcus exclaims, adjusting his drone controller. "The light is hitting just right." Corbin immediately shifts into performance mode, straightening his posture and brushing invisible dust from his shirt.

"We're ready to shoot, Riley," Marcus says, turning toward me. "I've got you mic'd up already, so there is no reason to yell, just act natural and speak in your normal voice."

I touch the small microphone clipped to my collar, suddenly hyper-aware of its presence. Acting natural is the last thing I'm capable of right now.

"Rolling in three, two …" Marcus gives the signal, and Corbin begins.

"Welcome back to Cross Claims History! I'm standing atop the majestic Temple of the Jaguar at Tikal, one of the ancient world's most impressive structures." His voice takes on that familiar cadence I've heard in countless videos, confident and pleasantly mysterious. "But what if I told you that everything you think you know about Tikal—about all ancient Maya civilization—is wrong?"

I hang back, watching him work. He's good at this—captivating, authoritative. The drone buzzes overhead, capturing the sweeping vista behind him.

"History books tell us Tikal was built around 200 CE,"

he continues, gesturing dramatically, "but new evidence suggests these structures could be thousands of years older. The stones here contain astronomical alignments that wouldn't have been possible during the classic Maya period," Corbin explains to his invisible audience. "They're lying to us, folks—the historians, the archaeologists, the textbooks."

The word *lying* lingers. I feel a chill despite the sweltering heat.

Lying? I think. *Like you're lying to me about having an assistant.*

"And today," Corbin says, turning toward me with a practiced smile, "I'm joined by Dr. Riley Donovan, an expert Egyptologist, who's going to give us a global perspective of these amazing structures."

Marcus swings the camera toward me, and suddenly I'm on. Despite the churning in my stomach, years of academic presentations kick in—my posture straightens, my voice steadies.

"The Maya were remarkable astronomers," I begin, falling back on solid facts rather than Corbin's theories. "Their calendar system was incredibly precise. In fact, they—"

"Before we get to that," Corbin interrupts smoothly, "would you agree that these structures bear striking similarities to those found in Egypt? Maybe even suggesting contact between these civilizations long before Columbus?"

The question throws me for a loop. Corbin has put me on the spot. If I contradict him, I'll look foolish on camera. If I support his questionable theories, I'm betraying my academic integrity. I choose my words carefully.

"There are certainly some interesting parallels between the ancient architectural achievements across different cultures," I say diplomatically. "The use of precise stonework, astronomical alignments, and pyramid structures appears in multiple civilizations. Traditional archaeology attributes this to parallel development—similar solutions to similar problems."

"But you're writing a book about knowledge that was lost during tumultuous periods in Egyptian history," Corbin presses. "Couldn't some of that knowledge have traveled further than the academic establishment wants to admit?"

The camera's unblinking eye waits for my answer. I'm acutely aware of how this will look to my colleagues, to potential publishers, to the academic world I've fought so hard to be a well-respected part of.

"My research focuses on recovering information that was deliberately erased from history," I clarify. "Using new technologies like LiDAR and advanced imaging to reveal what was intentionally hidden or destroyed. It's about filling in gaps, not rewriting the timeline."

I can see Corbin's frustration in the slight tightening around his eyes, but his camera smile never falters. He smoothly transitions back to his own theories, moving me to the background of the shot. Marcus gives me a subtle thumbs-up—apparently my diplomatic dodge worked well enough for their purposes.

For the next hour, we film segments all around the temple complex. Corbin presents increasingly wild theories about ancient technology transfer between continents, mysterious power sources, and hidden chambers beneath the temples. When he asks for my input, I stick to verifiable facts, pivoting away from his more outlandish claims while trying not to directly contradict him on camera.

During a break while Marcus changes his drone's batteries, Dr. Garcia approaches me.

"You're doing well," she says quietly, her voice carrying what sounds like condescension masked as sympathy. "It's difficult to navigate these ... creative interpretations while maintaining professional integrity."

The way she says "creative interpretations" gives me pause. Part of me completely agrees with her; part of me feels slightly defensive of Corbin. She gives me a wry smile and a shrug. But at this point, I'm happy to hear any positive feedback. Because whether I keep my academic integrity or not, I need viewers to like me. Or else my publisher's lawyers will eat me alive.

"What are your thoughts on Corbin's perspective?" I ask, tipping my head to the side.

She shrugs again. "Honestly? It doesn't really matter what I think. The park needs the exposure, and his fans bring tourist dollars. I just make sure my own research is published in peer-reviewed journals where accurate information can counterbalance the entertainment."

"One more segment, you two!" Marcus calls, waving us over to a particularly dramatic viewpoint where the temple rises against the jungle backdrop.

As we position ourselves for the final shot, Corbin places his hand on the small of my back, guiding me to stand beside him. The touch is intimate, and I can't help but think that not only is this my debut on Corbin's channel, but it's also a scene that will see us coming out as a couple.

"You're doing great," he whispers in my ear. "Just remember, two million subscribers will hear your name, see your face."

He's right, of course he is. This exposure could translate

to significant book sales, career opportunities, speaking engagements. Yet the thought brings no comfort as we smile side by side for the drone shot. Instead, one thought keeps circling in my mind:

If he's lying about something as basic as having an assistant, what else might Corbin be hiding?

CHAPTER TWENTY-ONE

"Need anything else for this shot?" Marcus asks as Corbin wraps up his monologue.

"Let's get some aerial footage of me pointing out the celestial alignments," Corbin replies. The two of them discuss shooting from the top of the temple, squarely in the beating sun. Corbin seems to notice my hesitation as I dab more sweat from my face.

"Riley, why don't you go check out the inner chamber? The carvings inside are incredible."

I retreat, grateful for the excuse to escape the punishing heat of the sun.

The interior chamber is cool and dim, a blessed relief. Stone walls rise around me, covered in elaborate carvings of jaguars, serpents, and human figures performing rituals I can only guess at. My eyes adjust slowly to the darkness, and I begin to make out the intricate details that have survived nearly a millennium.

The carvings tell stories of daily life—Maya nobility dressed in elaborate feathered headdresses, their faces painted with cinnabar and jade ornaments. These weren't just decorations; they were historical records, carved by artists who lived and breathed in this very space over a thousand years ago.

I trace the air above one particularly detailed panel showing a royal procession. The carver's hands shaped these figures with such precision, such care. Each feather in a headdress, each fold in a ceremonial robe was painstakingly chiseled into the limestone. That artist had a life, a family, probably worried about getting enough to eat, about whether the rains would come, about whether his children would survive to adulthood.

How fleeting our time really is. These people thought their civilization would last forever—their kings immortalized in stone, their gods eternally honored. Yet within a few centuries, the jungle swallowed their cities whole.

The thought hits me with striking clarity: Brody and I had so little time together. Four years together, gone in an instant. But maybe that's the point. Maybe the Maya understood something I'm still learning—that the time we have is precious precisely because it's limited.

Through the narrow doorway, I can hear Corbin and Marcus discussing camera angles, their voices carrying on the breeze. I pace the small chamber, the stone floor smooth beneath my feet. I'm lost deep in thought, savoring the quiet moment alone.

A sudden thunk echoes from above, followed by Corbin's muffled curse.

"Shit! Marcus, did you see where my phone went?"

"I think it fell through that gap in the stones," Marcus's voice calls back. "Sounded like it landed in the chamber below."

"I'll get it!" I yell up at them, my voice resounding within the carved walls.

I scan the chamber floor and spot the phone near the base of the wall, undamaged thanks to its toughened case, its screen flickering to life with an incoming notification. As I bend to pick it up, the text is impossible to miss.

The notification is from "K."

My finger hovers, wavering between an instinctive respect for Corbin's privacy and my own increasingly desperate need for truth. The choice is made for me when another message appears, lighting up the screen.

> Hey handsome. Don't forget our call tomorrow at 10.

But what really stops me in my tracks is the sequence of glittery pink heart emojis.

The blood rushes from my head so quickly I have to grip the stone ledge for support. *Handsome? Hearts? What the hell is going on?* The chamber spins around me.

It's one thing to suspect a lie, another entirely to see the proof illuminated in blue light against a darkened screen.

He's seeing someone else. All those calls, all those interruptions—they weren't work. They were another woman. A woman he's apparently close enough with to let her manage his schedule, to let her call him "handsome," to let her add a string of hearts to her name.

How could I have been so stupid?

The phone screen darkens, taking the damning message with it, but the words are branded into my mind. I stumble back from the wall, my breath coming in short gasps. The carved faces seem to mock me—all those ancient people who understood the brevity of life, while I'm standing here realizing I've wasted what little time I have on someone who's been lying to me.

"Riley?" Corbin's voice carries from the entrance, footsteps approaching. "You've got to come see this view. Marcus captured some amazing drone footage."

I swallow hard, forcing my features into what I hope is a neutral expression. "Coming," I call back, my voice steadier than I feel.

When he steps into the chamber, backlit by the bright sunlight outside, I search his face for signs of deception. Does he look like a man who's been lying? Does he look like a man who might be capable of worse?

Corbin's smile falters slightly as he takes in my expression. "Everything okay?"

"Fine," I say, the word clipped. "Just a bit lightheaded from the climb."

His concerned expression seems so genuine that once again I doubt myself. Maybe there's an innocent explanation.

But the "handsome" and the hearts tell only one story. And it's not innocent.

"We should head back down," he says, reaching for his phone. "You probably need a cold drink of water."

I watch his face as he glances at the screen, looking for any reaction to K's message. There's nothing –not a flicker of guilt, not a hint of concern. He simply pockets the device and offers me his hand.

Either he's an incredibly good liar, or ...

Or there's something else going on.

As we step back into the blinding sunlight, the temple looming above us, I can't shake the feeling that I'm not the first woman to be deceived by Corbin Cross.

CHAPTER TWENTY-TWO

As soon as we get back to the hotel, we have to rush off to dinner—leaving us barely five minutes to change. We've had zero time alone since leaving Tikal, and the questions in my head are multiplying like bacteria in a petri dish, building pressure until my skull feels ready to crack. I want answers, yes, but my mind is already made up.

I'll go through the motions for the rest of this trip. Let the video go live, make my peace with my publisher, salvage what's left of my career. Then I'll tell Corbin we're through. Because after what I saw in that message—*Hey handsome* with those damn heart emojis—I know he can't be trusted.

I let Corbin lead me by the hand down the hall, his fingers warm and familiar, while I do my best to mask the hurricane raging inside my chest. *Smile, nod, breathe.* We're the last to arrive at the restaurant, and I take in the scene with the detached precision of a forensic investigator documenting evidence at a crime scene.

The restaurant is a study in calculated luxury—polished mahogany and brass fixtures, with those enormous ceiling fans turning overhead like lazy vultures. They mock my inability to breathe properly, stirring the humid air without providing any real relief. The dining room buzzes with the low murmur of other guests, the clink of silverware against china, the soft pop of wine corks. Normal sounds of normal, albeit wealthy, people having normal evenings, while I sit here feeling like my world has just shifted off its axis.

Across the table, Corbin laughs at something Dr. Garcia says, his head thrown back. The sound grates against my nerves like nails on stone. A month ago, I might have found the sight endearing. Now, I wonder if everything about him—every gesture, every smile, every concerned look—is calculated for maximum effect.

When the waiter arrives, I tell her to bring me a large glass of wine and keep it coming. Once I'm a few glasses in, I reach down into my purse and pull out my phone with trembling fingers. I find Grace's contact and text her.

> I think Corbin is cheating on me.

I send the words to Grace before I can second-guess myself. The three dots appear almost immediately.

"Do you think so, Riley?" Corbin's voice cuts through my thoughts, and I realize everyone at the table is looking at me expectantly.

"I'm sorry, what?" I take a hasty sip of my water, buying time.

"Dr. Garcia was saying that social media has been a mixed blessing for archaeological sites," Corbin explains, his eyes narrowing as he studies my face. "More interest, but also more visitors who don't respect the distinctive cultural significance of each site."

"Oh. Yes, absolutely," I manage, nodding with what I hope looks like scholarly agreement rather than distracted panic.

Under the table, my phone buzzes against my thigh. I angle it to read Grace's reply.

> OMG! I knew it! That bastard!
>
> Want me to fly down?
>
> My partner owes me for covering his Christmas shift.

Dr. Garcia launches into a story about an influencer who tried to climb one of the temples at Chichen Itza for a photo op, and everyone's attention shifts away from me. I use the moment to type a quick response.

> No, I can handle it. Just needed to tell someone.

Three dots appear as Grace types her response, but I slip my phone back into my pocket as Corbin glances my way. His smile seems genuine, his eyes crinkling at the corners in that way that made my heart flutter when we first reconnected. Now, I search for cracks in the façade, for hints of the liar beneath.

"The real problem," Dr. Garcia continues, gesturing with her fork, "is that sites like Tikal become commodified. People come for the Instagram selfie, not the history."

"But isn't any interest better than none?" Corbin counters, leaning forward. "My channel may simplify things, but it gets people excited about the past."

"Even when your theories directly contradict established

archaeological evidence?" Dr. Garcia raises an eyebrow, the challenge clear in her voice.

"Especially then." Corbin grins, unruffled. "Controversy drives engagement."

As they debate, my phone buzzes again. I check it discreetly.

> Girl, be careful. If he's lied about this, what else is he hiding? Call me ANYTIME. I mean it. Doesn't matter what time of the day or night.

The evening drags on endlessly. I drink too much wine, hoping it might dull the sharp edges of betrayal cutting into me. It doesn't. Instead, it loosens my tongue.

"So, Corbin," I hear myself say during a lull in conversation, "how does a YouTube historian keep all his projects straight? Do you have help with scheduling?" The question sounds innocent enough, but I see Marcus glance up, confusion flickering across his face.

Corbin's smile doesn't falter. "Just good time management," he says smoothly. "And technology. My calendar app is my lifeline."

Not Kelly. His calendar app.

The lie slides off his tongue so easily that for a moment I doubt myself. Maybe I misunderstood. Maybe the text wasn't what I thought. But then I remember the hearts, the "handsome," and the sick feeling returns.

"Of course," I say, taking another sip of wine. "How efficient of you."

By the time we return to our room, my head is spinning —from the wine, from exhaustion, from the emotional whiplash of the day. I grab my nightclothes and retreat to the bathroom, rehearsing what I'll say when I confront him.

I saw the messages, Corbin. Who is Kelly, really?

Or maybe more direct:

Are you cheating on me?

My reflection in the mirror looks haggard, eyes too bright, cheeks flushed from wine. I splash cold water on my face, trying to clear my head. The confrontation needs to happen tonight. I can't spend another minute in this limbo.

But when I step back into the bedroom, the words die on my lips. Corbin is sprawled across the bed, his chest rising and falling in the deep, even rhythm of sleep. His face looks younger, vulnerable somehow, in the light from the bedside lamp.

"Corbin?" I say softly, but he doesn't stir.

I sink onto the edge of the bed, deflated. The confrontation will have to wait. I lie down beside him, careful not to touch him, staring at the ceiling fan as it cuts lazy circles above us. Sleep refuses to come. My mind races with scenarios, each worse than the last.

What else has he lied about? Who is Kelly? And most disturbing of all—the question I've been pushing away since Grace first planted the seed—what really happened to Meredith?

The minutes crawl by. One hour. Then two. Corbin's breathing remains steady, undisturbed.

His phone sits on the nightstand, face down. The glow of the charging light pulses like a heartbeat in the darkness.

Before I can talk myself out of it, I slide out of bed and reach for the device. Holding it above Corbin's sleeping face, I watch as the facial-recognition software does its work, the lock screen dissolving. I retreat to the bathroom, closing the door with a click before turning on the light.

My hands tremble as I open his messaging app, scrolling until I find the conversation with Kelly. Recent messages at the top.

There's those wretched heart emojis.

But what I find out next is like a knife in my own heart.

PART 2

MEREDITH

CHAPTER TWENTY-THREE

BEFORE THE FALL

I sit in the living room of our downtown Denver condo, reading the handwritten note over and over again, the afternoon sunlight catching the edges of the paper.

Dear Meredith,
Congratulations, you've made the New York Times bestseller list.

It came along with a box of cookies that were printed with the cover of my book, *Keepers of Earth: How Pueblo Women Shaped History*. The fragrant vanilla scent wafts up from the perfectly decorated treats, each one bearing a miniature replica of the cover where my name—Meredith Chin—appears in bold type beneath the title. I trace my finger across one of them, feeling the smooth, edible icing beneath my fingertip.

How is this possible? How is it possible that what felt like a relatively run-of-the-mill career in archaeology could turn me into a *New York Times* bestselling author? It's the privilege and the hope that every author has whenever they write a book—but very rarely is that dream fulfilled.

I chew on my lip, a habit my grandmother always scolded me for ("Aiyah, Meredith! You'll ruin your pretty face!"), debating on whether or not to run and tell Corbin. He's been in a—how do I say it?—*mood* lately. His *mood* has been about as steady as a rollercoaster ever since Netflix cancelled his second show after that disastrous expedition turned up nothing but empty caves.

Sure, he's still popular—two million YouTube subscribers isn't nothing—but the glory days of ten million views per video are long gone. And when you make your living solely off of viewership, that stinks. Not just for your bank account, but also your ego. I've discovered over the years that Corbin has quite an ego. It's not a bad thing per se. He has a lot to be confident about—good looking, charismatic, and he did make one of the most significant archaeological discoveries of the decade. But watching him deal with the slow fade from his peak shows a side of Corbin that I wasn't expecting.

I glance down at the engagement ring that sparkles in the light of our partially decorated condo. The two-carat princess-cut diamond catches the light, sending tiny rainbows dancing across my olive skin. It's tastefully expensive, and even my parents approved of it. The condo, on the other hand, is not exactly posh, but it works for us. And all of it is because of Corbin's hard work; I'd be an idiot not to recognize everything he's done for me. So, regardless of his mood swings, I love him, for better or for worse.

Corbin still dreams of moving back to Phoenix, but Denver is where I grew up. I like it here. My family's here. I have friends here I've known for literally decades. My grandparents moved here from Shanghai in the 1950s, determined to give their children opportunities they never had. That determination seems to have worked its way into my DNA.

"Who was at the door?" Corbin suddenly appears, slightly disheveled, wearing a knit Henley shirt and a pair of joggers. His hair sticks up at odd angles, as if he's been running his hands through it repeatedly. He has that look about him, the manic sort of state that he gets in when things aren't going well for the business. He'll spend days and nights analyzing numbers, trying to figure out a plan.

And now I'm at a fork in the road. Here I am holding my *New York Times* bestseller news, and Corbin, well, he's in a different place. I guess you could say I'm on the rise, and he's on the decline.

"Oh, it's just a package," I say, nodding toward the box of cookies on the coffee table.

"A package? From whom?"

Before I can even finish, Corbin's crossed the distance between us and is standing over me. "Are those cookies decorated with the cover of your book?"

"Yeah, I got them from my publisher." I try to keep my voice casual, though my heart is racing beneath my silk blouse. He picks one up, the scent of vanilla intensifying as he examines it.

"Wow, the details on these are amazing. What's the occasion?" He looks over my shoulder and sees the note that came along with the cookies. "*New York Times* bestseller? You made the list! Oh my gosh, Meredith, that's amazing!" He leans down and gives me a kiss on the cheek, cupping my face in both of his hands. I feel my shoulders relax, a sense of relief washing over me.

Maybe it won't be so bad sharing this with him after all.

"Thanks, I can't believe it," I say. "I never thought I would actually make the list."

The words come out breathier than I intended, betraying my excitement despite my attempts to downplay it for Corbin's sake. Corbin sits down next to me, the leather couch creaking under his weight. He puts his arm around me, but then pulls back slightly, studying my face.

"Wait—why didn't you say you made the list?"

The first words that spring to mind are sharp and defensive—*Because you sulked for a month after your Netflix special got canceled*—but I bite them back.

"I just ... I wanted to be sure it was real first. You know how these things can be."

His smile seems genuine, reaching his eyes, which crinkle at the corners in that cute way I've always found irresistible.

"Of course you did. I always knew you would."

"You know this is mostly because of you, right? The videos that we did together on your channel. If it weren't for that exposure, I wouldn't have had all those people buying my book in the first place."

Of course, I did pour three years of my life into researching it, spent months on interviews with Indigenous elders and late nights cross-referencing archaeological findings with oral histories. But I can't deny that the viewers on Corbin's channel brought everything past the tipping point into some kind of literary stardom.

"Well, we make a great team," he says, pulling me close. "Come on, we gotta celebrate tonight. Where do you wanna go?"

"I don't know! Anywhere," I say, still caught off guard by his supportive reaction.

"What about Jonathan's? The French place that you love. I'll call right now and make a reservation. I'm so excited for you, Meredith," he says, kissing me again before plodding down the hall and back into his office.

That wasn't so bad after all. Maybe there's been a change in his viewership. He said he'd gone back and updated all his videos with new thumbnails, shocking headlines that would grab people's attention and pique their curiosity. Besides, once I start doing interviews, I'll be able to bring a whole new audience to Cross Claims History.

Interview.

That word kills any sense of relief I was feeling. While I'm completely elated to have made the *NYT* bestseller list, there's something I haven't told Corbin yet.

I've been invited to do an interview with the number one podcast in the world. Rowan Johnson, comedian turned podcaster, who has an unbelievably massive following and an intense curiosity about ancient history. Corbin is a huge fan, listens to every one of his episodes. In fact, it's his dream to get invited on the podcast. He has no idea that my agent already set a date for me to go down to Austin and do the interview.

And Corbin wasn't invited.

He may have taken the news about the bestseller list in his stride, but I know Corbin. I know how his ego works. And I know when I tell him about the podcast interview, *it's not going to go over well.*

I sigh, tracing the embossed title on the cookie with my fingernail. This should be one of the happiest moments of my career, but instead, I'm calculating how to manage my fiancé's negative reaction. The thought makes me sit up straighter, a flicker of irritation igniting in my chest. My mother didn't raise me to make myself smaller for anyone—not even the man I love.

I grab my phone and text my best friend, Ling.

> Made the NYT list. Cookies arrived. Told C. No meltdown ... yet. Still haven't mentioned R.J. podcast.

Her response is immediate.

> OMG CONGRATS!!! 🎉 And, girl, don't you dare downplay this for him. Your badassery is not responsible for his insecurity.

She's right, of course. Ling has supported me throughout my entire career; plus, she's the only person I've confided in about Corbin. I've worked my ass off for this. Years of being the only Asian woman in rooms full of white male archaeologists, of having my research questioned and my findings dismissed, of pushing through anyway because I believe in the importance of telling these forgotten stories.

From down the hall, I hear Corbin on the phone, his voice animated as he makes dinner reservations. He sounds sincerely happy for me, and I feel a pang of guilt for assuming the worst. Maybe I'm not giving him enough credit. Maybe he's grown beyond the man who sulked for days when my first book got a better review than his documentary series.

I stand up, my reflection catching in the floor-to-ceiling windows. My hair is pulled back in a sleek black ponytail, emphasizing my refined cheekbones and elegantly shaped eyes—features my mother always said made me look "distinguished." At thirty-five, I've finally grown into the confidence that I used to only pretend to have. I straighten my silk blouse, smooth my fitted slacks, and decide that tonight, I'm going to enjoy my success. I'll tell Corbin about the podcast tomorrow.

"Reservation's at eight!" he calls from the office.

"Perfect," I reply, my voice steady. "I'm going to call my parents and tell them the news."

As I press my mother's number on my phone, I take a deep breath. Whatever happens with Corbin and his ego, I've earned this moment. The girl whose grandparents couldn't afford museum admission fees is now a *New York Times* bestselling author, illuminating hidden histories for the world to see. And I'm not about to let anyone—not even the man I'm going to marry—dim my light.

CHAPTER TWENTY-FOUR

I adjust the pen in my hand, flexing my fingers to ward off a cramp. The line at Tattered Cover still stretches to the door—I've been signing books for over two hours now. When I first walked in and saw the life-size poster of myself alongside my book cover—announcing the signing to a line of at least forty people—I was stunned.

My first signing, and this kind of turnout. So even though my cheeks ache from smiling, I can't complain—this is more than I hoped for. Not to mention, I'm still on a high after my celebratory dinner with Corbin last night. I can almost taste the rich wine we shared, feel the warmth that spread through my chest when he raised his glass to toast my success. He was so supportive and seemed genuinely happy for me. I actually felt guilty for even doubting he would be.

"Could you make it out to Anna? She's my daughter who's studying archaeology at CU Boulder," says the gray-haired woman in front of me, sliding my book across the table.

"Of course," I reply, uncapping a fresh marker. "Is she specializing in any particular area?"

As the woman launches into a proud explanation of her daughter's research interests, I notice a figure at the end of the line. A woman wearing a navy-blue baseball cap pulled low over her face stands motionless, staring directly at me with an intensity that sends a shivery chill down my spine. Unlike the other attendees, who chat excitedly among themselves—their voices creating a low, pleasant hum—or browse their phones with soft screen glows illuminating their faces, she remains perfectly still, her gaze unwavering.

"... and your work has been so inspiring to her," the gray-haired woman concludes.

I drag my attention back to my new friend in front of me. "That's wonderful to hear. Please tell Anna to reach out if she ever has questions." I sign with a flourish, adding a small note of encouragement. I look up again, and the woman is still there, but this time she's shaking her head at me. I switch my attention to the next person in line, feeling awkward and uncertain.

After finishing with the next few signings, I glance back toward the end of the line. The woman in the baseball cap is gone. I scan the crowded bookstore but see no sign of her. She must have jumped out of line and left. I furrow my brow, wondering where she went and why she was just standing there staring at me. The whole thing gives me the creeps.

"Last one, Dr. Chin," the bookstore manager says, guiding a teenage boy forward for a signature.

After the final fan departs, I stand and stretch, my lower back protesting from hours of sitting. The bookstore staff begin breaking down the event space as I gather my things, folding chairs with metallic clangs that echo through the area as it empties.

"Great turnout tonight," the owner says, helping me with my jacket. She hesitates, wringing her hands. "Though I need to tell you about something that happened during the event."

I pause, sensing the tension in her voice. "What happened?"

"Your promotional poster—the one we had displayed at the entrance—someone vandalized it while you were signing." Her face flushes with embarrassment. "One of my staff noticed it about halfway through the evening. Someone had written across your photo in red marker. Large letters saying, 'Her fiancé is a liar.'"

My blood turns cold. "During the signing?"

She nods miserably. "We took it down immediately, but ... I can show you the security footage if you'd like. Maybe we can identify who—"

"No." The word comes out sharper than I intended. The thought of watching someone deface my image, of seeing those words scrawled across my face, makes my skin crawl. Plus, I'm sure I know who it was, that woman in the hat ...

"Just throw it away," I say.

"Are you sure? We could file a report—"

"I'm sure." I force some much-needed calmness into my voice. "Thank you for handling it so discreetly and thoughtfully."

She nods, clearly relieved not to be obliged to pursue it farther. "I'm so sorry this happened. In twenty years of hosting events, I've never ..."

I barely hear the rest of her words. "Thanks for hosting

tonight," I finally manage, my voice hollow. The unsettled feeling follows me all the way to the parking lot.

I turn on some classical music on the way home, and by the time I return to our condo, the tension in my shoulders has eased. The lights of Denver glitter through our vast windows, and I kick off my heels with a sigh of relief. Corbin is out filming a segment for his channel, leaving the space blissfully quiet.

I pour myself a glass of pinot noir and settle onto our leather couch, opening my laptop to check the social media response to tonight's event. My publisher insisted I become more active online to promote the book, and as much as I initially resisted, I can't deny the strategy is working.

The notifications are overwhelming—hundreds of comments, shares, and messages across platforms. I scroll through them, smiling at the enthusiastic responses, until I notice a pattern. On nearly every post I've made in the last two weeks, the same username appears: @LostHistory_Fan.

Unlike the supportive comments from other followers, these messages have a subtle edge.

> *Where's your other half tonight? The famous YouTube star too busy to support his fiancée?*

> *The perfect archaeology power couple strikes again! Though one of you is hiding a little secret ...*

> *Too bad Corbin's Netflix show got canceled. Ever wonder how he discovered the royal chamber in Peru? Think that was his idea?*

> *That engagement ring looks expensive. Wonder if he*

can still afford flashy gifts like that with his declining views?

My finger hovers over the screen. These comments aren't just rude—they're personal. I check the profile, but it's sparse—created recently, no photo, no personal information. *Ugh, internet trolls.* Why do people have to be so mean?

I close the laptop just as I hear Corbin's key in the door.

An hour later, the two of us are sitting at the dining table, eating carry-out.

"So, I've been getting some pretty nasty comments across my social media."

"Oh, like what?"

"Comments about us, like asking why you weren't at my book signing, your canceled show ... your declining numbers on YouTube."

"Multiple people or just one?"

"One."

Corbin spears a piece of grilled salmon, not looking up from his plate. "Ignore them. It comes with the territory. People like to hide behind their computer screens and pile on the barbs, anonymously like a coward."

"But these were personal," I insist, pushing my rice around on my plate. "The person made a weird comment about how you found the site in Peru. Like you were hiding a secret."

Corbin looks up. "No secret. I just followed the clues that no one else was paying attention to ... most of which came from the LiDAR scans."

"But that's just it," I say, setting down my fork. "She talked about you like you were some kind of ... I don't know, idea thief?"

Corbin laughs, but there's a hint of discomfort in it. "That's ridiculous. Ideas are everywhere. Everyone I meet has some big idea." He says 'big' in air quotes. "Listen, Mer, there are two types of people in this world, those who act on their ideas and those who don't. I just happened to create a series of videos about mine."

I chew on my lip. He's not taking this seriously.

"And that's not all," I continue. "There was this woman at the signing tonight, wearing a baseball cap, just … staring at me. Not like a fan—it was hostile. Unsettling. When I looked back later, she was gone."

"A fan got starstruck by the great Dr. Chin," Corbin says with a smirk. "Can't say I blame her."

"This wasn't admiration, Corbin. And someone vandalized my promotional poster during the event. Right there at the entrance while I was signing books." My voice rises slightly. "They wrote 'Her fiancé is a liar' across my face in red marker."

Corbin's fork pauses halfway to his mouth. "What?"

"The bookstore owner found it halfway through the signing. Someone had been close enough to deface my image while I was sitting right there." I set down my fork, my appetite completely gone. "What if it was that woman who was staring at me?"

Corbin swallows his bite of food and sets down his fork too, his expression more serious now. "That's … weird. But, Meredith, this is part of being in the public eye. People get obsessive about public figures—trust me, I get strange stuff all the time."

"This felt different." I pull out my phone and show him the string of comments. "Look at what they're saying about us. About you. The same type of thing that was written on my poster."

He skims them quickly, his jaw tightening. "It's someone trying to get a rise out of us. Probably jealous of our success."

"You're not taking this seriously," I say, unable to keep the edge from my voice.

"I am, but I don't want you getting paranoid just as things are taking off for you." He reaches across the table to take my hand. "You've worked so hard for this recognition. Don't let one weird fan ruin it."

I withdraw my hand, frustration building. "If you'd seen the way this woman was looking at me—"

"Did she approach you? Threaten you in any way?" When I shake my head, he continues, "Then she's just a fan, Meredith. Probably nervous to meet you."

"But the comments—"

"Block them," he says simply, returning to his meal. "If it happens again, we can look into it more. But right now, you're letting one creepy fan overshadow our success."

I fall silent, knowing further argument will only entrench his position. Maybe he's right. Maybe the strain of the book tour, the interviews, and the sudden recognition are suddenly overwhelming me.

Nothing serious has happened. Just one weirdo on the internet is no big deal—*Right?*

CHAPTER TWENTY-FIVE

The ride home from my parents' house is suffocatingly silent. It's been nearly a week since the book signing, and Corbin has been unusually distant. He usually enjoys dinner with my parents, but this evening went in a completely different direction.

"Are we going to talk about what happened tonight?" I finally ask, my voice cutting through the silence like a nail on glass.

"There's nothing to talk about," Corbin replies, not taking his eyes off the road.

I let out an exasperated sigh. "Nothing to talk about? You practically bit my father's head off when he started telling us about his Brussels trip."

"He was droning on and on about Belgian architecture. I've heard it all before." His dismissive tone makes my blood simmer.

"He was excited to share with you. And the way you brushed off my mom when she asked about your Netflix show—" I stop myself, remembering how his face darkened when Mom innocently enquired about his latest videos.

Corbin's jaw tightens further. "I don't want to talk about my canceled show with your parents."

"They're just showing interest in your work," I say, softer now, trying to defuse the situation. "They've always supported you."

"Yeah, well, I don't need their support right now."

The rest of the ride passes in an oppressive silence, the raindrops intensifying against the windshield, matching my growing frustration. By the time we pull into our parking garage, the concrete pillars casting long shadows under the fluorescent lights, I've mentally rehearsed a dozen ways to confront him about his behavior.

Inside our condo, I kick off my shoes by the door, my feet aching after hours of tension. The familiar scent of sandalwood from our diffuser should be comforting, but tonight it just feels inane. Corbin heads straight to the kitchen, the sound of ice clinking against glass telling me he's pouring himself a whisky.

"Do you want one?" he asks, a peace offering of sorts.

"No, thanks. I'm going to get ready for bed." I'm too tired, too annoyed, for a drink.

In our bedroom, I remove my gold hoop earrings and the jade pendant my grandmother gave me before she passed, placing them carefully in my jewelry box. I unzip my dress, the soft pink fabric pooling at my feet. As I catch my reflection in the full-length mirror, I expect to see what I usually see, the woman my mother always wanted me to be—successful, poised, engaged to a promising man. But tonight, all I see is the uncertainty in my own eyes.

Over the past few days, the comments from @LostHistory_Fan have been escalating. I blocked the original account, but they keep popping back up as @LostHistory_Fan1, then 2, then 3.

> Trust is such a fragile thing, isn't it?

This appeared under a photo from my university lecture last week.

> Some secrets have a way of surfacing, like unearthed artifacts.

I found this comment on my post announcing my book. When I finally worked up the courage to check the profile earlier today, my blood ran cold—there were photos from last week's signing when my poster was vandalized. Grainy shots of me at the table, the crowd, even one of me walking to my car afterward. Someone has been watching me. @LostHistory_Fan isn't some random internet troll, it's someone who has been following me in real life.

I want to tell Corbin, show him the evidence, but between his filming schedule and my book tour, there hasn't been a moment where it felt right to talk about it. And when we are together, like tonight on the way to dinner, he dismisses my concerns so quickly that I lose my nerve.

After a hot shower that does little to ease the knot of tension between my shoulder blades, I slip into a silk chemise—the emerald green one that Corbin says brings out the amber flecks in my eyes. Maybe I can salvage this night, turn it around. After all, we've never let an argument fester before.

When Corbin finally enters our bedroom, his expression

is softer, the whisky having taken some of the edge off his mood. He unbuttons the top few buttons of his shirt but keeps the rest of his clothes on. I'm sitting on the edge of our bed, running a wide-toothed comb through my damp hair.

"That dinner was really something," he says. "Your mom still doesn't understand that I'm allergic to cilantro."

I laugh softly. "She forgets. But you know how she is—feeding people is her love language."

He nods, a small smile playing on his lips, and for a moment, I think we might be okay. I set my comb down and move toward him, sliding my hands up his chest as he removes his shirt.

"I've been thinking," I murmur, pressing a kiss to his collarbone, "maybe we should make up properly." My fingers trail down to his belt.

To my surprise, Corbin gently takes my hands and steps back. "Not tonight, Meredith. I'm tired."

It's the first time he's ever rejected my advances. The sting of it hits harder than I expected.

"Seriously? That's it—you're 'tired'?" The air quotes I make with my fingers are childish, but I can't help it.

"What do you want me to say? It's been a long day." He turns away, heading to the bathroom.

Something in me snaps. "What is with you lately? You've been moody for weeks, you were rude to my parents tonight, and now you won't talk to me about what's really going on."

Corbin whirls around, his eyes suddenly ablaze. "You want to know what's going on? Fine. When were you going to tell me about Rowan Johnson?"

My blood runs cold. "What?"

"The podcast, Meredith. The biggest freaking podcast in

the world. The one I've been trying to get on for three years. When were you going to tell me you're going to be a guest?" His voice rises with each word.

I feel the color drain from my face. "How did you find out?"

"He mentioned you in his upcoming interview line-up."

I close my eyes briefly. Of course, why didn't I think of that? "I was going to tell you," I say softly. "I just wanted to find the right time."

"The right time?" Corbin laughs, but there's no humor in it. "When would that be? The day before? Or maybe after you've already done it?"

"That's not fair. I've been trying to figure out how to approach this because I know how much you wanted that interview."

"And yet somehow, you're the one who got it. The archaeologist who's been on camera, what, three times? And I've been building my channel for two years." The bitterness in his voice cuts deep.

"It's because of my book," I say, defensive now. "It's not like I went behind your back and pitched myself to them."

"Didn't you, though?" His eyes narrow. "Because it seems awfully convenient."

"Are you seriously suggesting I orchestrated this to one-up you?" I say, hot anger coursing through me. "Is that how little you think of me?"

Corbin runs a hand through his hair, frustration evident in every movement. "I don't know what to think anymore. All I know is that everything's been coming up roses for you lately, while my career is tanking."

"And that's my fault?" I cross my arms, the silk of my

chemise cool against my skin. "I should hide my success because you're struggling?"

"No, but you could have told me! You could have been honest instead of sneaking around."

"I wasn't sneaking! I was waiting for the right moment because I knew you'd react exactly like this!" My voice echoes off the walls of our bedroom.

Corbin falls silent, his face a mask of hurt and fury. When he speaks again, his voice is dangerously quiet. "Did you even try to get me on the show with you?"

"Of course I did," I reply, my tone softening. "My agent said they were only interested in discussing my book, the archaeological findings, the Indigenous perspectives. But," I hesitate, "he did say you could come with me. Sit in during the interview."

Corbin's laugh is hollow. "Sit in? Like what, your cheerleader? Your personal photographer?"

"That's not what I meant—"

"No, I get it," he interrupts. "They want the brilliant Dr. Chin, not her YouTuber fiancé. The message is pretty clear."

I reach for him, but he steps back. "Corbin, please. This doesn't have to be a competition between us."

"Easy for you to say when you're winning." His words hit like a slap.

We stare at each other across the bedroom, the distance between us suddenly insurmountable. I see the man I fell in love with—passionate, ambitious, kind—but I also see something new: a smallness I never noticed before, a fragility that both breaks my heart and infuriates me.

"I'm going to sleep in the guest room tonight," he finally says, grabbing his pillow from our bed.

"Corbin—"

"I need space, Meredith. And honestly, so do you. Think about what really matters to you—your rising star or us."

The unfairness of his ultimatum leaves me speechless. As he walks out, closing the door behind him, I sink onto the edge of our bed, tears welling in my eyes.

Outside, the rain has turned into a downpour, water streaming down the windows. I stare at my reflection fragmented by the raindrops on the glass. Tomorrow I'll have to decide—fight for Corbin to understand that my success doesn't diminish him, or start questioning whether the man I'm planning to marry can truly celebrate my achievements.

For now, though, I let the tears fall, their warm tracks on my cheeks a stark contrast to the cold emptiness of the bed beside me.

CHAPTER TWENTY-SIX

The last few days have been a whirlwind of camera lights, microphones, and perfectly timed smiles. I've given interviews from a sleek downtown studio that my agent Derek rented out—its minimalist furnishings and exposed brick walls serving as the backdrop to my sudden rise to fame. My voice has traveled through podcasts, reaching thousands of listeners. I even sat across from the hosts of *Good Morning America*, trying not to fidget under the harsh studio lights while millions of Americans sipped their morning coffee and listened to me talk about ancient civilizations.

Suddenly, Dr. Meredith Chin is the story everyone wants a piece of. "The archaeologist bringing Indigenous American history to the mainstream," they call me. My phone buzzes constantly with notifications from social media, messages from colleagues, and emails from publishers interested in my next project. It's everything I've worked for, yet there's a hollowness at the heart of it all.

Because at home, things with Corbin remain painfully civil. We orbit each other like cautious planets, exchanging pleasantries about the weather, asking if the other wants coffee. He sleeps in our bed again, but the careful distance he maintains might as well be miles. We haven't spoken about the Rowan Johnson interview scheduled for Tuesday. His name hangs between us, unmentioned and enormous.

The only good piece of news is that I haven't heard anything from @LostHistory_Fan since the night Corbin and I fought. No comments, no weird messages. It should feel like a weight lifted from my shoulders, and in some ways it does. But something else is lurking beneath the relief, a cold knot of unease that settles in my stomach each time I check my phone.

Friday afternoon finds me exhausted after a morning radio interview. My throat feels raw from talking, and my cheeks ache from smiling. The elevator ride up to our condo is a welcome moment of silence. All I want is to kick off my heels, change into sweatpants, and possibly order takeout. Maybe tonight Corbin and I can actually talk about something real.

When I unlock our door, the scent hits me first—rich tomato, garlic, and basil intermingling in a familiar aroma that immediately triggers memories. Corbin's grandmother's pasta sauce. He only makes it on special occasions.

I step farther into our condo and stop short. The kitchen and dining area are transformed. Vases of flowers cover every surface—peonies, my favorite, their lush pink blooms spilling over crystal vases; elegant calla lilies standing tall in slender glass containers; cheerful yellow sunflowers brightening the countertop. Candles flicker throughout the space, casting a warm glow as afternoon sun streams through the windows.

And there's Corbin, stirring a pot at the stove, dressed in a crisp blue button-down with the sleeves rolled up to his elbows. He looks up when he hears me, and the smile that spreads across his face is the one I fell for years ago—open, warm, slightly crooked.

"You're home early," he says, setting down his wooden spoon.

I'm still standing in the entryway, my bag dangling from my fingers. "What is all this?" I gesture at the flowers, my voice coming out softer than intended.

Corbin walks around the kitchen island, wiping his hands on a dish towel. "This," he says, sweeping his arm to encompass the transformed space, "is my best attempt at an apology." He stops a few feet from me, uncertainty flickering across his features. "Could you ever forgive me?"

I look at him—really look at him—and see again the Corbin I fell in love with. Insanely handsome with his strong jawline and those hazel eyes that change color depending on what he wears. Confident in the way he stands, shoulders straight but relaxed. Charismatic in how he's orchestrated this entire gesture, knowing exactly what would touch my heart.

"You didn't have to do all this," I say, though the tightness in my chest is already loosening.

"Yes, I did." He takes a step closer. "I've been an ass, Meredith. A jealous, insecure ass who couldn't see past his own ego to celebrate the most important person in his life. Can you forgive me?"

There are a thousand things I want to say in this moment—rehashing every wrong, every snide remark he's made. But the earnest tone in his voice gives me pause. I swallow.

"It's okay," I say.

"I love you." He leans in and kisses me lightly on the lips

before turning back to his pasta, which has started to boil over. I set my bag down on the console table.

"The pasta smells amazing," I say, sidestepping any further discussion. I know everything will boil over again later, just like the pasta he's cooking, but for now, I'm going to enjoy the peace between us.

"Are you hungry? It's almost ready." He reaches for my hand, and when our fingers touch, the familiar electricity is still there, despite everything.

"Starving," I admit.

He leads me to our dining table, already set with our best china and crystal wineglasses. A bottle of my favorite pinot noir breathes next to a small, gift-wrapped box.

"What's this?" I ask, nodding toward it.

"Later," he says with a smile. "First, food."

We sit down to steaming plates of pasta, the sauce rich and complex, exactly like his grandmother used to make. The first bite transports me back to the early days of our relationship, when he'd cook for me in his tiny apartment kitchen, eager to impress.

"Remember the first time you made this for me?" I ask, twirling pasta around my fork.

"How could I forget? The smoke alarm went off because I was so busy trying to look cool for you that I forgot about the garlic bread."

We both laugh, and for a moment it feels like us again.

"Meredith," he says, setting down his fork, "I need to say something."

I nod, waiting.

"I was wrong. Not just about how I reacted to the podcast, but about everything. I've been so caught up in my own career struggles that I couldn't see what was happening to yours for the amazing achievement it is." He reaches across the table for my hand. "I'm so incredibly proud of you. You've worked harder than anyone I know to get to where you are, and you deserve every bit of this success."

The sincerity in his eyes makes my throat tight. "Thank you," I manage.

"And that's not all." He pushes the box toward me. "Open it."

I carefully unwrap the package to find a velvet box inside. When I open it, there's a small shard of pottery, not the jewelry I was expecting.

"What's this?" I ask, confused.

His eyes are bright with excitement. "You don't recognize it? It's from your favorite place ..."

I turn the pale rock in my hand, squinting in the light. Then I realize it's Puebloan ...

"Mesa Verde?"

He smiles. "That's just a hint of what's to come. I got us private access. I want to make it up to you with a trip to your favorite place—where you've been going since you were a little girl."

My mouth falls open. "Mesa Verde? But how—"

"I talked to the park manager, pulled some strings through a contact at the National Park Service. We're able to camp just a few yards away from Cliff Palace. We'll have private access before any tourists arrive in the morning and after they leave in the evening."

I'm stunned into silence. Mesa Verde isn't just any archaeological site—it's where my father first took me when I was eight years old, it's where I decided to become an archaeologist. To have private access to Cliff Palace, one of the most significant cliff dwellings in North America, is beyond anything I could have imagined.

"Corbin, this is ..." I struggle to find words adequate to express myself. I gently place the pottery shard back in the box.

"Is it too much? Not enough? I can—"

I cut him off by standing up, walking around the table, and pulling him to his feet. "It's perfect," I whisper before pressing my lips to his.

The kiss deepens quickly, weeks of tension dissolving into something else entirely. His hands find my waist, pulling me against him as mine slide into his hair.

"The pasta," he murmurs against my mouth.

"It can wait," I reply, already working on his buttons.

Later, much later, we lie tangled in our sheets, my head on his chest, listening to his heartbeat steady beneath my ear. His fingers trace lazy patterns on my bare shoulder, sending pleasant shivers down my spine.

"We leave for Mesa Verde in the morning," he murmurs into my hair. "I've already packed most of what we need."

I prop myself up on one elbow to look at him. "When will we be back? I fly out on Monday—"

"Sunday night," Corbin says simply. "We'll have plenty of time."

As I lie back down, fitting myself against the familiar contours of his body, I wonder if this is possible—if we can heal the rift between us so completely.

Doubt pulls at the edges of my mind, but for now, I enjoy being wrapped up in Corbin's arms.

CHAPTER TWENTY-SEVEN

The morning light filters through the towering pines as Corbin expertly secures the last tent stake. His movements are fluid and practiced, revealing a side of him that always surprises me—the outdoorsman. We've set up camp just fifty yards from Cliff Palace, close enough that I can see the intricate stonework through breaks in the trees.

I watch him work, trying to summon the contentment I should feel. We've made up, said all the right words, promised to try harder. But standing here in this sacred place, I can't shake the feeling that we're just going through the motions. The problems are still there—our fights, his jealousy of my success, the way he dismisses things that matter to me. Those problems haven't surfaced in our conversations since we reconciled, but I can still feel them surging like an undercurrent beneath our interactions.

Maybe this trip was a mistake. Maybe I'm fooling myself, thinking a grand gesture and change of scenery could fix what's fundamentally wrong between us. I take a deep breath. Regardless, we're here, and I'm determined to make the most of it.

"Not bad for a city boy," I say, forcing lightness into my voice as I hand him a water bottle.

"Eagle Scout, remember?" Corbin winks, taking a long drink. "My dad would disown me if I couldn't pitch a decent tent."

I wince at the casual reference to living up to his father's expectations, something that has plagued him since he was a kid. Everything with Corbin comes back to proving himself, to meeting some invisible standard. I used to find his drive attractive, but now I wonder if that's all there is. I turn toward Cliff Palace, its sandstone structures glowing golden in the morning light, and I try to push the negative thoughts away and enjoy the moment.

"I still can't believe we have this view all to ourselves."

Corbin smiles, clearly happy with himself for bringing me here. "Come on, let's go for a hike; you can show me around."

As we hike around the cliffs, I grow silent. Mesa Verde has always pulled at me, ever since my father first brought me here. I remember standing on the overlook, my small hand in his larger one, gazing down at the ancient city built into the cliff face. "The people who built this were master architects," he told me, his voice filled with reverence. "They understood their environment in ways we've forgotten."

That first visit planted a seed that grew into my life's work. While other kids collected dolls or baseball cards, I gathered books about the Ancestral Puebloans. I made clay models of their dwellings and wrote school projects about their agricultural techniques. The mystery of why they left—

abandoning these spectacular homes they'd carved from the very cliffs—became my personal obsession.

"You're doing it again," Corbin says, irritation creeping into his voice.

"Doing what?"

"Completely zoning out on me. I've been trying to talk to you for the past five minutes, and you're just staring off into space."

I feel heat rise in my cheeks. "Oh, sorry, I was—"

"You were ignoring me," he cuts me off. "We've come all this way to spend time together, remember?"

"Yes, I remember!" I snap back, my voice rising.

"Lower your voice," he hisses. I'm suddenly aware of a family with young children who've appeared on the trail nearby, the parents shooting us concerned glances. Corbin follows my gaze, and his jaw tightens, but he drops his volume. "Fine. Whatever. I just thought maybe for once you could focus on the present. On us."

The silence stretches between us, heavy and uncomfortable. The family passes by, giving us a wide berth, and I watch the children point excitedly at the historical structures, their wonder untainted by adult complications.

After a long moment, Corbin runs his hand through his hair and lets out a frustrated sigh. "Look, I'm sorry. I didn't mean to ... this isn't how I wanted today to go."

I cross my arms, still stinging from his dismissal of everything that matters to me. "No, I'm sure it isn't."

"I have a surprise for you tonight," he says suddenly, his voice taking on a forced brightness. "Something special. Why don't we head back to camp, and you can freshen up while I get things ready?"

"A surprise?" I raise an eyebrow, not sure if I want to be surprised by him right now.

"If I told you, it wouldn't be a surprise," he replies, attempting his usual charming wink. But it falls flat. "Just ... let me try to make this better, okay? We've got the whole evening ahead of us."

I grab my toiletry bag and a change of clothes, heading toward the small solar shower setup we've rigged near the tent. The warmth of the water is heavenly after a day of hiking, washing away the dust and sweat. As I'm drying off and changing into fresh clothes, I hear Corbin moving around the campsite, clearly preparing something.

When I return to the tent to drop off my things, Corbin is nowhere to be seen—probably setting up his surprise elsewhere. I kneel to tuck my toiletry bag into my backpack, but as I turn, my elbow catches on Corbin's duffel bag, sending it toppling from the camp chair where it was precariously balanced.

"Damn it," I mutter as the contents spill across the tent floor. Quickly, I begin gathering his things—a sweater, a flashlight, his toiletry kit. As I reach for a small leather-bound notebook that slid under my sleeping bag, something larger and heavier catches my eye.

Partially hidden beneath Corbin's extra clothes is a weathered leather journal—much larger and clearly much older than the pocket notebook I was reaching for. The leather is cracked with age, the corners worn smooth from handling. It's secured with a leather strap wrapped around a tarnished brass button.

I hesitate. This must be his private journal. I shouldn't pry. But something draws me to it. I glance over my shoulder, confirming I'm still alone, then carefully lift the journal from the bag.

The weight of it surprises me—it's substantial, filled with what I can now see are hundreds of pages, many of them dog-eared or marked with colorful sticky notes. The leather feels butter-soft against my fingers, the kind of softness that comes only from decades of handling.

I know I shouldn't, but I unwrap the leather strap and open the cover.

CHAPTER TWENTY-EIGHT

In faded ink, in careful, scholarly handwriting, is the title "Theories of the Past: H.L." Below it, in smaller text: "Private Research Journal of Henry Lawrence, Ph.D. 1963–1978."

Henry Lawrence. The name registers immediately in my archaeological memory—a controversial figure from the early twentieth century, known for his radical theories about ancient civilizations. His ideas were widely dismissed by the academic community during his lifetime; though in recent years, some have been reconsidered as new evidence has emerged.

As I carefully turn the pages, my breath catches in my throat. Here, meticulously documented with hand-drawn maps, detailed notes, and careful citations, are all the theories that have made Corbin famous. The Richat Structure as the true location of Atlantis. The purpose of the Great Pyramid as an ancient power generator. The prehistorical civilization that built Göbekli Tepe. Every revolutionary "discovery" that Corbin has presented as his own original research is here, laid out in exacting detail by Henry Lawrence many decades ago.

Page after page reveals the true source of Corbin's "genius."

I flip through sections on lost technologies, astronomical knowledge, forgotten migration patterns. Each theory I recognize from Corbin's videos, often presented word for word as Lawrence had written it.

I am shocked, appalled. But what I find next nearly stops my heart.

A detailed sketch of a mountainous region with precise coordinates scrawled in the margin. Lawrence titled this section "Royal Burial Sites—Theoretical Locations Based on Inca Astronomical Alignments." The handwriting becomes more excited here, less controlled, as if Lawrence was on the verge of something momentous. He calculated the exact position where an undisturbed royal tomb should be located, based on star charts and ceremonial pathways. The coordinates are a near perfect match with the remote Andean location where Corbin made his "miraculous" discovery.

My hands shake as I read Lawrence's final notes in this section: "If my calculations are correct, this site should contain an intact burial chamber of significant importance. The astronomical alignments suggest royal status. Expedition planned for 1979."

The implications hit me like a physical blow. Corbin's career-defining discovery, the find that launched him to international fame, wasn't luck or intuition or even his own research. It was Henry Lawrence's forty-year-old findings and calculations. I keep flipping the pages, my hands frantic now, only to discover that the last portion of the journal pages has been torn out.

Footsteps crunch on the gravel outside. Corbin is returning.

My heart racing, I wrap the journal and shove it back into his bag, arranging his clothes around it exactly as they were. I make a show of gathering my toiletry kit as he calls my name from outside the tent.

"In here," I call back, my voice miraculously steady despite the adrenaline pumping through me. "Just finishing up."

When he pokes his head into the tent, I'm sitting calmly on my sleeping bag, brushing my hair. If he notices the slight tremor in my hands or the flush in my cheeks, he doesn't mention it.

"Ready for your surprise?" he asks, his eyes bright—the eyes of the Corbin I thought I knew. Not the man who has built his entire career on stolen, unacknowledged work.

I force a smile. "Sure."

I clench and unclench my fist, my palms sweating as I follow him down the path. Everything about him now seems performative—his enthusiasm, his charm, the way he takes my hand so tenderly. How much of the man I fell in love with is in any way real?

And why wouldn't he tell me about the journal?

I follow him, my mind racing. The sun has nearly set now, the cliff dwellings cast in deep shadow. Realizations roll across my brain like a stock ticker ... the connection between Atlantis and the Richat Structure, the burial chamber in Peru. All of which he claimed were his ideas. And I stood next to him, on camera, supporting him. But off camera, nothing was true—everything was a lie.

I follow silently as he leads me down the trail toward Cliff Palace. In the central plaza, he's laid out an elaborate meal on a Navajo blanket, lanterns casting a warm glow over the ancient stones. Under different circumstances, it would be breathtakingly romantic.

We sit across from each other, the ruins surrounding us like silent witnesses. I can hardly breathe at this point, the swirl of thoughts in my head nearly suffocating me. Corbin unwraps a charcuterie board full of artisanal cheeses, fruit and crackers he surely must have picked up before the trip. I struggle to reconcile the man before me with the fraud I now know him to be.

I can barely taste the food as questions burn on my tongue. I wait until he's poured us both steaming cups of tea, until the moment feels intimate and sacred—just as he planned it. Then I set down my barely touched plate and look directly into his eyes.

"I found Henry Lawrence's journal in your bag," I say quietly.

Corbin freezes, cup halfway to his lips. For a split second, shock registers on his face before he carefully sets the cup down, his movements deliberate.

"Journal?" he says, but there's a new tightness around his eyes.

"A leather journal," I continue, my voice steady despite my pounding heart. "With 'Theories of the Past: H.L.' written on the first page. The source of every 'original' theory you've ever presented," I say, aware of the shake in my voice. "The location of the burial chamber in Peru."

Corbin stares at me in the flickering lantern light, his face unreadable. When he finally speaks, his voice is unnervingly calm. "It was given to me—a gift. I took what he wrote and shared his ideas with the world."

"Shared? You didn't even name him," I counter. "You've

been passing off his theories as your own original research. And that discovery in Peru—you let the entire world believe you found it on your own. Why would you do that? It's worse than plagiarism, Corbin."

His laugh is sharp and humorless. "Plagiarism? There are no new ideas under the sun, Mer. You study history, you should know that."

"It's not about originality. It's about attribution. Academic integrity. Something you'd understand if you'd—" I stop myself, but the implication hangs between us.

"If I'd what?" His voice drops. "I'd gotten some fancy degree? Spent eight years accumulating debt just to put PhD after my name?"

"That's unfair."

"No, what's unfair is how Lawrence was ridiculed by the academic community. His theories were buried, dismissed. Even his Peru expedition was denied funding. I gave them new life."

"You gave yourself fame and fortune using another man's work. You claimed credit for one of the most significant archaeological discoveries of the decade—and it wasn't even yours to claim!"

"I gave his work the platform it deserved!" Corbin's voice rises, bouncing off the ancient walls. "Do you think anyone would have listened to these theories coming from a dusty old journal? Would Netflix have funded an expedition to follow Henry Lawrence's forty-year-old research? I made people care. I made them see."

"By lying," I say, my own anger rising to match his. "You took full credit for finding that tomb. Does anyone else know about this? Corbin, this is fraud!"

Corbin's face transforms, a mask of anger taking over his features.

"Careful, Meredith," he says, his voice dangerously soft. "Very careful."

"Or what?" I challenge, rising to my feet. "You'll leave me? For telling the truth?"

He stands too, matching my stance. "Don't be so self-righteous, Meredith. Remember, you're as much a part of this as I am. If you go public with the journal, you can say goodbye to your bestseller. Your career will be over."

He's right. Chilled, I shift my weight from side to side, trying to think of what to say next.

"Where did you get this journal, anyway?"

Corbin looks away for a moment, then back at me. "It's a long story for another time," he says firmly. I open my mouth to object and then close it. Do I even want to know?

And if he told me, would it be the truth?

"So, what now?" I ask, suddenly exhausted. "You expect me to forget what I saw? To keep your secret?"

"Yes," he says simply. "That's exactly what I expect. Because the alternative …" He lets the sentence hang unfinished, the threat clear enough.

We stand in tense silence, the lantern flames flickering between us, casting bizarre, elongated shadows against the stone walls. Shadows that seem to move of their own accord, as if the amassed centuries of inhabitants are gathering to witness our confrontation.

"I think I want to go back to the hotel," I say finally, my voice barely above a whisper.

"We have special permission to camp here tonight," Corbin reminds me, his tone reasonable again, as if the explosion of anger never happened. "It would be a shame to waste it."

"I'm not spending the night here with you," I say, gathering my resolve. "Not after this."

Something dangerous flashes in his eyes. "And how exactly do you plan to leave? We're miles from anywhere, Meredith. The rangers won't be back until morning."

As his words sink in, I realize my predicament. We're alone in the wilderness, the journal that could destroy his career now safely back in his possession, and I've just made it very clear that I can't be trusted with his secret.

The ancient walls of Cliff Palace feel less like protection and more like a trap, with no way out until dawn.

PART 3

RILEY—PRESENT

CHAPTER TWENTY-NINE

I perch on the edge of the ornate bathtub, the porcelain smooth and cold against my thighs. I've been in here for nearly twenty minutes, my heart pounding so loudly I'm certain it must be audible through the heavy wooden door. The shower drips steadily, each droplet hitting the marble with a rhythmic *plink* that marks the passing seconds.

I *should* feel guilty about this invasion of privacy.

I should put the phone down, walk away, pretend I never saw anything. But Grace's warnings echo in my mind, mingling with Marcus's confusion about Kelly's existence. Something isn't right, and my instincts won't let me stop.

My fingers tremble as I scroll through the messages between Corbin and his supposed "assistant." Each exchange makes my stomach tighten further.

I scroll back as far as I can, trying to read them from the beginning.

> Where's the money from the Netflix deal?
> You promised payment by Tuesday.

> Working on it. I'm still waiting for them to wire the money. You'll get it Friday.

Not acceptable. I've kept my end of the bargain. I expect you to keep yours.

> I'm doing everything I can, I promise. We can celebrate together. Champagne at my place?

Is that a booty call?

> I would never.

Money? Booty call? This doesn't sound anything like a relationship between an assistant and her boss. My mouth goes dry as I continue scrolling, a sick feeling spreading through my chest.

Your last video was exactly what we discussed. But I saw the view count. You can do better. Make it more controversial. Stir up some more conspiracy. Show that handsome face of yours. That's what sells.

> I'm trying to maintain some credibility here.

Credibility? Don't make me laugh. You know what would happen to your "credibility" if people knew the truth.

I shiver. *The truth about what?* I grip the edge of the tub with my free hand, suddenly dizzy. I scroll back farther, feeling like an intruder but unable to stop. It's like excavating a burial site you know you shouldn't disturb but can't turn away from.

> You didn't answer my call. Again.
> Remember our agreement. I OWN you.

> I was filming. Can't we move past this? What we had is over. The arrangement is strictly business now.

What we had? So they were involved romantically. The jealousy that flares within me is immediately tempered by confusion. If they were together, why the elaborate ruse about her being his assistant? Why hasn't he ever mentioned her?

> It's over when I say it's over. The journal stays with me unless you want everyone to know exactly where your "brilliant theories" come from.

My breath catches. What journal? What theories? What else is Corbin hiding? The thought makes me physically ill—after all, I've just allowed myself to be filmed for his channel, lending my academic credibility to whatever house of cards he's constructed. I keep reading.

> We need to talk about the missing pages.

> What missing pages?

> Don't play dumb, Corbin.

> I've told you a hundred times, I didn't remove any pages from the journal.

I can't stop scrolling. Message after message that makes my stomach clench. Each one revealing a relationship I didn't know existed. Finally, I land on a text from right around the time when we started dating.

> You're speaking at Arizona State? Without consulting me first? Bold move. Stupid, but bold.

> It's just a speaking engagement. Standard material. Nothing new.

> I'd better not see anything I don't approve of.

I shiver despite the humid air filtering through the small window. The relationship is clearly toxic, controlling. Nothing that I'm reading feels like messages from an assistant at all. This person, whoever they are, seems to have Corbin trapped in some kind of blackmail situation. My mind races with possibilities, each more disturbing than the last. *What have I gotten myself into?* The man I've been sharing a bed with, whose touch I've welcomed, whose grief I thought mirrored my own—was any of that even real? I frantically scroll back and forth amid their history of messages. I keep reading, desperate to find something that shows me Corbin hasn't been doing nothing but lie to me since I've known him. The most recent exchanges are from today, and my hands begin to shake more violently as I read them.

> I saw your teaser ... who is this Riley woman, and why is she coming on your channel? I never agreed to this.

My name on the screen sends a chill through me. This person knows who I am. This person has been watching us.

> Just a colleague. Adding credibility to the Tikal segment.

Just a colleague. The casual dismissal stings more than it should, given what I'm discovering. But in the next message he defends his right to a personal life—that has to count for something, doesn't it?

> A colleague? I know you, Corbin. Are you sleeping with her?

> My personal life isn't part of our agreement.

> EVERYTHING about you is part of our agreement. Get rid of her, or I swear I'll tell her everything. About the journal. About Meredith. About what really happened at Mesa Verde.

I nearly drop the phone, my fingers numb. The bathroom tilts around me as blood rushes in my ears. *What about Meredith? What about what really happened at Mesa Verde?*

Oh God. Grace's warning comes back full force. *The police wanted to make sure it was actually an accident, not a murder.*

I grip the cold edge of the tub harder, willing myself not to pass out. Could it be true? Could Corbin have done something to Meredith? The man who held me through the night, the man who kissed away my tears when I spoke of Brody—could he be capable of that?

The message continues.

> You think she'd still look at you the same way if she knew what you did? How you REALLY became famous? She's an actual archaeologist. She'd despise you. And that's if I'm feeling generous enough to tell only HER and not the whole world.

My stomach lurches. I swallow hard against the acidic taste of fear rising in my throat. Whatever Corbin did—whatever this mysterious K is holding over him—it's serious enough to destroy him professionally. And it has something to do with Meredith's death.

I scroll frantically through more messages, looking for explanations, for answers, but find only more veiled threats and Corbin's increasingly desperate attempts to placate K. My mind spins with terrible possibilities. What if Grace was right? What if Corbin did push Meredith?

What if I'm sleeping with a murderer?

The room spins as I look up from the phone. I silently curse myself for the wine at dinner; it's making my thoughts sluggish, so that I'm seeking rationality as if I were wading through thick mud.

And what of this K person? Someone from Corbin's past, clearly, someone with power over him, someone dangerous enough to make him live a double life. Someone who is watching us even now, here in Guatemala. The thought sends another wave of nausea through me.

I need to leave.

I need to get out of here, away from Corbin, back to Phoenix. I'll call Grace, tell her everything. She warned me, and I should have listened. I should have—

The bathroom door handle turns with a soft click. I freeze, the phone clutched in my trembling hand, as the door swings open to reveal Corbin standing in the frame, his expression shifting from sleepiness to confusion as he takes in the sight of me with his phone.

"Riley," he says, his voice dangerously quiet, "what are you doing?"

Too late.

CHAPTER THIRTY

"Riley," Corbin repeats, "what are you doing with my phone?"

He stands in the doorway, backlit by the bedroom lamps. His hair is disheveled, eyes heavy with interrupted sleep, and he's wearing only a pair of boxer shorts. In another context, I might have found the sight of him endearing—vulnerable even. Now, with his phone clutched in my trembling hand, a piece of damning evidence, he looks like a stranger.

The dripping shower provides a steady rhythm that matches my racing heartbeat. I realize I've been holding my breath and exhale shakily, the sound unnaturally loud in the tense near-silence. The cool porcelain of the bathtub rim presses against my thighs as I grip it for support.

"Who is K?" I ask, my voice steadier than I expected. I hold up the phone, screen illuminated with those damning messages. "The person you've been pretending is your assistant Kelly?"

Corbin's gaze flicks between my face and the phone. He takes a hesitant step into the bathroom, the floor creaking slightly beneath his weight. The scent of his sleep-warm skin—familiar just hours ago when I curled against him in bed—now seems foreign.

"You've been going through my messages." It's not a question but an accusation. The bathroom feels smaller with him in it, the walls pressing in.

"I wasn't snooping," I lie, the words bitter on my tongue. "But the notification came through when I was in here, and I saw ..." I stop, remembering the veiled threats, the references to Meredith, to Mesa Verde. I suppose I should ease into such a delicate topic, but the alcohol swimming through my brain compels me to summon a single question. "What happened at Mesa Verde, Corbin?"

His face pales, the tan he's acquired during yesterday's filming in the Guatemalan sun suddenly ashen. He runs a hand through his hair.

"Riley, it's nearly two in the morning," he says as he gestures toward the bedroom. "Let's go back to bed. We can talk about this tomorrow."

"No." The word comes out sharp, hollow against the marble walls. "I want to know now. These messages ..." I scroll quickly, finding one particularly damning exchange. "This person is threatening you. About a journal? About Meredith's death? And they're angry about me being on your channel."

The words feel thick in my mouth as they spill out, my tongue not quite cooperating. I can hear it too—the way my consonants blur together, how "threatening" became "threa'ning." *Damn it, I've got to stop drinking so much.*

Corbin sighs heavily. The humidity from the shower has created a sheen of moisture on his bare chest, glistening in the dim bathroom light.

"You've been drinking," he says, nodding toward the empty wineglass sitting on the bathroom counter—evidence of the nightcap I brought in with me when I first came in to remove my makeup.

"What?" The accusation catches me off guard. "Just a few glasses with dinner." I straighten my posture. "I'm not drunk, Corbin."

"Three," he corrects, his voice gentle but firm. "Three glasses at dinner, then another when we got back. It's okay. I understand." His tone shifts, becoming softer, more concerned. "But the alcohol might be affecting your judgment right now."

I blink, momentarily confused. *Did I really have four glasses?* The dinner is somewhat foggy—the wine flowed freely as we dined with Dr. Garcia and Marcus. And yes, I poured another when we returned to the room. But I'm not drunk. *Am I?*

The cool marble countertop suddenly seems necessary for balance as I push myself up from the bathtub's edge. My reflection in the mirror shows flushed cheeks, bright eyes—signs I've learned to recognize from too many nights alone with the bottle. The realization sends a rush of doubt through me.

"This isn't about the wine," I insist, but my voice lacks conviction even to my own ears. "These messages—someone is blackmailing you. Someone who knows about Meredith's death."

Corbin takes another step toward me, close enough now that I can feel the heat radiating from his body. His eyes—those hazel eyes that change color with his moods, now dark with concern—hold mine steadily.

"Let's go sit down and talk," he says as he extends his

hand to me. I'm uncertain whether to hand him back the phone or take his hand in my own. I choose the former. He takes the phone from me and gestures for me to head back to the bedroom. I oblige, sitting on the edge of the bed. He follows and turns on a side lamp before settling down next to me.

"K is my ex," he says simply. "Katherine. We were together before Meredith. It ended badly. She's ... unstable. She helped me with research early in my career, and now she thinks she owns part of my success."

I chew on my lip. *Okay ... so far, so good.* The explanation is plausible. Simple even. But it doesn't account for the references to Mesa Verde, to what "really happened" with Meredith, or why he owes her money.

"She mentions Mesa Verde," I press. "She says she'll tell me what really happened there. What is that supposed to mean?"

A muscle twitches in Corbin's jaw. "It means nothing. Katherine was jealous of Meredith and me. And when the accident happened, she saw an opportunity to lash out at me. Create problems that aren't there."

"That doesn't explain—"

"Riley," he interrupts, his voice gentler now, "you've had a long day. The heat, the filming, the wine. You're exhausted, and finding these messages has upset you. I get it." He sets the phone on the counter, face down, then takes my hands in his. They're warm, steady. "I promise I'll explain everything tomorrow. When we're both clear-headed."

I search his face, looking for signs of deception, of manipulation. But all I see is the man I've come to care for—tired, concerned, a little hurt by my suspicion. The man who understands my grief because he carries his own. Could Grace have been wrong?

Could I be misinterpreting the messages, the interactions between him and K?

The room tilts as I move, confirming what I've been trying to deny—the wine has affected me more than I realized. The familiar sensation of alcohol-induced paranoia creeps along the edges of my consciousness.

"I'm just trying to understand," I murmur, suddenly feeling foolish. "These messages seemed so threatening."

"Katherine *is* threatening." Corbin sighs. "She's threatened lawsuits, exposed private details about my life, even followed me to events. That's why I don't talk about her. That's why I use a generic name for her when people ask about messages or calls." He pauses. "I should have told you. I'm sorry."

The explanation hangs in the air between us, almost convincing. *Almost.*

"Then why does she talk about a journal? And money?" My voice sounds distant, fatigue and alcohol blurring the edges of my thoughts.

Corbin sighs. "Early in my career, Katherine helped me research some topics. She thinks that entitles her to credit, to compensation. We've been negotiating a settlement for months." He brushes a strand of hair from my face, his touch tender. "It's boring legal stuff, Riley. Not some dark conspiracy."

I want to believe him. God, how I want to believe him. The alternative—that I've fallen for a man who might be involved in his fiancée's death, who might be building a career on lies—is too painful to contemplate.

"And tomorrow you'll tell me everything?" I ask, hating the pleading note in my voice.

"Everything," he promises, pressing a kiss to my forehead. "No more secrets."

As he tucks the blankets around me, his movements careful, I find myself yielding to exhaustion. The room spins when I close my eyes, a telltale sign that perhaps Corbin was right about the wine.

In the darkness beyond my closed eyelids, I hear the soft tap of his fingers on his phone screen, sending a message to someone. A final thread of suspicion winds through my mind as sleep overtakes me. Who is he texting at this hour? And what is he saying?

But my questions evaporate as consciousness fades, leaving only the distant sound of tropical insects beyond the window and the steady rhythm of Corbin's breathing beside me. My last thought before sleep claims me is of Grace's warning: *Just be careful.*

CHAPTER THIRTY-ONE

Sunlight breaks through the gauzy curtains of our hotel room, painting golden stripes across the bed. I wake to an empty space beside me, my hand instinctively reaching for Corbin before memory floods back—the phone, the messages, the confrontation in the bathroom. My head throbs with a dull, insistent ache, and my mouth feels like I've been chewing cotton.

"Morning." Corbin's voice carries from the patio adjoining our room. "Coffee's ready when you are."

I sit up slowly, fighting a wave of dizziness. The clock on the bedside table reads 9:37—hours later than we planned to start filming today. Through the open patio doors, I can see Corbin lounging at a table laden with covered dishes, reading something on his tablet. He's already showered and dressed in lightweight khaki pants and a blue button-down with the sleeves rolled up, looking refreshed and relaxed. The sight is jarringly normal after the tension of last night.

I slip into the bathroom, avoiding my reflection in the mirror as I splash cold water on my face. The events of last night feel dreamlike in the harsh morning light—was it all real? *K is Kelly, or is K Katherine? The blackmail? The ex-girlfriend?* The headache intensifies.

When I emerge from the bathroom in the hotel robe, Corbin looks up with a warm smile. The morning sun catches in his hair, highlighting those silver strands at his temples that make him look distinguished rather than simply old.

"I thought you had an early filming session scheduled," I say, my voice raspy from sleep as I join him on the terrace.

"Pushed it back," he replies, pouring me a cup of coffee from an elegant carafe. "Thought we could use some time to talk."

The patio offers a breathtaking view of Lake Atitlán, its surface glittering in the bright morning light, each ripple seeming to mirror my churning thoughts. Beyond it, the jungle stretches toward distant mountains, a lush carpet of emerald green that I should appreciate, though my hangover makes it hard to focus on natural beauty. I pick at the breakfast, which is waiting beneath silver domes, the once-enticing aromas of tropical flowers and rich coffee now turning my stomach.

Corbin smiles and hands me the coffee cup, and I suddenly feel despicable for snooping through his phone. The world surrounding us only amplifies my guilt—paradise corrupted by my own suspicion.

But I still have questions.

"How are you feeling?" he asks, his tone gentle with concern.

"Like I've been trampled by a herd of jaguars," I admit, sipping the coffee gratefully. The rich, slightly bitter liquid warms me from the inside, beginning to cut through the fog of my hangover.

"Try this," Corbin says, pushing a small glass filled with a murky reddish liquid toward me. "Local hangover cure. The restaurant manager swears by it."

I eye the concoction skeptically. "What's in it?"

"Better not to ask," he says with a smile. "Something about chili peppers, tomato juice, and a few Mayan secret ingredients."

The memory of last night's wine consumption—apparently more extensive than I told myself—compels me to take the glass. I down it in one gulp, wincing at the burning, spicy flavor that sears a path down my throat.

"That's horrible," I gasp, reaching for my coffee to chase away the taste.

"But effective," Corbin promises, gesturing to the fresh fruit and pastries. "Eat something. It'll help."

We eat in silence for a few minutes, the awkwardness between us growing heavier with each passing moment. I empty two glasses of water, the contents sloshing in my stomach. Finally, I set down my fork and meet his eyes directly.

"About last night—"

"I owe you an explanation," he says simultaneously.

We both stop, an uncomfortable laugh escaping me. Corbin reaches across the table, his hand covering mine in a gesture that feels both reassuring and possessive.

"Katherine Lawrence," he begins, withdrawing his hand to refill our coffee cups. "We met a several years ago at a bar. I was still trying to make it as an engineer, and she was in graduate school." He gazes out at the lake, his profile sharp against the blue backdrop. "We were together for about a year. It was … intense."

"She helped with your YouTube channel?" I prompt, remembering the messages about a manuscript, about theories.

Corbin nods, his expression darkening. "I was between jobs—and honestly, I was pretty lost about what to do next. We were watching some documentary one night, and I mentioned how I'd always dreamed of being a history professor instead of following the family tradition into engineering. Katherine got this look in her eyes and told me about some ideas her grandfather had shared with her. She suggested I start a YouTube channel and pitched all these sensational theories—even claimed she knew the location of a burial chamber in Peru. I didn't have anything to lose at that point, so I listened."

He runs a hand through his hair, a gesture I've come to recognize as his tell when he's stressed. "I offered to put us both on camera, but she wanted to be a silent partner, stay behind the scenes. By the time I made the discovery in Peru, things between us had gone south. Like I said, Katherine was intense. Extreme highs, crushing lows. When I tried to end things, she completely lost it. Started threatening to go public, telling everyone I'd stolen her grandfather's work unless I kept paying her as a consultant."

"So you broke up?"

"Yes. We were on and off again for a while. Then I met Meredith. And everything changed. I had to cut things off completely. Even though we had an agreement, Katherine never got over our breakup. When Meredith and I got engaged, she became ... unhinged. Started sending threatening messages, showing up at Meredith's book signings."

The explanation sounds plausible, and from everything I read last night, his story tracks with the messages. But there is still the issue of Meredith's death. "In her messages, she mentions the accident at Mesa Verde."

Corbin's jaw tightens, a muscle twitching beneath the tanned skin. He takes a deep breath. "After Meredith's accident, Katherine implied online that it wasn't really an accident. It was cruel, opportunistic. Disgusting, really. She saw a chance to hurt me at my most vulnerable."

My hand trembles as I reach for my coffee cup. "The police investigation—"

"Was standard procedure for any unwitnessed death," Corbin finishes firmly. "I wear an Apple watch to track my sleep cycles—and I wore it that night too. The data showed I never moved from the tent, never got up, nothing. My sleep patterns were completely undisturbed until morning." His jaw tightens. "The police never suspected me. They concluded exactly what I told them: Meredith was sleepwalking, wandered too close to the edge." His voice cracks. "I woke up, and she was ... gone."

The pain in his eyes seems genuine, raw. I think of my own loss, how even now, the memory of Brody's final days can bring me to my knees. Grief can't be faked—at least, not like that.

"I'm sorry," I say softly. "For snooping, for doubting you."

Corbin's smile is sad but warm. "I should have told you about Katherine from the beginning. Why it was so important that I quickly respond to her messages ... I was always afraid she would go public and ruin me in one of her moods."

He shakes his head. "But it's humiliating, you know? Being blackmailed by your ex. Paying her to keep quiet about ideas that aren't stolen like she claims—they were given to me with permission."

As I consider his explanation, Corbin shifts the conversation, his tone changing subtly.

"Riley, can I ask you something now?" When I nod, he continues, "How long have you had issues with alcohol?"

The question hits like a slap. I open my mouth to deny it automatically, then close it again. After last night—waking up with fragments of memory missing, letting paranoia overwhelm reason—I can't credibly claim I don't have a problem.

"Since Brody died," I admit, my voice barely audible over the rustle of palm fronds in the morning breeze. "At first, it was to help me sleep. Then to numb the pain. Then ..." I shrug helplessly. "Then it was just what I did. And sometimes I'd drink so much I couldn't remember what happened the night before."

"You mentioned memory gaps," Corbin says gently. "Does that happen often?"

Heat rises to my cheeks. "More than I'd like to admit. There have been entire evenings I don't remember. The night I lost my job ..." I trail off, the humiliation of that memory—or lack thereof—still too raw.

"You need help, Riley," Corbin says, covering my hand with his again. "Professional help. Not just for the drinking, but for your grief. I understand what you're going through. After Meredith ..." He swallows hard. "Well, I had some dark days too."

Tears prickle at my eyes. "I know. I've been seeing someone, actually. A therapist that Brody's mother recommended." Of course, this is only partially true because I haven't been seeing him consistently. Not yet anyway.

"That's great," he says, squeezing my hand. "That's really great."

We sit in companionable silence for a moment, the

tension between us dissipating like morning mist over the lake. The hangover cure must be working—my headache has receded to a dull background throb, and the world feels sharper, clearer.

As I watch Corbin's earnest expression, something settles in my chest—not quite peace, but it's close to acceptance. His story makes sense. The Katherine I glimpsed in those messages matches the woman he's described: volatile, manipulative, clinging to past grievances. And his grief over Meredith ... that can't be manufactured.

I know grief intimately now, and what I see in his eyes is real.

The guilt of going through his phone still burns, but maybe it was necessary. We've both laid our cards on the table now—his troubled ex, my drinking problem, the shadows we've been carrying. It feels liberating to have our secrets exposed, like lancing an infected wound. We can move forward now, both of us damaged but honest about it. I reach across the table and squeeze his hand, offering what I hope is a reassuring smile.

But as I settle back in my chair, watching a fishing boat cut across the lake's surface, a chill snakes down my spine despite the morning sun. If Katherine Lawrence is as unstable as Corbin claims, and if she's still obsessed with destroying him ... how long before she comes after me?

CHAPTER THIRTY-TWO

Less than an hour later, I emerge from the shower feeling like a new person. I wrap the robe from the hotel room tightly around my waist as I return to our table on the terrace. Corbin has his laptop open, looking intense as he taps away at the keys.

"So, what's on the agenda today?" I ask.

His face lights up. "Actually, Marcus found the perfect location for filming the eclipse. There's a temple called El Mirador that's perched right at the edge of a deep ravine with a river running through it. The Maya built it specifically for astronomical observations."

"Sounds remote," I say, reaching to pour myself a fresh cup of coffee.

"It is," he confirms, his enthusiasm infectious as he leans forward. "That's why we've arranged for a helicopter to drop us about an hour's hike from the site."

"A helicopter?" My cup freezes halfway to my lips. "You didn't mention anything about flying."

Corbin shrugs. "It was a last-minute arrangement. The

pilot is a friend of Dr. Garcia's. While the crowds gather for the eclipse at the main plaza in Tikal, we'll have this incredible spot practically to ourselves."

"I'm not great with heights," I admit, remembering my white-knuckled grip on the armrest during our flight to Guatemala.

"It's a short trip," he assures me. "Twenty minutes, tops. And the view will be worth it. There's evidence that the ancient Maya held their own eclipse festivals at this exact spot."

The thought of the helicopter sends a wave of unease through me. While I'm not terribly afraid of heights, helicopters have always made me nervous. Commercial planes feel insulated—more like riding in a bus than actually flying. Helicopters, however, hover precariously, the ground always visible and seemingly within reach. I still vividly recall the violent turbulence I experienced during a research expedition after graduate school—the tiny aircraft bucking wildly as we flew over the Sahara, my knuckles white from gripping the seat, certain we were about to crash into the rocky, sandy hillsides below.

"And there's no other way to get there in time for the eclipse?" I ask, already knowing the answer.

His eyes soften. "Not unless you want to hike for eight hours through dense jungle. But if you're really uncomfortable ..."

I sigh, relenting. "No, it's fine. I'll manage."

"That's my girl," he says with a grin. "Trust me, this is going to be amazing. Everyone loved you in yesterday's clips."

Pride swells in my chest despite myself. "Really?"

"Absolutely. You brought exactly the credibility the

channel needs." He reaches across the table, tucking a strand of hair behind my ear in a gesture that makes my heart flutter. "What do you say? Up for another adventure?"

I'm about to answer when my phone buzzes. Glancing down, I see Grace's name on the screen and feel a momentary flicker of guilt for ignoring her.

"Just a minute—" I open the message, expecting another check-in from my overprotective friend.

> Surprise! Just landed in Guatemala City. Don't worry, we can sort this whole thing with Corbin out over margaritas. Getting a car to Tikal now. Where are you staying?

I stare at the screen in disbelief, my mouth suddenly dry despite the coffee I've just swallowed. I know Grace is worried about me, but flying down here? Really?

"Everything okay?" Corbin asks, head tilted in concern.

I look up from the phone to meet his questioning gaze, unsure how to explain that my best friend—the one who suspects him of murder—has just shown up unannounced in Guatemala.

My hands shake as I type back a response, trying to keep my voice level. "Yeah ... just give me a second," I say, forcing what I hope is a casual smile. He gives me a polite smile and looks back down at his computer.

> What do you mean you're HERE? Like, actually in Guatemala?

The response comes back almost immediately.

> Took a few days off work. I was worried about you after all those text messages you sent me last night. You said you were trapped, that you need to get out of there. Are you okay? Send me your hotel info.

I feel beads of sweat form on my nose. *Messages?* I remember sending her some messages at dinner, but most of that is now a blur. I scroll back through my phone and she's right. My messages are erratic, panicked. *Great, I've brought this on myself.*

Still, Grace doesn't take impulsive trips. She's the most methodical, planned person I know—the type who books restaurants three weeks in advance and keeps detailed spreadsheets for vacation itineraries.

> I'm fine. Really. You didn't need to come all this way.

> Riley, you wouldn't answer any of my calls last night. What was I supposed to think?

> I'm sorry. I should have spoken to you. But seriously, you flying here is insane. Everything's fine.

> I know you, Ri. Something's wrong.

I glance up at Corbin, who's pretending to read something on his computer, but he's clearly watching me out of the corner of his eye. The morning sun catches the concern etched in his features, and I realize this fragile peace we've just rebuilt—this tentative trust after last night's confrontation—is about to shatter completely.

Grace doesn't know about my drinking problem getting

worse. She doesn't know about the memory gaps, the paranoid episode with Corbin's phone, or the emotional breakthrough we just had over breakfast. All she knows is that I'm in a foreign country with a man she's convinced is dangerous, and after reading through my increasingly drunken and distressed messages from yesterday, I've given her plenty of ammunition. From her perspective, this probably looks like a classic case of an abusive partner isolating his victim.

> Look, I'm already here. At least let me see that you're okay with my own eyes. Then I'll leave if you want me to.

My chest tightens. There's no way Grace will leave quietly once she actually meets Corbin. She'll take one look at him—charming, wealthy, pleased with himself and his own success—and all her suspicions will crystallize. She'll remember every true-crime podcast we've ever listened to together, every story about women who have vanished on romantic getaways. And when she inevitably brings up Meredith's death, which I know she will, everything will unravel. Another message pops up.

> Riley? Hotel name and room number. I'm not taking no for an answer.

"Bad news?" Corbin asks, finally abandoning the pretense of reading.

> Hotel Casa Santo Domingo.

I hit send, then start to type back. *But Corbin and I are about to leave for—*

She responds before I can even hit send.

> Great, I'll grab a cab.

I stare at the message, and a new thought occurs to me. We're supposed to leave for El Mirador in less than thirty minutes. The helicopter, the eclipse filming—it's all planned, and Corbin's team is counting on us. There's no way Grace will get here before that; the hotel is more than two hours away. Which means ... I'll have to deal with her interrogation later, after we return from our trip to the remote temple.

"No, just some questions from my publisher about the book." I stand up from the table and walk around to face him. "I'll get dressed and meet you out front?"

"Sounds perfect."

I lean down and give him a long kiss before leaving the terrace. My heart beats faster as I walk away. Because the careful framework of understanding we've built this morning —about Katherine, about my drinking, about moving forward together—now feels as fragile as spun glass.

And Grace, for all her good intentions, is about to take a hammer to it.

CHAPTER THIRTY-THREE

The jungle grows denser as we follow Dr. Garcia along a narrow path that winds between massive ceiba trees and tangled vines. My legs still feel shaky from the drop—the terrifying moment when we had to climb down the ladder for the last ten feet while the helicopter hovered above. We only have one hour to get to El Mirador and set up for the eclipse.

The humidity wraps around us like a living presence, causing my shirt to cling uncomfortably to my back. I sent Grace a text while we were over the jungle, telling her we had a tour scheduled and we'd have to connect later. The signal has been dodgy since then, so I haven't seen her response.

"You okay back there?" Corbin calls over his shoulder, pausing to let me catch up. Sweat gleams on his forehead, catching the dappled sunlight filtering through the canopy.

"Fine," I lie, tucking my phone back into my pocket. Guilt gnaws at me for keeping Grace's arrival secret, but telling Corbin now would only complicate our filming schedule. Better to deal with it afterward. "Just taking in the scenery."

The path narrows farther as we ascend, rocks jutting from the earth like ancient bones. Marcus leads the way, camera equipment balanced expertly on his shoulders, while Dr. Garcia points out notable flora and fauna. My boots slip occasionally on the muddy ground, the rich scent of decomposing vegetation rising with each step.

"Almost there," Dr. Garcia announces. "El Mirador is just beyond this ridge."

As we crest the hill, the temple reveals itself—not simply a structure, but a mountain of human creation emerging from the jungle. El Mirador's La Danta temple dwarfs anything I've seen before, even in my years studying the monuments of Egypt.

"Incredible, isn't it?" Dr. Garcia says, noting my awestruck expression. "Most visitors think it's built on a natural hill, but recent excavations proved something remarkable—the entire 'hill' is manmade. The Maya constructed this on completely flat ground."

"It's massive," I breathe, trying to comprehend the scale of the sight before me through the verdant canopy that's partially covering the structure.

"While Egypt's Great Pyramid of Khufu stands at 139 meters tall, La Danta reaches an astonishing 172 meters," Corbin adds, pointing to the sections where stone peeks through vegetation. "And they built this around 400 BCE, with nothing but stone tools and human labor."

I shake my head in total disbelief. The pyramids of Giza have always been my benchmark for monumental architecture, the standard against which I measure all other ancient constructions. Yet here, hidden in the Guatemalan jungle, stands something significantly more ambitious—a testament to human determination that has remained concealed for centuries beneath a blanket of tropical growth. I wipe my brow, suddenly feeling like a wimp for barely making it through this short hike without struggling.

"It's amazing," I murmur, momentarily forgetting my worries about Grace.

"Wait until you see what's below," Corbin says, a mysterious smile playing at his lips as he gestures toward the ravine. "That's where the real magic is."

Dr. Garcia leads us around the temple to a stone staircase carved into the cliff face. The steps descend steeply, their edges worn smooth by centuries of use and weather. From here, I can hear the gentle burble of water far below.

"So," Corbin begins, his excitement palpable, "here's the plan. The Maya believed that during eclipses, the sun was being devoured by a celestial jaguar. Looking directly at this sacred battle could blind you—physically and spiritually."

I nod, familiar with the mythology. "Many ancient cultures had taboos against directly viewing eclipses."

"Exactly," he continues, "but the Maya had a unique solution. Dr. Garcia, would you explain?"

My phone vibrates in my pocket, distracting me. I'm sure it'll be Grace, letting me know she's almost at the hotel. I wince, pressing the silence button on the side of my phone while it's still in my pocket. *Grace will have to wait.*

Dr. Garcia steps forward, brushing dust from her hands. "Below us is a cenote—a sacred well. The Maya would observe eclipses through its reflection in the water, believing this protected them while still allowing them to witness the celestial event."

"And that's where we'll film the eclipse segment," Corbin adds triumphantly. "Inside. Looking up through the water at the darkening sky."

My stomach drops. "Inside? As in ... swimming?"

"Not exactly," Dr. Garcia clarifies. "We'll descend into the cenote using ropes. There's a ledge about halfway down where you can stand and observe the reflection safely."

Marcus begins unpacking climbing equipment—harnesses, carabiners, ropes. The sight sends a wave of anxiety through me. I've done some basic climbing over the years, but descending into a dark water-filled cave is entirely different.

"You didn't mention this part," I say quietly to Corbin, trying to keep the tremor from my voice.

He squeezes my shoulder. "I wanted it to be a surprise. Don't worry—it's perfectly safe. We'll have you harnessed securely."

I glance down at the steep drop, the dark water barely visible at the bottom of the cenote. The circular opening resembles a gaping mouth ready to swallow us whole. Memories of childhood swimming lessons flood my brain—my panic whenever water closed over my head, the instructor pulling me sputtering to the surface. I've avoided deep water ever since.

While Marcus sets up the equipment, I step away, finally checking my phone. One bar of signal—enough to receive Grace's latest message.

> At the hotel. They said you're at El Mirador.
> Getting a ride with some locals headed
> that way. See you soon!

My heart races. *What is she doing?* I know Grace cares about me, but her insistence on "helping" my situation is doing the exact opposite. Regardless, she'll be here soon enough, and there's no telling how she'll react when she sees Corbin. *How am I going to explain this to him?* I know she means well, but I can't help but feel deeply irritated. The conversation between me and Corbin this morning feels like a tenuous truce. One that could easily be broken by Grace showing up and giving Corbin a hard time. I type hurriedly:

> We're filming. PLEASE wait at hotel. Will explain later.

The message fails to send, the signal flickering out as I stare at the screen. *Perfect.*

"Riley, you're up," Marcus calls, holding out a harness. "We need to get down there and set up before the eclipse begins."

I force a smile, tucking my phone away. "Coming."

I slip into the harness, which feels strange and constricting against my body, the straps digging into my thighs and waist. Corbin checks my equipment twice, his fingers moving with practiced precision as he secures carabiners and adjusts straps.

"I'll go first," he says, squeezing my hand. "Then you, then Marcus with the equipment. Dr. Garcia and the rest of the team will stay up here to feed us the rope."

I nod, not trusting my voice. Clouds have moved in front

of the sun, blocking the view of the water below. It's like plunging into an endless black hole.

Corbin backs toward the edge, then leans back into the empty air, supported only by the ropes, and begins his descent with smooth, confident movements.

"Your turn," Dr. Garcia says gently, guiding me to the edge. "Remember—lean back into the harness and trust the rope."

At this point, it feels like my life is in Corbin's hands requiring me to have complete trust in him. I chew on my lip. Our conversation went as well as it could this morning. He explained the entire Kelly/Katherine situation to me so smoothly, but still. It's hard to let go.

Corbin glances up, flashing me a confident smile. I guess, at this point, I have no choice but to put my faith in him. The first step is the hardest—forcing myself to lean backward into nothingness. The rope catches, the harness tightens, and suddenly I'm suspended, the temple growing smaller above me as I descend into the cenote's watery embrace.

Halfway down, the walls glisten with moisture, covered in delicate formations that have taken millennia to create. Stalactites hang like stone daggers from rocky overhangs, catching what little light penetrates the depths. The air rising from it is cool and damp, carrying the mineral scent of water.

"You're doing great," Corbin calls from below, his voice echoing. "Just a little farther."

I focus on my breathing, on the feel of the rope in my gloved hands, on anything except the dark water waiting below. The ledge comes into view—a narrow stone shelf jutting from the cenote wall, only just wide enough for three people to stand side by side.

My feet touch solid ground, relief flooding through me as Corbin helps me onto the ledge. The surface is slick with moisture, requiring careful footing. Above us, Marcus begins his descent, the camera equipment dangling from a separate line.

The water below is eerily still, a perfect obsidian mirror reflecting our silhouettes. In Mayan cosmology, cenotes were entrances to Xibalba, the underworld—portals between worlds. Standing here, I can understand why they believed that.

"This is perfect," Corbin whispers, his breath warm against my ear. "The eclipse will begin in about twenty minutes. The light will change, and—"

A sharp cracking sound cuts him off. Marcus shouts from above, his voice echoing in the confined space.

"Shit!" Marcus yells, now dangling precariously from his own line.

Before anyone can react, his rope swings wildly, the camera equipment slamming into the rock wall. The rim of the rock above him crumbles, sending him tumbling farther into the cavern. Corbin and I watch as his body plummets to the ground, his shoulder taking the brunt of the fall as he hits an outcropping about twenty yards below us.

"Marcus!" Corbin shouts, moving dangerously close to the ledge's edge.

I grab his arm. "Don't! We need to—"

The rest of my warning is lost as our ledge shifts beneath us, ancient stone giving way. A section crumbles, sending chunks of limestone tumbling into the water. The remaining portion—barely large enough for one person—trembles ominously.

Dr. Garcia's panicked voice crackles over the two-way radio. "What happened, are you okay?"

Corbin is breathing heavily next to me as I grip his arm like a vise. The silence that follows is deafening, broken only by the distant drip of water and our ragged breaths. The cenote feels alive around us, its limestone walls seeming to pulse in the dim light filtering down from above. I hear Marcus moaning below us.

No, we are very definitely *not* okay.

CHAPTER THIRTY-FOUR

"We're okay!" Corbin calls into his walkie-talkie, his voice bouncing off the damp walls. "Marcus fell below us, but I can hear him. We're going to climb down to him now!"

My hand fumbles against the wall, seeking stability as my eyes strain uselessly against the perfect darkness. Suddenly, I feel Corbin pull away from me, his arms reaching for his head.

"Headlamp," he mutters. "Where's the damn button on my headlamp?"

I hear him patting himself down, then a click, and blessed light floods the cenote. The beam from his forehead cuts through the darkness, illuminating swirling dust particles and Marcus's slow movements on the ledge below.

"Turn yours on too," Corbin urges.

My fingers tremble as I reach for the switch on my own headlamp. A second beam joins his, and suddenly we can see the extent of our situation. The ledge we're standing on has indeed crumbled, but only partially—a four-foot section remains intact, pressed against the wall. Marcus moans.

"I think I dislocated my shoulder," he calls up, his voice tight with pain.

Corbin's light scans the walls, stopping at another ledge about fifteen feet below us, much wider and seemingly more stable. "There." He points. "Marcus, can you make it to that platform?"

Marcus nods, grimacing as he begins a one-armed climb toward the lower ledge. The camera equipment bounces roughly against the wall as he ascends.

"Dr. Garcia!" Corbin calls into the radio. "We're going to move to a lower ledge. We need light down here!"

"I'm calling for help!" she responds, her voice fading in and out. "The emergency team from the park is coming, but it might take them an hour!"

"We'll be fine. Just don't leave us down here!" He's half joking, but I can see the stress in his temples. He begins to pull the rope we were connected to until he comes to a frayed end. He holds it up to the light. "Must have split on a sharp rock."

I eye the torn end. "Does that happen often?"

He shakes his head. "No. It was my fault. I should have double-checked the rope."

I say nothing, not wanting to make him feel worse. Even though I'm increasingly terrified of what else he might have forgotten to "double-check." Corbin turns to me, his face half illuminated, half in shadow.

"We need to get down to that lower ledge. I'll go first."

I nod, trying to mask my terror. The wall looks slick with moisture, the handholds few and far between. But staying on this crumbling ledge isn't an option.

Corbin shifts his equipment bag to his back and begins his descent, finding tiny crevices for his fingers and toes, moving with an easy confidence that suggests this isn't his first impromptu climb. I watch his progress, memorizing each handhold, trying to calm my racing heart.

"Your turn," he calls once he reaches the wider ledge. "Take it slow. I'll guide you."

I turn around, pressing my body against the damp stone, feeling for the first handhold. The rock is slippery and cold beneath my fingers, chilling my already trembling body. Carefully, I lower myself inch by inch, Corbin's light and voice directing me.

"Left foot—there's a small ledge about eight inches down. That's it. Now right hand to that crack beside your hip."

The descent feels eternal, my muscles screaming with tension as I cling to the wall. Finally, Corbin's hands find my waist, guiding me the last few feet until I stand beside him on solid stone.

By this time, Marcus has pulled himself into a sitting position and flipped on his headlamp. His face is pale with pain, and his right arm hangs limply. He sits with his back against the wall, breathing heavily.

"The equipment," he gasps, nodding toward the cases below us. "We need it."

"I'll get it," Corbin says. The beam from his headlamp catches on the water's surface as he turns, creating eerie patterns against the cenote walls. He makes his way farther down and scoops up the bundle of electronics.

I kneel beside Marcus, examining his shoulder in the dim light. "How are you feeling?" I ask, lightly touching his good shoulder.

"It's dislocated. Happened to me once before," he says grimly. "Corbin will need to set it."

By the time Corbin returns, Marcus and I have positioned ourselves for the procedure. Marcus relays the situation to Corbin.

"Ready?" Corbin says, his hands reaching out to grasp his colleague's shoulder. I hold Marcus steady while Corbin takes his arm, rotating it slowly, carefully, until with a sickening pop, the joint slides back into place.

Marcus's cry of pain echoes off the walls as Corbin pulls, followed by a string of creative curses. "Thanks," he gasps finally. "Much better."

The three of us crouch in silence. Corbin gazes around the cavernous space, then looks at his watch. He looks at Marcus.

"Listen, buddy, I know this is a lot to ask, but ... we have ten minutes until the eclipse. Would you still be up for filming?"

Marcus rubs his shoulder, then stretches it in a small circle. "I'm fine. Let's do it."

Dr. Garcia's voice cuts through the cavern. "Good news, the rescue team is closer than I thought. Fifteen minutes. Can you wait?"

"The eclipse starts in ten minutes," Corbin says. "We will film with what we have!"

"Got it," she responds.

He turns to Marcus, who, despite his injury, has begun unpacking the cases. "Is any of it salvageable?"

Marcus nods. "The housing protected most of it. The drone's toast, but the main cameras are fine."

As they set up tripods on our ledge, I step back, watching them work with routine efficiency despite our precarious situation. The cenote feels a little less threatening with the solid stone beneath my feet. I pull out my phone, praying for a signal now that we're in a different position.

To my surprise, two bars appear. Almost immediately, the phone begins to vibrate, then erupts into a ringtone that bounces off the cave walls like an electronic banshee. The sound is so startling in the space that I nearly drop the device into the water.

In my fumbling attempt to silence it, my thumb accidentally swipes to answer.

"Riley? Riley!" Grace's voice blares from the speaker, filling the cenote. "Are you okay? I found a helicopter pilot who can take me straight to El Mirador! We're just about to take off—"

Corbin turns at her words, his eyebrows drawing together in confusion. "Who's that?"

I press the phone to my ear, backing away as far as the ledge allows. "Grace, I can't talk right now. We're in a bit of a situation—"

"What situation? Are you hurt? Is it him? Riley, I'm coming—"

"No! Don't come here! We're fine, just—"

"Who is that?" Corbin asks again, stepping closer, moisture from the cavern making his skin glisten.

I cover the microphone with my hand. "It's just Grace. My friend from Phoenix."

"In Guatemala?" His expression is a picture of confusion.

"Riley!" Grace's tinny voice continues from the phone. "Are you there? I can't hear—"

The phone cuts out. "There's something I need to tell you," I begin, my voice barely audible over the water dripping from the ceiling.

Before I can continue, Marcus interrupts. "Guys, look at the water!"

Marcus points upward with his good arm. "The opening—it's not directly above us." Following his gaze, I can see he's right. What I had assumed was the main entrance is actually just one of several openings in the limestone ceiling. About thirty feet away, partially hidden by an overhang, sunlight streams down through a much larger aperture, creating a natural spotlight that hits the water at an angle.

"That's why we couldn't see it from our original position," Corbin says, turning off his headlamp now that the sun's rays provide enough illumination. "The cenote must have multiple openings—and it's that one that is positioned perfectly to catch the eclipse."

Marcus nods, already adjusting his camera angle toward the illuminated section of water.

We turn to see a perfect circle of light with a small black crescent on the black surface of the cenote pool. Above, through the opening, a sliver of the sun has already disappeared behind the moon's shadow.

"It's starting," Corbin says, his voice filled with wonder. He turns to me, his expression unreadable in the strange, diminishing light. "Whatever it is, it might just have to wait. We have about three minutes before totality."

As he turns away to adjust the cameras, I watch his back, the self-assured set of his shoulders. While my brain is bouncing around in a hundred different places, Corbin is in his element.

Above us, the sun continues its disappearance, the light in the cenote growing stranger by the second. I take a deep breath, trying to calm myself as we edge into darkness.

CHAPTER THIRTY-FIVE

"We're here in the temple of La Danta inside the city of El Mirador, about sixty-five miles north of Tikal. Here, the ancient Mayans created a structure taller than even the pyramids of Egypt ..." Corbin's voice resonates against the damp stone walls as we stand on a wide limestone ledge inside the cenote beneath the temple.

Our headlamps cast eerie, dancing shadows across the cave's interior while Marcus has his lighting equipment trained on us, capturing every moment. Corbin regales his prospective audience with the history and significance of this old Mayan city. The humidity clings to my skin like a second layer, and the rich mineral scent of the underground water fills my nostrils with each breath.

I should be savoring this moment. Standing here, present for a celestial event inside a temple built by a civilization that prized astronomical observations—this is everything the archaeologist in me signed up for. The childlike wonder of something so full of portent that it's hard to conceive of its true meaning.

That's what I *should* be doing. *Savoring*.

Instead, all I can think about is how everything in my life is hanging precariously by a thread. What am I going to tell Corbin when Grace gets here? That I've been talking about him behind his back? That my best friend thinks he killed his ex-girlfriend? That my publisher wants the advance back, or that I spent every last cent while I was on a drunken bender? That I'll probably be tied up in a lawsuit for the next year and likely declaring bankruptcy shortly after?

I need to get my act together. Nearly tumbling down into the depths of the cenote has made me realize how fragile my life really is.

"Riley, what is your take on the building of the temple?" Corbin's question pulls me from my spiraling thoughts. His eyes gleam in the artificial light, expectant. "Do you truly believe that the temple was built by hand, that the study of celestial movements was really nothing more than part of a primitive group's customs?"

I shove all of the internal ping-pong my brain is playing to the back of my mind and straighten my posture for the camera. The cool stone beneath my palm grounds me as I lean a little against the wall.

"The Mayans were anything but primitive. Evidence suggests they built these massive structures through coordinated community effort," I begin, my academic voice taking over. "This included thousands—sometimes millions—of laborers working together over several generations to complete their work. So, while in our modern framework we think of buildings going up in a year or two, the ancient people had a much longer-term commitment to finishing what they started."

I can see Corbin's face fall slightly; there is a pleading

look in his eyes for me to support or even open up to the possibility of some of his more controversial theories. A drop of water falls from the ceiling, landing with a soft plink near my foot. I smile and continue.

"But there is a lot we don't know, a lot that still brings out a sense of wonder and raises questions about how any of this spectacular architecture was actually accomplished. We're constantly refining our understanding of Maya engineering techniques, social organization, and astronomical knowledge through new technologies like LiDAR and isotope analysis. The truth is ... we don't know everything."

Marcus gives me a wink, then turns away from the camera, adjusting something on his equipment. The faint mechanical whirr of the camera is almost soothing in the otherwise silent cave.

Corbin's smile returns, the tension in his shoulders relaxing. "You heard it here—a doctor in the field of archaeology admitting the truth; we don't know everything. And all we need is that little thread of doubt that might suggest that a different, new theory is even possible." He checks his watch, the face glowing in the dim light. "Now, enough of me talking. We're just a minute away from a full eclipse. We're going to see what happens to the water below us."

His voice drops lower. "The Mayans had the foresight to build an oculus—a rumored opening around the top of this temple. And if my theory is correct, we should be able to stare down at the water below and see the eclipse in all its glory."

Corbin turns off his mic, the small click echoing in the chamber, and the three of us turn toward the water below. We're standing at the rim of a huge cavern probably thirty yards in diameter. The shape is roughly circular, with ledges, tight passages, and rocks jutting out from the sides. The water below glows faintly from the remaining sunlight filtering through from the hole high above.

And to my utter amazement, I can see the ring of the eclipse forming in the water's reflection. I witnessed an eclipse when I was a little girl, watching it in the sky, but this is something else entirely. It's otherworldly, the way it glows in the dark water below—a perfect circle of light with a growing black center, surrounded by shimmering ripples.

Corbin grabs my hand, his palm warm and slightly rough against my fingers. We stand close together, our shoulders touching, breath mingling in the cool air.

"This is amazing," I say breathlessly, unable to tear my eyes from the spectacle below.

Corbin glances over at me, just for a moment. "I'm glad you're here," he says, his voice barely above a whisper.

I feel something well up inside me then, a connection with him I didn't even realize was there—something deeper than physical attraction or shared grief. The cave around us grows darker as the eclipse reaches totality, the water now glowing with an unearthly light that bathes our faces in a silvery blue hue. We stand there in reverent silence for the full three minutes, watching the cosmic dance reflected in ancient water. Marcus's camera captures everything, the muted mechanical sounds the only disruption in our sacred moment.

After the eclipse has passed, the chatter above us returns, voices bouncing down to us off the stone walls.

"Did you get it? Did you guys get that?" Dr. Garcia's voice crackles over the radio. "Is everyone still doing all right?"

"We're good!" Corbin replies, his voice reverberating through the cenote. "We got it!"

The sunlight returns gradually, filtering down through the opening and causing the water to sparkle once more.

"The rescue team is coming up now," Dr. Garcia announces through the radio, the static crackling in the otherwise silent cave. "We'll have you out of there in just a few minutes. Hang tight, guys."

"Sounds good," Corbin replies.

A few minutes later, fresh ropes drop down through one of the tunnel openings. Marcus heads up first with the equipment tied securely to his back, wincing as the movement pulls at his injured shoulder. I follow, the rough fibers of the rope burning against my palms despite the gloves. Corbin is the last to ascend.

Once we reach the surface, the light is starting to return to its normal brightness, as the eclipse has passed completely. I emerge from the entrance on the side of the temple where our group waits for us—about a dozen people including the rescue team, their equipment scattered across the stone platform.

Before I can even thank Dr. Garcia, I'm thrown into a barrel-like hug, the familiar scent of her perfume surrounding me.

"Grace?" I gasp, pulling back to look at her flushed face.

"Riley, I'm so glad you're okay," she says breathlessly, her blue eyes wide with concern. "Listen, there's something I need to tell you before—"

But as she's about to finish speaking, I hear Corbin's voice behind me, sharp and cold as ice.

"What the hell are you doing here?"

CHAPTER THIRTY-SIX

The temperature seems to have dropped ten degrees as Grace and Corbin lock eyes over my shoulder, the tension between them palpable.

What is going on?

Corbin's words are as sharp and cold as a blade. The celebration around us fades away, voices becoming distant and muffled as I look between him and Grace.

"What are you talking about?" I ask, confusion washing over me like cool water. "This is Grace. My friend from Phoenix."

Corbin's face has transformed completely from the man who held my hand during the eclipse. His jaw is tight, eyes narrowed to dangerous slits, shoulders rigid with tension. He looks at Grace with such naked hostility that I instinctively take a step back.

"Is that what she told you?" he says, his voice low and controlled, though I can hear the rage simmering beneath. "That her name is Grace?"

Grace meets his gaze without flinching. Her chin lifts, a gesture of defiance.

"Corbin," Dr. Garcia calls, rushing over with a medical kit in hand. Her face is flushed with concern as she approaches our tense triangle. "Are you all right? We were so worried when we heard the ledge collapse!"

Marcus trails behind her, his injured arm now supported by a makeshift sling fashioned from someone's bandana. "I think I should probably see a doctor," he says, grimacing. "The shoulder's back in place, but it hurts like hell."

Corbin doesn't even turn to look at them. His eyes remain locked on Grace, as if she might vanish if he glances away. "We're fine," he says dismissively. "A minor setback."

"You don't look fine," Dr. Garcia observes, her eyes sweeping between the three of us. "Is everything okay?"

"I'm perfectly fine," Corbin says, his smile not reaching his eyes. "But Riley, our visitor and I need to have a private chat. Marcus," he says, looking over at the group around him, "I'll catch up with you later. Dr. Garcia, thank you again for your incredible support today. We can discuss the footage tonight."

Before anyone can object, he gently but firmly takes my elbow and gestures for Grace to follow. We move away from the group, down the temple steps and toward a narrow path that leads deeper into the jungle. The silence between us is suffocating as we walk, broken only by the calls of tropical birds and the distant sounds of the rescue team packing up their equipment.

We stop in a clearing near a stream, the water rushing over smooth stones. In another context, it would be peaceful, beautiful even. Now it feels like the menacing calm before a storm.

"Do you want to explain what you're doing here, Katherine?" Corbin asks, his voice dangerously quiet.

I look at Grace—my best friend, my support system through the darkest days after Brody's death—and see a stranger in her familiar face. Her eyes hold mine for a moment, then drift away, and that small gesture tells me more than any words could.

"Katherine?" I repeat, the name feeling foreign on my tongue. "What is he talking about?"

She sighs, running a hand through her blonde ponytail—a gesture I've seen a hundred times before. "My full name is Katherine Grace Lawrence," she says finally. "Sometimes I go by Grace."

"Sometimes?" I say weakly. The ground seems to shift beneath my feet.

Katherine Lawrence. K. The blackmailer. The ex-girlfriend.

The woman Corbin claimed was unstable and dangerous.

The person threatening to expose his secrets.

My supposed best friend.

I take a step backward, the world suddenly off-kilter.

"How long have you known her, Riley?" Corbin demands, his eyes never leaving Grace's face.

"About eight months," I answer automatically, my mind racing to recalibrate everything I thought I knew. "We met at a café. She's a pediatrician. She—"

"Was a pediatrician," he interrupts, his voice harder than I've ever heard it. "She lost her license because she was stealing prescription drugs. Another thing *Grace* conveniently left out of her story, I'm sure."

Grace's face flushes. "I made mistakes. I paid for them. That doesn't change the truth about you."

My eyes dart between them, noting their body language, the way they stand like fighters sizing each other up. There's history here—complicated, toxic history that I have stumbled into blindly.

And then it hits me with stunning clarity—that night at Arizona State. The lecture. Grace practically dragged me there. *You're not gonna believe who's speaking at the ASU tonight*, she texted. She insisted I come with her. Pushed me to talk to him afterward.

Did she orchestrate our reunion?

"Did you plan this?" I say, my voice a whispered hush. "That night at the lecture ... you knew who he was."

Grace's eyes flicker with something—guilt, perhaps, or simply confirmation.

"Riley," she begins, taking a step toward me.

I back away farther. My mind is racing, reassessing every moment of our friendship. The way she'd ask casual questions about Corbin. How interested she was in my growing relationship with him. The "concerned" warnings about his past.

It was all calculated.

"Will someone please explain what the hell is going on?" My voice sounds strange to my own ears, higher than normal. "Grace– Katherine—whoever you are, did you deliberately befriend me because of Corbin?"

Her expression softens as she looks at me. "Not at first. We met at that café on Camelback Road—you were crying into your laptop, remember? I felt sorry for you."

The memory stings. Months ago, when I was struggling to write after Brody's death, Grace bought me a latte, and we became friends from there on.

"One night I came over for wine," Grace continues, her

tone sharper now. "You had that photo of Meredith on your bookshelf. I recognized her immediately." She glances at Corbin with disdain. "That's when I casually brought up her fiancé. Don't you remember? You confessed to me you'd had a crush on him."

My stomach drops. I do remember—hazily, through wine-soaked grief. Grace asking about the photo, and me admitting, shame-faced, that I'd had a crush on Meredith's fiancé. How wrong it felt to confess that with Meredith barely cold in her grave.

"When I learned he had just moved to Phoenix, I knew I had to stay close. To protect you."

"Protect me? From what?" I ask, although I already suspect the answer.

"From him," she says with a nod toward Corbin. "From what happened to Meredith."

"This has nothing to do with Meredith!" Corbin's voice rises, ringing out among the trees. He takes a step toward Grace, his finger pointed at her face. "This has nothing to do with her, and you know it."

She takes a step back, stumbling on a large tree root and then catching herself. "It has to do with the truth. The truth about the past. About the videos you blast across the internet. About the pages you stole from me."

The jungle closes in around me, the air thickening with unspoken accusations.

"Corbin, what is she talking about?" I ask, my voice as steady as I can possibly make it.

Grace looks at me, and I can discern something like genuine concern in her eyes. "Riley, you need to know who he really is. Who this man is you've been sleeping with."

"And who is that?" I ask, my mouth dry.

"A fraud," she says simply. "A man who built his entire career on stolen work. A man who—"

"Shut up," Corbin interrupts, his voice harsh and commanding. "You have no idea what you're talking about."

"I have every idea," Grace counters.

I look at Corbin, searching his face for the man I thought I knew. The man who held me, who understood my grief, the man who made me feel alive again after a year of numbness. But his expression is closed, unreadable, his eyes hard in a way that frightens me.

The bird calls that provided a constant background to our conversation suddenly stop, as if the jungle itself is holding its breath. In the silence, I can hear my own heartbeat, the rush of blood in my ears.

I need to get out of here.

The realization washes over me with crystal clarity. I'm in a foreign country, isolated in the jungle with two people locked in some kind of psychological war I don't understand. One of them lied about who she was for months. The other might be hiding some terrible, violent secret. And between them stands the ghost of Meredith Chin, who fell—or was pushed—to her death at Mesa Verde.

I debate running. I could just run back to Marcus and Dr. Garcia, escape this madness. But no, I need answers this time. No more letting Corbin wave away my concerns.

"What happened with Meredith?" I ask, my voice barely above a whisper.

Corbin and Grace exchange a look I can't interpret—some shared knowledge passing between them that excludes me.

"Tell her," Grace says, her voice suddenly quiet. "Tell her the truth, Corbin."

Time seems suspended as I wait for his answer, my body tense and ready to run if needed.

"It's complicated," Corbin finally says, his voice almost pleading now. "Riley, you have to understand—"

Grace makes a disgusted sound. "Are you going to tell her the truth, or should I?"

CHAPTER THIRTY-SEVEN

I stand frozen between them, my body tensed and ready to flee. The jungle surrounds us, dense and watchful, the rushing stream providing its burbling soundtrack to this moment of terrible revelation.

Corbin meets my eyes, and for a moment, I see a flicker of that Corbin who held me through the night, who understood my grief, who made me feel alive again. But he's already lied to me once. *Who is he really?*

"Meredith died exactly the way I told the police, exactly the way I told you. She was sleepwalking, Riley. She had done it since college it got worse with stress. We were camping near Cliff Palace, and sometime in the night, she left the tent. I woke up, and she was gone." His voice breaks with emotion. "By the time they found her, it was too late."

"You're leaving out the good parts, Corbin," Grace says immediately.

"What parts?" I ask.

Grace hesitates for a fraction of a second. "The circumstances might be true, but he's leaving out context. He's leaving out what I know."

"Which is what?" I ask.

"Meredith and I ... we had an argument. She broke off the engagement."

"Why?"

"She figured out his entire career is built on intellectual theft," Grace says, her eyes never leaving Corbin's face. "And if she lived, she would have exposed him."

Corbin shakes his head, his expression darkening. "You're twisting everything, as usual."

"Tell her about my grandfather's journal," Grace demands. "Tell her where all your brilliant theories really came from. How you found that burial chamber in Peru."

A muscle twitches in Corbin's jaw. "Your grandfather's journal has nothing to do with Meredith's death. Stop trying to connect them."

"What journal?" I prompt.

Corbin closes his eyes briefly, then opens them with a resigned sigh. "Katherine's grandfather was Henry Lawrence, an unconventional archaeologist who was laughed out of academia in the 1970s for his theories about ancient civilizations. Theories that, decades later, turned out to have some merit."

"My grandfather was brilliant," Grace interjects. "He was ahead of his time, and the establishment crucified him for it."

"The journal contains his research?" I ask, my mind piecing the puzzle together despite my emotional turmoil.

Corbin nods. "Katherine's family kept his journals after he died. When we were together, she showed them to me. I found them fascinating—groundbreaking, even. With her permission, I started building videos around some of his concepts. And then we decided to follow the trail he'd left for us to Peru."

I look between them, letting my gaze land on Grace. "You were there? When Corbin discovered the burial chamber?"

"Yes," Grace says bitterly. "And once he got what he wanted, he tried to dump me."

"What about Meredith?" I ask Corbin, trying to keep my voice steady. "Did she know about the journal?"

A heavy silence falls between them. The jungle closes in yet further, the air thickening with unspoken truths.

"No," Corbin finally says. "I never told her about it. But that night at Mesa Verde, she found the journal."

"And if she found out Corbin was lying about finding the burial chamber on his own," Grace adds, "not to mention all of his theories, don't you think she would have felt a moral obligation to tell someone?"

I turn to Grace, studying her face—a face I thought I knew so well. "So you're saying Corbin had a clear motive to push her."

Grace raises her eyebrows, saying nothing.

"That's exactly what you've been implying!" Corbin explodes, his voice echoing through the clearing. "Ever since it happened, you've been dropping hints, making insinuations, torturing me with the idea that I had something to do with her death!"

"I never said—"

"You didn't have to say it! It was in every message, every threat, every time you demanded more money for your silence, even though you gave me the journal!" Corbin's face is flushed with pent-up anger, his control finally shattering.

"I deserve half of everything you've made, and you know it," Grace retorts.

"So this is about money?" I interject, desperate to untangle their complicated history.

"It's about justice," Grace insists. "About getting what I deserve."

Corbin laughs. "It's about control. She couldn't stand it that I moved on. That I built something successful. That I found happiness with Meredith."

"And then with me," I add quietly, the pieces falling into place. "That's why you befriended me, isn't it? Not to protect me, but to sabotage Corbin."

Grace's expression flickers. "No, I was trying to keep history from repeating itself. I didn't want you to get hurt like Mere—"

"By lying to me? By manipulating me?" The betrayal cuts deep, all those nights we spent talking, all the confidences we shared, the support during my darkest moments—was it all strategic?

"Meredith died in a tragic accident," Corbin says firmly. "Katherine has been using that tragedy to manipulate me, to extort money from me, to keep me under her control. The journal and Meredith's death are entirely separate issues that she's deliberately conflated."

I look between them, these two people I thought I knew.

Both liars, in their own ways.

"I need to get out of here," I say suddenly, taking another step toward the path. "I can't be around either of you right now."

"Riley, wait—" Corbin reaches for me, but I pull away.

"Don't." I hold up my hand. "I need time to think. I need to get back to the group."

"You can't trust him," Grace insists, desperation edging into her voice.

"I can't trust either of you," I reply, my voice breaking despite my efforts to stay composed.

As I turn to leave, I hear the two of them as they continue to bark hostilities at each other. "I don't have the pages, Katherine, I told you!"

I try to block out the rest of their conversation as I hurry down the path, the jungle closing around me, hiding me from their sight. But their voices, their accusations, their tangled and toxic history follow me like a shadow I can't outrun.

CHAPTER THIRTY-EIGHT

I stumble back toward the main temple site, jungle branches catching at my clothes as if trying to hold me back. My breath comes in ragged gasps, my mind reeling from the confrontation I've fled. The ground beneath my feet feels utterly unstable—much like everything else in my life right now.

Grace. Katherine. *Whatever her name is.*

The woman who held my hand through tears, who brought me soup when I was sick, who dragged me out of my apartment when all I wanted was to drink myself into oblivion—she never existed. She was a construction, a calculated façade designed to infiltrate my life. For what? Revenge against Corbin? Some twisted form of justice for her grandfather?

And Corbin—the man whose touch brought me back to life after a year of numbness—what secrets is he hiding behind those hazel eyes? A stolen career? A suspicious death?

I break through the tree line, the bright sunlight momentarily blinding me after the filtered green glow of the jungle. The rescue team is packing up their equipment, their voices carrying across the cleared area in front of the temple. Dr. Garcia stands nearby, deep in conversation with Marcus, whose arm is now properly bandaged and supported in a sling.

"Riley!" Dr. Garcia calls, spotting me. "We were getting worried. Where are the others?"

I wave my hand vaguely behind me. "Still talking." My voice sounds distant, disconnected from my body.

She studies my face, her archaeologist's eye for detail clearly extending to human expressions. "Is everything all right?"

"Fine," I lie, the word bitter on my tongue. "When is the helicopter returning? I'd like to go back to the hotel."

Dr. Garcia checks her watch. "About twenty minutes. We radioed ahead. They're sending two choppers, enough for everyone if we split into two groups."

"Great," I say, relief washing through me. "I'd like to go back on the first one, if possible."

"Of course." She nods, her eyes still curious. "The footage from the cenote is remarkable, by the way. Marcus showed me what you captured during the eclipse."

Marcus gives me a weak smile, his face pale from pain and shock. "It's going to make an incredible segment."

I nod absently, unable to summon any enthusiasm for the video now. The footage, the channel, the whole trip—it's all tainted: poisoned by lies and manipulation.

"The helicopter is on its way," someone calls from the communications tent. "ETA fifteen minutes!"

The next quarter of an hour passes in a blur. I help pack equipment, my movements mechanical, my responses to questions minimal. My mind is elsewhere, cycling through memories of the past months, reexamining every interaction with Corbin and Grace through this new, terrible lens of suspicion.

Was Grace—Katherine—only my friend because of Corbin? Was she counting on me dating him after the night I ran into him at the symposium? And Corbin's gentle patience with my drinking—was that genuine concern or a calculated indifference?

The helicopter's approach saves me from my spiraling thoughts, the rhythmic thump of rotors growing louder until it appears above the jungle canopy. Wind whips through the clearing as it descends, forcing us to shield our eyes from flying debris.

"Ready?" Dr. Garcia shouts over the noise, gesturing toward my escape vehicle.

I nod, ducking low as we approach. Marcus is helped aboard first, wincing as the movement jostles his injured shoulder. I climb in after him, strapping myself into the seat without looking back at the path where I left Corbin and Grace.

The journey back to the hotel passes in a haze. I stare out the window at the vast expanse of jungle below, the canopy occasionally broken by the gleam of water or the jutting stone of the Mayan temples. The pilot attempts to engage with me, pointing out landmarks visible from the air, but I respond with monosyllables until he gives up.

By the time we land on the hotel's helipad, the sun is setting, painting the landscape in shades of orange and gold.

Marcus is whisked away to the medical center, leaving me alone with my thoughts and an overwhelming need to numb them.

I wonder for a moment about Corbin and Grace riding back together in the second helicopter, contemplating whether they made it back okay, but then I dismiss the thought. I don't have the energy to care at this point.

I head straight for the hotel bar—an open-air affair tucked between the main building and the pool. Hanging lanterns sway in the evening breeze, but I barely notice their warm glow over the polished mahogany and leather. My attention fixes solely on the back wall lined with hundreds of bottles—amber, clear, and green glass glinting with allure.

The bartender raises an eyebrow in silent question, and I already know I'll be ordering something stronger than my usual.

"What can I get you?" he asks. He's a local man, perhaps in his fifties, with kind eyes and hands that move with practiced efficiency.

"Tequila," I say. "Straight. Your best."

He tilts his head at me but reaches for a bottle on the top shelf. "Rough day?"

"You could say that." The first shot burns a path down my throat, a familiar fire that promises temporary oblivion. I push the empty glass toward him. "Another."

Three shots later, the edges of the world have softened pleasantly. The bar has filled with other guests—a couple arguing quietly in one corner, a group of German tourists laughing over some shared joke, two businessmen discussing deals in hushed tones. Their voices wash over me like distant waves.

"American?" the bartender asks as he pours my fourth shot. I nod, running my finger along the rim of the glass.

"First time in Guatemala?"

"Yes." I down the shot, welcoming the burn. "Might be my last."

He chuckles, though there's concern in his eyes. "That bad, huh?"

I stare at the empty glass, memories surfacing through the haze. Brody's smile on our first date, the way his eyes crinkled at the corners when he laughed. The quiet dignity with which he faced his diagnosis. The terrible emptiness of the hospital room after he was gone.

And then newer memories: Corbin's hand in mine as we watched the eclipse reflected in cenote water. Grace—no, Katherine—holding my hair back after a night of too much wine, never judging, always there. Was any of it real?

"My name is Miguel," the bartender says, gently interrupting my thoughts. "Perhaps you would like some water with your next drink? And maybe something to eat?"

I look up at him, at the kindness in his face, and feel tears threaten. "I don't know what's real anymore," I whisper, more to myself than to him.

Miguel disappears for a few minutes and then returns with a glass of water and a small plate of empanadas. "On the house," he says. "Food helps in times of confusion."

I manage a weak smile and take a bite, grateful for this act of human kindness from a stranger when those I trusted have proven false. As the alcohol flows through my veins, loosening my grip on pain and reason alike, I wonder if I'll remember this moment of compassion in the morning.

What I know with certainty is this: I cannot stay in Guatemala. I cannot face either Corbin or Katherine again.

As soon as the sun rises, I'll book the first flight back to Phoenix, back to a home that, while empty, at least contains no fresh betrayals.

The empanadas coat my stomach as Miguel pours me another shot. This one, I promise myself, will be the last.

It isn't.

CHAPTER THIRTY-NINE

Pain lances my skull as consciousness returns, an ice pick driving into my temples with every heartbeat. My mouth tastes like something died in it—cotton-dry with traces of stale tequila and bile. I'm sprawled facedown across the hotel bed, still wearing yesterday's clothes, my arm hanging numbly over the edge.

For one blissful moment, I exist only in this physical discomfort, my mind a blank slate of hangover misery. Then the memories crash in—the confrontation in the jungle, the revelations, the betrayals.

Grace is Katherine.
Corbin lied about his research.
Nothing is what I thought it was.

I groan and roll onto my back, staring at the ceiling fan rotating above me. Sunlight filters through half-drawn curtains, suggesting it's well into the morning. Maybe afternoon. I have no idea how long I've been unconscious.

The room is eerily silent. Corbin's side of the bed is

untouched, his luggage still neatly arranged in the corner. Did he come back last night? Did Grace?

The thought of them turns my stomach, and I close my eyes against a fresh wave of nausea. My head throbs in time with my pulse, a metronome of shame and misery. What I wouldn't give for one of those local hangover concoctions right now.

A sharp knock at the door jolts me upright, sending a fresh stab of pain through my temples. I freeze, waiting.

The knock comes again, more insistent. "Riley? Corbin? Are you there? It's Marcus."

Relief floods me. *Not Corbin. Not Grace.*

Just Marcus, who, as far as I know, is still actually Marcus.

"Coming," I rasp, my voice like sandpaper. I stumble to the door on unsteady legs, pausing to check my reflection in the mirror—a mistake. My mascara has migrated halfway down my cheeks, my hair is a tangled mess, my skin is sallow and my eyes bloodshot. I look like I've been exhumed. I wipe the mascara from my cheeks with a tissue and look again; only slightly better.

I unlock the door to find Marcus standing in the hallway, his right arm supported in a medical sling. His face is drawn with exhaustion, dark circles shadowing his eyes. Whatever has brought him here, it's not good news.

"Is Corbin here?" he asks, glancing nervously down the corridor.

I shake my head. "No, I haven't seen him."

"Have you spoken with him? Since yesterday?"

I shake my head. "No."

"May I come in?"

I step aside wordlessly, suddenly aware of how the room

must smell—stale alcohol, unwashed human, a miasma of desperation.

"Let's talk on the patio," I suggest, leading him through the sliding glass doors. The fresh air is a blessing despite the humidity that immediately coats my skin in a sheen of moisture. The view of Lake Atitlán stretches before us, its surface a mirror casting sharp reflections that seem to spike my headache.

Marcus settles into one of the wicker chairs, wincing as the movement jostles his injured shoulder. I take the chair opposite, fighting the urge to rest my pounding head against the cool glass-topped table between us.

"What time is it?" I ask, squinting against the brightness.

"Almost two," Marcus replies. "I've been trying to reach Corbin since this morning. We were supposed to meet, but he never showed up." Marcus leans forward, his expression grave. "Riley, I'm worried about him. It's not like him to miss a meeting. He was extremely upset the last time I spoke to him. And now he's missing."

His words take a moment to penetrate my alcohol-fogged brain. "Missing? What do you mean missing?"

"He never came back from El Mirador."

A cold sensation spreads through my chest, displacing the discomfort of my hangover. "What? There was a second helicopter …"

"Yes, but he wasn't on it." He pauses. "Nor was Grace."

My stomach twists at her name. "Maybe they came back on another chopper."

Marcus shakes his head. "No one at the hotel has seen him. I've called the police."

"The police?" My voice sounds detached and faraway, as if coming from someone else.

He nods. "And I received some strange messages from him last night. I'm worried he might be in trouble."

My stomach twists even more. "What did the messages say?"

Marcus looks away as he speaks. "That he needs my help. He's in trouble. To call him ASAP."

I swallow, my throat dry. Where could Corbin and Grace have disappeared to? Despite my anger at Corbin for his lies, I suddenly feel concerned for his safety.

"Riley," Marcus continues, "the police want to talk to you. Just to answer a few questions. You were the last person to see him."

"Of course. I just need to clean up first," I say, rising unsteadily to my feet. "Where did they say to meet them?"

"In the lobby. Or I could have them come here—"

"No," I say. I can't imagine anyone official seeing me or this room in this condition. "Give me ten minutes, and I'll be down."

Marcus nods, standing carefully to avoid jolting his injured shoulder. "I'll tell them you'll be down soon."

I walk him to the door and gently close it behind him, leaving me alone with my thoughts. I'm not surprised Corbin didn't come back to our room last night, after what happened at El Mirador. He probably booked another room. But even if he'd come here, to gather his things, I'd still have no memory of it. I curse myself for drinking too much, *again*.

Regardless, I need to shower and clear my head before going downstairs to speak with the police. I make my way toward the bathroom. As I get closer, I notice a splash of red wine spilled on the floor, along with a few shards of glass. I kneel and pick one up. It's green, the color of a wine bottle.

Funny, I don't remember drinking any red wine last

night. Of course, all my memories of the evening are gone. I pinch my temples. *Another night lost to a blackout.* I vow for the hundredth time to get my act together.

Once in the bathroom, I begin stripping off yesterday's clothes, throwing them in a heap back toward the bedroom floor. The marble feels shocking against my bare feet, sending a shiver up my spine that I attribute to the hangover. The two sinks sit in a separate room from the bathtub and shower, their brass fixtures gleaming in the harsh light streaming through the frosted window.

I notice a few more chunks of the wine bottle scattered across the floor, emerald fragments catching the light like broken promises. The largest pieces have been swept aside, but smaller shards glitter dangerously in the grout lines. I have to step carefully around them, my toes curling instinctively away from the glass. I wonder for a moment how much the hotel will bill us to clean up this mess.

I step into the inner section of the bathroom, eager to get in the shower and wash away the pounding in my head and the sour taste coating my mouth. What I see next freezes me in place.

My entire body goes rigid, every muscle locking as if someone has poured concrete into my veins. It takes my brain several seconds to process what I'm seeing—like trying to solve a puzzle when half the pieces are missing.

No.

Corbin is lying in the bathtub, his shoulders hunched forward at an unnatural angle, his body twisted as if he'd tried to climb out but couldn't manage it. His dark hair is matted and wet, not with water but with something darker, stickier. His eyes stare upward at nothing, vacant and glazed like marbles, reflecting the bathroom light in a way that makes my stomach lurch. His mouth hangs slack, and there's a thin line of dark red trailing from the corner of his lips down to his chin.

And there's blood.

So much blood.

Sticking out of his neck at a grotesque angle is a shard of green glass—the neck of a wine bottle, the cork still impossibly, absurdly intact. The bottle's jagged edges are embedded deep into his pale skin, and around the wound his flesh has turned a sickly purple-gray. More glass fragments glitter in the congealed blood on his chest, as if someone repeatedly pressed the broken bottle against him.

My knees give out. I hit the bathroom floor hard, the marble freezing against my bare skin, but I can't look away. Can't breathe. Can't think.

This isn't real. This can't be real.

A scream builds in my throat, trapped behind the paralysis of shock. I back away, my bare feet slipping on the tile, sending me crashing into the bathroom counter. The sound of my own ragged breath fills the small space as reality crashes down around me.

Corbin is dead.

CHAPTER FORTY

The world stops spinning. My lungs freeze mid-breath. Time fractures around me as I stare at Corbin's lifeless body in the bathtub.

This can't be real.

I crouch against the bathroom wall, my bare legs touching the cold tile. The room tilts and sways around me as if I'm still drunk, though the shock has burned away any remaining alcohol in my system.

Corbin. *Dead.*

The scene before me is a nightmare painted in crimson and emerald. The pristine white bathtub is stained dark with blood, so much blood that it's pooled thick and congealed in the bottom. Jagged shards of green glass—are they remnants of last night?—are scattered across his chest and embedded in the porcelain around him. Again, I notice how the largest shard juts from his neck at an obscene angle, the cork still grotesquely intact at its base.

I can't get close. Can't make myself step forward. The

scene is too horrific, too visceral. Instead, I press myself against the bathroom wall, my whole body trembling.

"Corbin," I whisper, my voice breaking. Despite everything—the lies, Grace's accusations, the confrontation in the jungle—seeing him like this shatters something inside me. He was alive yesterday, vibrant and real, holding my hand as we watched the eclipse reflected in the water.

The tears stream hot and fast down my face. A sob is ripped from my throat, raw and primal. But I can't move toward him, can't bring myself to get any closer to the carnage.

Time loses meaning as I kneel beside the tub, tears running down my face, my hand stroking his cold cheek. I remember the way he held me through the night when memories of Brody became too much to bear. The way he understood my grief because he carried his own. Was any of it real? Either way, does it matter now?

Gradually, the shock ebbs enough for rational thought to return in fragmented bursts.

I've seen enough true-crime documentaries—the same ones Grace forced me to watch during our girls' nights together—to know exactly how this looks. A dead boyfriend. A hotel room. No witnesses. No alibi.

The realization hits me like a physical blow: Corbin was murdered. This wasn't some tragic accident with a wine bottle. You don't accidentally stab yourself in the neck with glass. Someone did this to him—someone with rage, with intent, with enough strength to drive that shard deep enough to kill.

And I can't remember anything after leaving the bar.

My memory of last night stops with Miguel the bartender placing another drink in front of me. After that—

nothing. A terrifying blank void where hours should be. Hours when I was apparently here, in this room, while someone was butchering the man I was falling for.

Images flash through my mind unbidden: myself in an orange jumpsuit, shuffling through a Guatemalan prison. Months, maybe years, of appeals while I rot in a stinking cell. My unfinished book. My reputation destroyed. The headlines would write themselves: *Archeologist Murders Boyfriend in Hotel Room.*

I stumble back into the bedroom, my legs numb and unsteady. The bed is unmade, sheets twisted from my restless sleep. My clothes from yesterday are scattered on the floor—my sundress, my sandals, my underwear. I don't remember getting into bed. The gaps in my memory feel like gaping wounds.

I need help. I need to call someone.

My hands shake as I reach for my phone, Miranda's number already pulled up. My book agent, my former mother-in-law, the closest thing I have to family. She'll know what to do. She always knows what to do.

But as my finger hovers over the call button, the words die in my throat. What would I even say? *Hi, Miranda, I woke up next to a dead body, and I can't remember if I killed him?*

I set the phone down, staring at my trembling hands.

That's when I see it—dried blood under my fingernails. Dark crescents that definitely weren't there yesterday.

Oh God.

My knees give out, and I sink onto the unmade bed. The evidence is literally on my hands. How do I explain that away?

The police are waiting in the lobby, Marcus said. They'll

come looking for me when I don't show up. I need to think. I need options.

Option one: Go to the police immediately and tell them the truth. Walk downstairs right now and confess that there's a dead body in my bathtub, and I have no memory of how it got there. Show them the blood under my nails and hope they believe my story about blacking out.

This is obviously a terrible idea. I have no alibi, no explanation, and physical evidence links me to the scene. They'd arrest me on the spot.

Option two: Talk to the police as planned and pretend I haven't made any discoveries yet. Act surprised when they tell me Corbin is missing. Play the concerned girlfriend. Buy myself time to figure out what really happened last night.

Option three: Make a run for it. Pack my bags right now and try to get to the airport before anyone realizes Corbin is dead.

Let's face it—I wouldn't get far. A blonde American woman fleeing Guatemala the day after her boyfriend's murder? They'd stop me in my tracks before I cleared customs.

The weight of what I'm about to do presses down on me with each passing second. I'm about to lie to the police. I'm about to conceal a crime scene. Even if I didn't kill Corbin, I'm about to become complicit in covering up his death.

But what choice do I have? Option two is the only one that gives me any chance at all.

I hurry to the bathroom sink—the one outside the murder scene—and scrub the blood from under my fingernails until my skin is raw. I splash cold water on my face, trying to erase any trace of my tears and shock. In the mirror, I practice looking surprised, concerned, but not panicked.

The worried girlfriend, not a potential suspect. That's me.

After pulling on clean clothes, I slip out of my room, careful to lock the door behind me and hang the "Do Not Disturb" sign firmly on the door handle. We had already requested a late check out, so I'm hoping that's enough for the staff to leave our room alone. The hallway is mercifully empty.

I take the service stairs instead of the elevator, trying to avoid running into anyone who might recognize me. As I descend, my heart pounds so hard I'm sure it must be audible.

Here goes nothing.

CHAPTER FORTY-ONE

When I arrive in the lobby, I expect everyone to turn and look at me as if the scene from my hotel bathroom is branded across my forehead. Thankfully, no one even spares me a glance. Tourists mill about with their cameras and guidebooks, blissfully unaware that I'm walking among them with a terrible secret burning in my chest.

I spot the police officer immediately—he's impossible to miss in his crisp uniform, standing near the reception desk. My heart hammers against my ribs as I approach him. The marble floor seems to echo with accusation. *Act natural,* I tell myself. You're just Riley, the concerned girlfriend who hasn't seen her boyfriend since yesterday.

"Excuse me," I say, surprised by how steady my voice sounds. "I'm Riley Donovan. My friend Marcus said you wanted to speak with me?"

The officer straightens, his attention immediately focused on me with an intensity that makes my skin crawl. I can feel him cataloging every detail—my red-rimmed eyes, the way my hands shake slightly, the forced casualness of my posture.

"Ms. Donovan, yes. Thank you for coming down." His English is perfect, with only the slightest accent. "I'm Officer Morales. We have a few questions about your friend Corbin Cross."

Friend. The word stings, but I nod anyway. "Of course. Is everything okay?"

"Would you mind if we spoke privately?" Officer Morales gestures toward a small conference room just off the lobby. "It won't take long."

The conference room is sterile and windowless, designed for business meetings and wedding planning consultations. A large wooden table dominates the space, surrounded by leather chairs that squeak when we sit down. The walls are painted a soothing beige that now feels suffocating. I choose a seat facing the door—I need to see my escape route.

Officer Morales settles across from me, pulling out a small notebook and pen. The scratching of his pen against paper sounds unnaturally loud in the quiet room. Behind him, a motivational poster shows a sunset over the ocean with the words "Dreams Come True" in flowing script. The irony makes me want to laugh hysterically.

"What is your relationship with Corbin Cross?"

"He is my boyfriend."

"The two of you came to Guatemala together?"

"Yes."

"And you are staying in a room together?"

"Yes."

So far, so good.

"When was the last time you saw Mr. Cross?" he asks, pen poised.

The scene flashes in my mind for a moment: *the broken glass, the blood, the gruesome scene in the bathroom.* I force myself to breathe normally. Morales studies me from across the table, a concerned look on his face.

"Miss, are you all right?"

I nod. "Yes, just a little too much to drink last night."

He pushes a bottle of water toward me. I open it and take a drink. "I saw him yesterday afternoon. We were at El Mirador—the ruins—with a tour group."

"And after that?"

"He stayed behind when the rest of us came back to town."

Officer Morales makes a note. "Oh? Why did you come back alone?"

Heat rises in my cheeks, and I wonder if Morales knows about our fight. I debate whether or not to tell him the truth —the entire truth, but immediately decide against it. How do I explain that I discovered my boyfriend was living a lie? That the woman I thought was my best friend was deceiving me about her identity? That everything I thought I knew about my life crumbled to dust in the span of a few hours?

"I was tired," I say finally. "Corbin still had work to wrap up at the site."

He nods. "Did you see him at all after returning to the hotel?"

"No. I went to the bar downstairs, had a few drinks. Then I went back to my room alone."

"What time was that?"

My mind races. *What time did I leave the bar?* The last thing I remember is Miguel placing another drink in front of me, the condensation on the glass catching the light. "I'm not sure exactly. Maybe around midnight?"

The scratching of his pen continues. "And you haven't seen or heard from Mr. Cross since yesterday afternoon?"

Blood. Bathtub. Death ... The images come unbidden. I clench my jaw, trying to stay focused.

"No."

Officer Morales leans back in his chair, studying me with those dark, kind eyes that see too much. "Ms. Donovan, we have reason to believe Mr. Cross might be in trouble."

I force surprise into my expression, widening my eyes slightly. "Why is that?"

"His colleague Marcus received a text message from him late last night, which said he needed help, but then his phone went dead. When Marcus tried to call back, it went straight to voicemail."

I keep my face neutral while cursing Marcus in my head. "That's strange. Have you tried calling him this morning?"

"Multiple times. His phone appears to be turned off." Officer Morales makes another note. "Marcus also mentioned that Mr. Cross was supposed to meet him for breakfast this morning but never showed up."

Of course he didn't show up. He's dead in my bathtub. The thought comes unbidden, sharp and awful. I swallow hard, tasting bile.

"That is weird," I manage. "Corbin's usually pretty reliable about stuff like that."

Was he? I realize I don't actually know. How well did I really know him? Grace's accusations echo in my mind—all the lies, the fabricated stories, the carefully constructed persona. Maybe reliability was just another part of his act.

"When you last saw him, did he seem upset? Worried about anything?"

Other than the fact that I'd just discovered he was a total

fraud? Other than the way his face crumpled when I walked away from him in the jungle?

"Just the usual work stuff," I say carefully. "But nothing beyond that. He seemed like himself otherwise."

Officer Morales nods, but I can see the wheels turning behind his eyes.

"What about Grace Lawrence? When did you last see her?"

My stomach drops. "Grace? Why are you asking about Grace?"

"Marcus mentioned she was part of your group. We'd like to speak with her as well."

I shake my head, genuine confusion mixing with my manufactured concern. "I haven't seen Grace since yesterday either ..." I trail off, letting him draw his own conclusions.

Grace is gone? I haven't really given her a thought since last night. The last time I saw her was with Corbin. They were fighting. My train of thought is interrupted by Morales clearing his throat.

"Have you tried contacting her?"

"No."

Officer Morales makes more notes. The sound is beginning to grate on my nerves like nails on a chalkboard. How much longer can I keep this up? How long before he asks the wrong question or I slip up and reveal what I know?

"Ms. Donovan, is there anything else you think we should know? Anything at all that might help us locate Mr. Cross?"

I shake my head, perhaps too quickly. "I really don't know where he could be. We had made plans to fly back to Arizona separately. He wanted to stay for an extra few days to shoot some additional footage for his show. I'm supposed to fly out this afternoon." I glance down at my phone, pretending to look at the time. "In fact, I should be packing now. Do you have a card or a number you can give me? I can call you as soon as I hear from him."

True enough. I do have a flight, and I do need to pack. What I don't mention, of course, is that Corbin won't be calling me, given the gruesome scene in my blood-drenched bathroom. For a moment, I think I might be sick to my stomach. I reach for my water and take a long gulp.

Officer Morales closes his notebook and stands. "Of course. Thank you for your time, Ms. Donovan. Here's my card." He slides a small white rectangle across the table. "If you hear from Mr. Cross or Ms. Lawrence, please contact me immediately."

"I will," I promise, though I probably won't be able to keep that promise.

We stand together, and he extends his hand. I shake it, hoping he can't feel the tremor in my fingers. I follow him back to the lobby, forcing myself to maintain a normal pace even though every instinct screams at me to run. I can feel his eyes on my back as I cross the lobby.

Only when I'm safely outside in the fresh air do I allow myself to exhale.

What just happened? Did I really just lie to the police ... in a foreign country?

I glance around the outdoor courtyard, the sign for the bar catching my eye. I need to find out what happened to me last night. What happened to me after I blacked out. And I think I know who might have some answers.

The weight of my situation feels like it's crushing the breath out of me. I'm in deep trouble—deeper than I've ever been in my life. Officer Morales was polite, even kind, but I could see the calculation in his eyes. He's already building a case in his mind, and I'm the obvious suspect. The girlfriend who fought with the victim. The last person to see him alive. The one with no alibi and a convenient, alcohol-induced blackout.

I need more than mere ignorance to protect me now. I need an alibi, or at least information about what really happened in those lost hours. Because one thing is crystal clear—when they find Corbin's body, and they will find it, the police are going to come straight back to me. And next time, Officer Morales won't be asking polite questions in an airless conference room. Next time, I'll be in handcuffs.

Miguel the bartender spent time with me last night. He might be the only person who can help me piece together those missing hours—or confirm that I was too drunk to have killed anyone. It's a long shot, but it's the only shot I have.

CHAPTER FORTY-TWO

The hotel bar is quiet in the afternoon lull—just a handful of tourists nursing cocktails, their laughter and conversation creating a surreal backdrop to my internal chaos. Miguel, the bartender from last night, is wiping glasses behind the bar, his movements precise and methodical.

He looks up as I approach, recognition dawning in his eyes.

"Señorita," he says with a gentle smile, "feeling better today?"

I slide onto a stool, leaning forward to keep my voice low. "Miguel, I need your help. I ... I can't remember much about last night. After I was here."

His smile fades, replaced by concern. "You had many drinks. Too many. This happens sometimes."

"Was I alone? The whole time?" The question comes out more desperately than I intend.

Miguel studies me, his brow furrowing. "You don't remember?"

"Please, it's important. Was I drinking alone?"

He places a glass of water in front of me. "Yes, mostly alone. A few men tried to talk to you, but you were ... not interested. You just wanted to drink."

"What about my friends? The man I was traveling with? Or the woman who arrived yesterday?"

Miguel's expression shifts subtly. "The man—your boyfriend?—he came looking for you. Very worried. But you had already gone."

My heart hammers against my ribs. "Corbin was here?"

But Marcus said ...

"Did he leave alone?"

Miguel nods. "He was upset. Said he would wait for you upstairs."

"And did a woman come by? Blonde, blue eyes, about my height?"

"This woman came later. Asking for you. I told her you took a bottle of wine to your room."

I freeze. "I took wine to my room?"

"Sí. You insisted. Said you needed it to sleep." His expression grows more concerned. "Señorita, are you in trouble?"

No, no, no. The wine bottle. Likely the very same bottle Corbin was murdered with.

My vision blurs as the implications hit me. When the police question Miguel—and they will question him—he'll tell them exactly what he just told me. That I was drunk, belligerent, insisted on taking wine upstairs. Wine in the same bottle that's now embedded in Corbin's neck.

My hands start shaking so violently I have to grip the edge of the bar to steady myself. *This is so much worse than I imagined.* It's not just that I can't remember what happened—it's that I was literally seen carrying the murder weapon to the scene of the crime.

"The blonde woman," I press, my voice barely steady. "Was she alone? Did she speak to anyone?"

Miguel wipes his hands on a towel, his movements slowing as he considers. "She sat at the far end, watching the entrance. She seemed ... nervous. She drank only water. Left after maybe thirty minutes."

"Did you see where she went?"

He shrugs. "She left through there. Probably went back to her room. It was late." He points toward the path leading to the hotel gardens and the lake beyond.

"Miguel, this is really important—do you remember what time I took the wine upstairs?"

He considers, tilting his head. "Maybe eleven thirty? Midnight? You were very insistent. Said you needed it to help you sleep."

I can see the police report now, with terrible crystal clarity: American woman, mid-thirties, takes wine bottle back to room and shatters it. Uses broken bottle neck as murder weapon. It's so obvious, so textbook, that any jury would convict me without hesitation. The bartender's testimony alone would seal my fate.

"Señorita?" Miguel's voice cuts through my spiral of panic. "Would you like something to drink? You look very pale."

The offer is tempting—God, is it tempting. I want nothing more than to order the strongest thing he has and drink until Corbin's glassy stare fades from my memory. Until the image of that green glass shard disappears. Until I can't feel the phantom stickiness of blood under my fingernails. I want to drown in my grief, to wash away every complicated feeling I had for him—the love, the betrayal, the confusion, the loss.

But I can't. There will be time for falling apart later, assuming I'm not in a Guatemalan prison cell. Right now, I need answers more than I need oblivion.

"No, thank you," I manage.

The timeline doesn't make sense. If I took the wine upstairs around midnight, and Corbin came looking for me after that, then someone else had to have been involved. There's no way I could have killed him in my blackout state and arranged his body so precisely in the bathtub. Now that I scrutinize it, I realize the scene is too deliberate, too staged.

But that raises an even more terrifying question: how did someone come into my room and murder Corbin without me knowing? Was I really that out of it? Or was there something else in those drinks—something that made sure I wouldn't wake up no matter what happened around me?

The thought makes my stomach lurch. Someone could have drugged me, then used me as the perfect fall guy. *Get Riley drunk enough to black out, make sure she's seen with the murder weapon, then kill Corbin while she's unconscious upstairs.* It's almost elegant in its simplicity.

I think about Officer Morales mentioning Grace, how she's missing too, but somehow not a concern. Just a witness they want to interview, not a suspect. The last time I saw Grace was with Corbin in the jungle, and they were fighting. Fighting over some old journal and who knows what else.

A dark thought creeps into my mind. Could Grace have something to do with this? Could she have hired someone to take Corbin out? She clearly knew more about his background than she'd let on. Maybe she knew something that made him dangerous to her, something worth killing him for.

But even as the thought forms, I dismiss it. This is Grace—my best friend, my confidante, the woman who held my hand through my grief. There's no way she could be capable of something like this. *Right?*

Or am I being naïve? Despite all the time we've spent together, there is so much she omitted or straight up lied about. I chew on my lip. The fact remains that she's missing too. And, unlike me, she's not being treated as a suspect.

I realize I'm gripping the bar so tightly my knuckles have gone white. Miguel is watching me with increasing concern, probably wondering if he should call hotel security.

Corbin is dead. Nothing I do can change that fact. The man I thought I loved, the man I thought I knew, is lying in my bathtub with his throat slashed open. Whether he was the person I believed him to be or not, he didn't deserve to die like that. And despite everything—all the deception, all the unanswered questions, all the elaborate lies—part of me is genuinely grieving for him.

But grief is a luxury I can't afford right now.

"Thank you," I tell Miguel, forcing myself to straighten up. "You've been very helpful."

As I walk away from the bar, my mind races, trying to piece together a solution. When I was little, my parents used to give me puzzles—jigsaw puzzles, logic problems, riddles that would keep me occupied for hours. I was good at them, really good. "Your mind is a powerful thing, Riley," my father would say whenever I'd solve something particularly challenging. "Never underestimate your ability to think your way out of a situation." Right now, I need that little girl's clarity, that unshakeable confidence that every problem has a solution if you look at it hard enough from the right angle.

My phone buzzes in my pocket—a text message.

> Where are you?

CHAPTER FORTY-THREE

My fingers are trembling so badly I can barely hold my phone. The message from Marcus stares back at me. It feels like the puzzle pieces are right in front of me, yet I can't quite fit them together.

I'm missing something, something very important.

I type a message back.

> At the hotel bar. Need to talk about last night. Can you meet me here?

His response comes almost immediately.

> On my way.

I pivot away from the exit, scanning the room for a quiet spot. The hotel bar is busier now, the afternoon crowd growing as tourists return from excursions. I choose a table in the corner, partially hidden by a large potted palm, and wait.

Miguel catches my eye from behind the bar and gives me a small nod. I wonder if he knows anything else that he hasn't told me. Marcus arrives five minutes later, sliding into the chair opposite, leaning forward with an urgency that makes my pulse quicken.

"Where have you been?"

"I needed to figure some things out," I say, keeping my voice low. "About last night."

"What about it?" His tone is casual, but I notice how his hand tightens around the edge of the table.

"I can't remember anything after drinking here," I admit, trying to keep my expression neutral despite the alarm bells ringing in my head. "Not a single thing."

Marcus's expression softens with what looks like genuine concern. "That doesn't surprise me. You were pretty wasted when I saw you."

"You saw me here? At the bar?" My heartbeat accelerates even more. Miguel didn't mention Marcus being here last night.

"Just briefly. I came down looking for Corbin and found you instead." He runs a hand through his hair—groaning as he rotates his shoulder.

Before I can comment on his injury, Miguel approaches our table, setting down two glasses of water without being asked. His eyes linger on Marcus for a moment longer than necessary.

"Can I get you something stronger?" he asks, but his question seems directed more at me than Marcus.

"Just water for now," I reply, not taking my eyes off Marcus.

The moment stretches uncomfortably as Miguel stands there, looking between us. Finally, he gives a brief nod and returns to the bar.

"So, have you heard from Grace?" I ask, trying to sound

casual despite the tension coiling in my stomach.

Marcus frowns. "Grace? You mean your friend who flew down here?"

"Yes."

"That's an odd question. Why would I have talked to her? I don't even know her."

"Oh, I just figured you two must have met before. Since she and Corbin used to date."

"Nope," he says and leans forward. "You feeling okay, Riley?"

"Just fine," I say, trying to hide the panic in my voice. I take a sip of water, buying time. Something about the way Marcus has been acting since I saw him this morning is gnawing at me. He seems off. Maybe it's worry about his friend, but I'm not convinced. Before I can open my mouth for another question, a voice calls from behind us.

"Marcus, Riley, there you are!"

I turn to see Dr. Garcia walking toward our table, her expression brightening when she spots us. Her eyes briefly meet mine before focusing on Marcus.

"Dr. Garcia," Marcus says, his smile not quite reaching his eyes, "join us."

She slides into the empty chair between us; then her gaze sharpens as she takes in Marcus's appearance. "Your shoulder—where's your sling?"

A flicker of something crosses Marcus's face before it's smoothed away. "Oh, it's feeling much better today. The hotel doctor gave me some pain medication and said I could take it off for short periods."

Dr. Garcia frowns, then turns to me. "Riley, have you spoken to Corbin? He was supposed to meet with me before he left today."

My stomach twists. And there are the images again —*blood, bathtub, empty eyes.* She doesn't know. No one knows except me. The knowledge sends a wave of nausea through me. I swallow hard.

"No." I shake my head.

"I haven't seen him either," says Marcus. "In fact, he sent me some strange message last night. He said that he needed help. That he wanted me to call him immediately. I was so worried, I called the police. They are looking for him too."

Dr. Garcia frowns again. "Oh no, that's terrible. I will ask around as well."

Miguel approaches, now setting down a glass of water for Dr. Garcia. His eyes meet mine briefly, and I see something there—caution, perhaps, or a warning.

"Señora Garcia," he says with a respectful nod, "your usual?"

"No, Miguel," she replies with a warm smile. "I will only be here for a moment."

Miguel straightens. "Señor Marcus, I meant to ask—did your friend find his way back to his room last night? The American gentleman you were helping?"

Marcus goes very still. "Excuse me?"

"Last night," Miguel continues, his expression almost comically innocent. "Very late. You were helping the American gentleman? He had too much to drink, I think."

I feel the blood drain from my face. Marcus helped Corbin to his room?

To *our room* ... that means ...

"You must be mistaken," Marcus says, his voice tight. "I wasn't with Corbin last night. You must be thinking of someone else."

Miguel shrugs. "As you say, señor." He walks away, leaving a silence heavy with implication.

Marcus shakes his head, looking between the two of us. "I'm not sure what the bartender is talking about. He must have me confused with someone else."

Ice spreads through my veins as I watch him. Shifting in his seat, not making eye contact. The beads of sweat on his nose. *He's lying.* I know it. Dr. Garcia nods, though she doesn't look convinced.

"It's a busy hotel," she says.

"Excuse me," I say abruptly, standing. "I need to use the restroom."

"Of course. We'll catch up with you later," says Dr. Garcia. Marcus looks at me, a strange expression on his face. I realize that what I have been missing may have been staring me in the face all along.

Before Marcus can say anything, I turn on my heel and make a beeline for the lobby. I might finally have an idea to help me figure out what happened last night.

CHAPTER FORTY-FOUR

The hotel lobby seems to stretch for miles as I race toward the front desk, my heart hammering against my ribs. I quickly scan the room for any signs of the police, who may or may not have paid a visit to my room. Thankfully, there's not a uniform in sight.

The front-desk attendant—Lucia, according to her name tag—looks up as I approach, her professional smile wavering slightly when she sees my expression. It's been over an hour since I met with the police. And even longer since I left the gruesome scene in my hotel room.

I'm running out of time.

"Señorita, are you all right?"

I lean over the counter, keeping my voice low and urgent. "I need your help. It's a matter of life and death."

Her dark eyes widen. "The police were just here. Perhaps you should speak with them?"

"I will," I promise, "but first I need to see your security footage. Please."

Uncertainty flickers across her face. "That is not possible. Hotel policy—"

I reach into my purse, fingers fumbling past my passport and phone until they close around the wad of cash I withdrew for the trip. Five hundred dollars—nearly all I have left. I pull out two crisp hundreds and slide them across the counter, keeping them hidden from view with my palm.

"Please," I repeat, my voice breaking slightly.

Her eyes dart to the money, then back to my face. For a terrible moment, I think she's going to call the police over. Then her hand covers mine, the bills disappearing.

"Follow me," she whispers. "Quickly."

She gestures to another attendant to cover the desk, then leads me through a door marked *Staff Only*. We hurry down a narrow hallway lined with supply closets and maintenance equipment before stopping at a nondescript door. She punches a code into the keypad, and it opens with a soft click.

"The security room," she explains, ushering me inside. "Carlos is on break for ten minutes. That is all the time I can give you."

The room is dimly lit, dominated by a wall of monitors showing different areas of the hotel—lobby, restaurant, hallways, pool area. A desk with three computer screens sits beneath them, various controls and keyboards arranged neatly.

"I don't know how to operate this system," I say, panic rising again.

Lucia hesitates, then moves to the desk. "What do you need to see?"

"First-floor hallway, last night. Starting around midnight."

She types quickly, and the center monitor switches to show the corridor—empty, silent, the timestamp in the corner reading 00:00:03.

"Can you make it go faster?" I ask, glancing nervously at the door.

She clicks something, and the footage begins to speed up, the digits in the corner blurring as minutes pass. At 00:47, I spot movement.

"Stop! There!"

She hits a button, and the footage returns to normal speed. My stomach drops as I watch myself stagger down the hallway, clearly intoxicated. *But I'm not alone.* I see Marcus next to me, holding what looks like a bottle. A green wine bottle. The same one that the bartender said I took back to the room. The same one that was shattered on the bathroom floor.

The revelation makes me sway on my feet. Marcus never mentioned he saw me last night, much less escorted me to my room. I watch in breathless silence as he takes the keycard from my hand and swipes it against the door lock. We disappear inside.

What is he doing in my room?

We patiently watch the screen, waiting for something to happen. "Can you fast-forward again?" I say, breaking the silence. "There, stop."

Three minutes later, Marcus emerges from the room and closes the door behind him. He looks directly at the camera for a split second, then walks briskly back toward the elevator. I feel the hairs rise on my arms.

"Still, this doesn't prove anything," I murmur, frustration building. Of course Marcus would know about the hallway cameras.

Of course he'd be careful.

We spend a few more minutes running through the footage of the hallway for the next couple of hours. There is no one in sight. I rack my brain. If Corbin didn't come in through the front door, then how did he get into our room?

"Is there more you need to see?" Lucia asks, glancing at the door. The walls seem to close in on me. I only have a few more minutes before Lucia runs out of patience. *Think, Riley.* How is it possible that Corbin was able to get into the room without being seen on the hallway camera?

A sudden thought strikes me. "Are there any outdoor cameras? Showing the balcony?"

"Yes, actually. For guest safety. We just installed them a few weeks ago. Hidden in the trees."

"Show me the first-floor balcony for room 114, same timeframe."

She taps more keys, and the view changes to an exterior shot of the hotel. The balconies stretch across the screen like dark mouths, most of the rooms dark at this hour.

We fast-forward again, the timestamp racing forward. 01:23 … 01:40 … 01:58 …

"There!" I grab Lucia's wrist, and she stops the footage.

The balcony door to my room slides open. A figure steps out—Marcus—looking carefully in both directions before returning inside. A minute later, he emerges again, this time dragging something heavy. No, not something. Someone.

My breath catches as a second figure appears—Grace, her white jumpsuit nearly glowing in the moonlight, unmistakable even in the dim lighting. There is no doubt it's her. Together, they maneuver a limp form over the balcony railing. *Corbin.* His head lolls back, his body slack.

"Oh my God," I whisper.

Grace and Marcus struggle with the weight, eventually managing to lower Corbin onto the balcony floor. Then Marcus climbs over the railing himself, dropping down beside the body while Grace disappears back into my room. He pulls the body inside.

A few minutes later, Marcus re-emerges alone, climbing over the railing and disappearing back into the trees surrounding the courtyard. Grace is nowhere to be seen.

"Keep going," I tell Lucia, my voice barely audible. "I need to see what happens next."

The timestamp continues racing forward: 02:15 … 02:28 … 02:45 …

Then, thirty minutes later, Grace finally appears on the balcony again. But this time, her white jumpsuit is covered in dark stains—surely blood. She's carrying what looks like a stained white towel, moving quickly and purposefully as she climbs over the railing and disappears into the darkness.

The air leaves my lungs completely. My hands fly to my mouth as the horrifying truth crashes over me.

Grace didn't just help move the body. She killed him. While I was unconscious upstairs, my friend—my *best friend*—murdered my boyfriend with that wine bottle and then spent thirty minutes staging the scene to frame me for it.

"*Grace …*" I whisper, her name coming out like a prayer, like a curse. "*Oh my God, Grace, what did you do?*"

The betrayal cuts deeper than any knife. This is the woman who held me while I sobbed over Brody's death. Who knew every secret, every fear, every vulnerable part of me. She used it all—every piece of trust I confided to her—to destroy my life.

My mouth gapes open, my body trembling with shock. *What did I just see?*

"Señorita!" says Lucia, her hand rising to her mouth. "We need to show this to the police."

"I know, but first, can I make a recording?"

Lucia hesitates, then nods once. "Quickly."

I film the key segments—Marcus and Grace with Corbin's body on my balcony, the transfer inside, Marcus's departure, then Grace's bloody exit thirty minutes later. My hands are shaking so badly I have to brace my wrist against the desk to keep the footage steady.

As soon as I've captured what I need, I message them to someone I know will be interested in seeing them.

"The police will be looking for me," I tell Lucia. "When they come, tell them—"

The door flies open, revealing a breathless hotel employee—a housekeeper, judging by her uniform. Her eyes are wide with shock, her face pale.

"Lucia! There's a body!" she cries in Spanish. "Room 114! A man—he's dead!"

Lucia and I exchange glances.

"Are you certain?"

The housekeeper nods frantically. "Yes! I've already called security!"

"We need to go," I say to Lucia. "Now."

We follow the housekeeper back through the staff corridors, emerging into the lobby as an almighty commotion erupts near the front door. The police burst into the lobby. Morales spots me first.

"Ms. Donovan, stay where you are."

I freeze in place, my gaze sweeping the room and landing directly across the hall.

Marcus is standing there, next to Dr. Garcia, glaring at me.

Let him glare. He has no idea what I just saw.

CHAPTER FORTY-FIVE

Officer Morales crosses the lobby with purpose, his boots clicking against the marble floor with the steady rhythm of inevitability. My heart pounds so hard I'm certain everyone can hear it echoing through the suddenly silent space. Tourists and hotel staff freeze mid-conversation, sensing the electric tension crackling through the air.

"Ms. Donovan, stay where you are," Morales repeats, his voice carrying the authority of someone who's used to being obeyed.

Marcus steps forward, his face a mask of confusion and concern. If I hadn't just watched the security footage, I might have believed his act. The worried friend, the loyal companion who did everything right by contacting the authorities when Corbin went missing.

"Officer, what's going on here?" Marcus asks, his voice pitched perfectly—just the right amount of confusion tinged with growing alarm.

Morales glances between us, his trained eyes cataloging our positions, our expressions, the invisible threads of tension connecting us. Dr. Garcia hovers behind Marcus, her weathered face creased with worry.

"Mr. Morrison, I'm sorry, but we need to speak somewhere private," Morales says, his tone professional but calming. "You as well, Ms. Donovan."

The walk back to the conference room is like a death march. My legs feel disconnected from my body, moving through sheer force of will. The video files burn like a secret fire in my phone, evidence that could destroy Marcus's carefully constructed façade.

The same beige walls and motivational sunset poster greet us as we file into the conference room. The leather chairs squeak in protest as we sit—Morales across from us, Marcus and me on the same side of the table like co-conspirators. The irony makes my stomach churn.

Marcus maintains his posture, hands folded on the table. But I can see the subtle signs of tension—the slight tightness around his eyes, the way his jaw clenches almost imperceptibly. He's worried, though he's hiding it well.

"Mr. Morrison," Morales begins, consulting his notebook, "I'm very sorry to have to tell you this, but your friend Corbin Cross has been found dead in his hotel room."

Marcus's reaction is flawless. His face goes through the textbook progression of emotions—confusion, disbelief, then dawning horror. His hands fly to his mouth, his eyes widening with what appears to be genuine shock.

"Dead?" he whispers, his voice breaking slightly. "How? What happened?"

I sit frozen, watching this masterful performance while bile rises in my throat. He should win an Academy Award for such a dramatic display. The concerned friend devastated by tragic news, when in reality he's a participant in the entire nightmare.

"We're still investigating the circumstances," Morales says carefully. "The initial examination suggests possible foul play."

"Foul play?" Marcus's voice climbs higher, and he turns to look at me with what appears to be shocked accusation. "You mean someone killed him?"

"We're exploring all possibilities," Morales replies neutrally. "Mr. Morrison, when you contacted us about Mr. Cross's distressed message, did he give you any indication of what kind of help he needed?"

Marcus shakes his head, his performance never wavering. "No, there was just that text saying he needed help, and then nothing. His phone went dead. I tried calling back immediately, but it went straight to voicemail." He pauses, swallowing hard. "I should have done something sooner. Maybe if I'd gone looking for him instead of waiting ..."

"You did the right thing by contacting us," Morales assures him. "Can you think of anyone who might have wanted to harm Mr. Cross? Anyone he had conflicts with recently?"

Marcus's eyes flick to me for a moment—so brief that if I hadn't been watching carefully, I might have missed it. But it's enough. He's laying the groundwork, preparing to point the finger directly at me.

"Well," he says hesitantly, as if the words are being dragged from him against his will, "he and Riley were having some problems. They had a pretty big fight yesterday at the ruins."

Morales makes a note, his pen scratching against the paper with ominous finality. "What kind of problems?"

"I don't want to speak out of turn," Marcus says, glancing at me with feigned reluctance. "But there were trust issues. Accusations about infidelity; lies about the past. Things got pretty heated."

My hands clench into fists under the table. Morales's radio crackles to life, the dispatcher's voice cutting through the tension. He holds up a hand apologetically. "Excuse me for just a moment."

He steps outside, leaving Marcus and me alone in the suffocating silence of the conference room.

The moment the door clicks shut, Marcus springs from his chair like a caged animal suddenly freed. He begins pacing the small space, his previous calm completely evaporating. He repeatedly runs his hands through his hair, and the careful mask he's been wearing finally cracks completely.

"Shit, shit, shit," he mutters under his breath, his movements sharp and agitated. The sight of him coming unraveled makes my pulse spike even higher. This is not the reaction of an innocent man.

"I know what you did, Marcus," I say quietly, my voice steady despite the fear coursing through my veins as I watch him pace.

He doesn't flinch. "I don't know what you're talking about." But his pacing intensifies, and I notice how the sweat beads on his forehead.

"The security cameras caught everything. You and Grace moving Corbin's body onto my balcony. Did you really think no one would figure it out?"

He stops mid-stride, turning to face me. For the first time, uncertainty flickers across his features. "And you're sure you saw us? On camera?"

"One hundred percent." I lean forward in my chair.

"The question is why? Why kill Corbin? And how do you know Grace?"

Marcus resumes his pacing, his steps more erratic now. "Grace is my cousin."

The pieces click into place with sickening clarity.

"Look, you have to understand," Marcus says, his voice taking on a desperate edge as he continues his restless movement around the room. "After Corbin found that first burial site, we realized what we were sitting on. The journal didn't just lead to one discovery—there were missing pages that described another site. A bigger one."

He pauses his pacing to look at me directly. "I was happy to keep taking my cut from Corbin's YouTube earnings. Steady money, you know? But Grace ..." He shakes his head. "Grace became obsessed. She wanted to find that second site herself, then claim the discovery. The money, the fame—she wanted it all."

"So you decided to steal from him?"

"Grace showed up in Guatemala out of the blue. That wasn't part of any plan we had." Marcus's voice becomes more frantic as he paces the room. "She was convinced Corbin had shared those missing pages with you. That's why she thought she could push the two of you together—then, if she got close to you as your friend, maybe you'd confess to having seen the pages."

My stomach drops as I realize how thoroughly I've been manipulated. "She never cared about our friendship." It's not a question.

"She thought if she couldn't get the pages from Corbin directly, maybe she could get them through you." Marcus's laugh is bitter and sharp. "But there's something you need to know about what really happened last night."

He stops pacing and grips the back of his chair. "We didn't kill him on purpose. Grace and I invited him for drinks in the courtyard—just casual, you know? I slipped something into his drink, GHB, just enough to make him compliant while I searched his room for the pages."

"But?" I manage to croak out.

"But when I got back to the courtyard, Corbin was practically catatonic. I mean, he was breathing, but he wasn't responding to anything. We had to carry him back to his room. I thought he'd sleep it off—but I must have massively misjudged the dose."

I feel the blood drain from my face. "So, what then? You just left him there?"

"We thought he'd be fine! I moved his unconscious body to your room while you were passed out, figuring when he woke up confused and disoriented, it would look like you two had simply had a fight. But he was supposed to wake up, Riley. He was supposed to be alive."

There's something Marcus doesn't know yet—something that will shatter his version of events completely.

"Marcus," I say slowly, needing to tell him, "Corbin didn't die from the drugs."

He turns to stare at me. "What do you mean?"

"He was stabbed to death. With a wine bottle. Someone drove a shard of green glass straight into his neck."

The color drains from Marcus's face. His mouth opens and closes wordlessly, like a fish gasping for air.

"That's impossible," he whispers. "Grace just helped me move him, and then she left. She said—" He stops, the horrible truth dawning in his eyes. "Oh my God. Grace stayed behind."

"She murdered him, Marcus. And then she tried to frame me for it."

Marcus staggers backward until he hits the wall, his face a mask of horror and disbelief. "She killed him? Grace actually killed him? I thought ... I thought he died from the overdose, a stupid mistake that we just had to cover up."

"No, Marcus," I say. "She spent thirty minutes in that room staging the scene. There's video evidence of her leaving, covered in blood."

Marcus's breathing becomes rapid and shallow. "I have to get out of here. If they think I know about the murder—if they think I was part of that—" He lunges toward the door, grabbing the handle and yanking.

Nothing happens. The door doesn't budge.

"It's locked," he says, his voice rising to a pitch of pure panic. He pulls again, harder this time, then pounds on the door with his fist. "They've locked us in!"

He throws his shoulder against the door once, twice, and on the third attempt, it bursts open with a splintering crash. But instead of an empty hallway, three uniformed officers stand waiting, their hands resting casually on their weapons.

"Going somewhere, Mr. Morrison?" Officer Morales asks, stepping forward with handcuffs already in his grip.

"Riley Donovan, Marcus Morrison, you're both under arrest for the murder of Corbin Cross," another officer announces.

As the cold metal closes around my wrists, I feel a strange sense of calm envelop me. Let them arrest me. I have the evidence. I have the truth. And unlike Marcus and Grace, I know I'm innocent.

This nightmare is finally going to end.

CHAPTER FORTY-SIX

THREE MONTHS LATER

The sunlight streams through the windows of my small Phoenix home, casting long rectangles across the hardwood floor. It's been three months since Guatemala, but sometimes I still wake up in a cold sweat, the vision of Corbin's body burned into my retinas like an afterimage from staring too long at the sun.

I sip my coffee—just coffee, no wine—and survey the organized chaos of my dining room table. My laptop sits open, surrounded by stacks of neatly arranged research notes. On the screen, the manuscript for *What Was Lost: The Intermediate Periods of Egypt* is open to the dedication page, my fingers hovering over the keys after I finish typing the name "Corbin Cross."

After what happened in Guatemala and the sensational headlines that followed—*Archeologist Framed for Murder by Best Friend, Discovery Leads to Deadly Betrayal*—Miranda had no trouble renegotiating my publishing deal and sidestepping even the hint of any type of lawsuit. What started as a single-book contract became a two-book deal that exceeded even my wildest expectations. The first book, my original work on Egypt, and the second, a real-life account of everything that happened in Guatemala and beyond.

"Strike while the iron is hot," Miranda instructed me during one of our weekly check-ins. "The public is fascinated by your story, Riley. Give them what they want."

The irony doesn't escape me—a book about recovering knowledge that was deliberately erased from history, written by a woman piecing together the deliberate erasure of truth in her own life.

Three months. It feels more like three lifetimes.

After they found Corbin's blood-drenched body in the bathtub in room 114, everything happened with dizzying speed. I spent a week in a Guatemalan jail cell while they investigated, the concrete walls and persistent, moldering dampness a constant reminder of how close I'd come to spending the rest of my life behind bars. But Marcus's confession, combined with the video footage of Grace in her bloodied white jumpsuit, ultimately led to my release without charges.

Marcus was convicted as an accessory to murder—a credible charge given that his actions directly led to Corbin's death, even if he hadn't intended murder. During his trial, the full scope of his involvement became clear. He hadn't just drugged Corbin that night; he'd drugged me too. A significant dose in my drinks at the bar, ensuring I'd be unconscious enough that I wouldn't hear Grace stabbing Corbin to death in the bathroom just twenty feet away.

"I never knew she was going to kill him," Marcus testified, his voice breaking during cross-examination. "I thought we were going to search his room for the journal pages and leave him confused when he woke up. When he didn't wake up, I panicked. I helped move the body because I thought I'd accidentally killed him with an overdose."

But, as the court learnt, Grace had other plans. While Marcus waited outside, she spent thirty minutes turning Corbin's accidental death into deliberate murder, then staging the scene in a determined attempt to frame me. The prosecution painted a picture of a woman so consumed by greed and obsession that she was willing to destroy anyone who stood between her and what she wanted.

Marcus received a jail sentence of twelve years, found guilty of the charges against him: accessory to murder and conspiracy. He'll be eligible for parole in eight.

Grace, meanwhile, vanished completely after her flight landed in Phoenix. The international arrest warrant hasn't yielded results yet. Sometimes I find myself looking over my shoulder, scanning crowds for a blonde ponytail, expecting to see her familiar face. The woman I once considered my best friend, who held my hand while I was suffering from panic attacks and who dragged me from the depths of grief, only to try to frame me for murder.

The month after Guatemala is mostly a blur in my memory. I checked myself into rehab as soon as I returned to Phoenix—thirty days of confronting my grief, my alcohol dependency, and the trauma of everything that had happened. Miranda visited weekly, her steady presence a lifeline when everything else felt like a murk of quicksand. It was during those quiet weeks that I was able to finish my Egypt manuscript, channeling my recovery into productive work.

When I emerged, clear-headed for the first time in over a year, I knew what I had to do. Corbin's final voicemails to me in Guatemala revealed he'd had a change of heart. He'd planned to credit Henry Lawrence publicly, to tell the truth about where his theories originated. His messages outlined his intentions, his regrets, his hopes to make amends.

While Corbin's channel, Cross Claims History, was lost, there was still a chance for me to set things right. I decided to start a new YouTube channel, my own way to honor his work. *Riley Reclaims History*—a deliberate play on words that I knew he would have appreciated. The channel serves multiple purposes: giving Henry Lawrence the credit he deserved, analyzing his theories from a legitimate archaeological perspective, and yes, telling the other side of the story about what really happened in Guatemala.

My first episode, "The Truth About Corbin Cross: Setting the Record Straight," reached five million views in its first week. In it, I explained everything—the journal, the stolen research, Corbin's death, and Grace's betrayal. I introduced Henry Lawrence to the world and promised that future videos would give his work the academic and popular recognition it deserved, examined through the lens of genuine archaeological evidence.

The response has been overwhelming. The second episode, where I analyzed Henry's Richat Structure theories, garnered another three million views. Comments pour in daily from amateur historians, archaeologists, and multitudes of people simply fascinated by the story. Publishers have been falling over themselves to secure the rights to my second book—the full account of everything that happened. Miranda takes great delight in informing them that no such rights are available, but a third book ... now, that might be on the table.

I take another sip of coffee and open my email. Another message from the FBI—they're still looking for Katherine

Grace Lawrence. She's become something of a ghost, leaving no digital footprint, no paper trail. It's as if she simply evaporated.

My phone chimes with a calendar reminder: Film Episode 4: "Henry Lawrence's Göbekli Tepe Theories—Archaeological Evidence vs. Speculation."

As I set up the camera and adjust the lighting, I catch a glimpse of myself in the reflection of the black screen—hair neatly styled, eyes clear, posture straight. No trace of the broken woman who once sat in this same house, drinking wine at three in the afternoon, drowning in grief and self-pity.

My gaze drifts to the corner of my desk where I keep two precious items: a signed copy of Meredith's book and a framed photo of us from graduate school, arms linked, grinning at the camera during a dig in Colorado. Meredith's death at Mesa Verde was what set this entire tragic chain of events in motion, her journal the catalyst that would ultimately lead to Corbin's murder and Grace's betrayal.

"I'm sorry I couldn't save him too," I whisper to her photo, as I do sometimes when guilt threatens to overwhelm me.

Brody would be proud, I think. And oddly enough, I believe Corbin would be too.

I'm about to press record when my phone buzzes with a text from Miranda.

> Still on for lunch at 1? Can't wait to hear about the latest episode numbers!

I smile and type back:

> Wouldn't miss it. See you soon.

It's a small thing, but it feels monumental—making lunch plans with a friend, looking forward to normal conversation about work and life. The simple pleasure of a healthy relationship built on trust and genuine care rather than manipulation and hidden agendas.

I press record and smile into the camera, ready to reclaim another piece of history that deserves to be told.

EPILOGUE
KATHERINE GRACE

I slap yet another fly from my sweat-slicked face, the humid air thick enough to choke on. The buzzing of insects creates a constant drone that mingles with the distant calls of howler monkeys echoing through the canopy above. Slapping flies in the middle of the Guatemalan jungle wasn't exactly the ending I was hoping for after what happened in Tikal, but here I am—following in my grandfather's footsteps through this green and sticky hell.

Of course, he craved the academic recognition that would make him famous. *And me?* Quite the opposite. I'm after the money. I'm already famous enough after what went down in Guatemala, leaving my dear cousin Marcus behind with his wrists in handcuffs.

The memory of what happened to Corbin still makes my stomach clench—not from guilt, but from something more complicated. I won't deny it. I had a thing for him, maybe the closest thing to love I've ever felt. But he was so damn difficult, even more so than his annoying girlfriend, Riley.

That night in the hotel room plays on repeat in my mind,

crystal clear despite the months that have passed. After Marcus left me alone with Corbin's unconscious body, I searched his room methodically. It didn't take long to find what I was looking for—the missing journal pages tucked inside his laptop bag, exactly where I suspected they'd be.

Six pages. Six pages that held the key to everything my grandfather worked toward.

But then I made the mistake of going through Riley's things. Seeing her lingerie, imagining her with Corbin—something snapped. The rage that had been building for months, maybe years, finally found its target.

I had what I needed. The pages were mine now. I didn't need Corbin anymore, and Riley didn't deserve her perfect little life either. So, while he was unconscious in the bathtub, I broke that wine bottle and jammed it in his throat. The sound it made, the way his body jerked once and then went still—it was almost peaceful, really.

I thought for sure Riley would spend the rest of her life rotting in a Guatemalan prison. The perfect frame job: her fingerprints on the bottle, her blackout preventing any alibi, their very public fight providing motive.

But those damn outdoor cameras were something I hadn't counted on.

I feel bad about Marcus, I really do. He went to prison for something he never intended to happen. But he'll understand when he makes parole in eight years and finds a very large sum of money mysteriously deposited in his bank account. Money I plan to make selling the artifacts from my grandfather's discovery. Marcus always understood that sometimes you have to make sacrifices for the benefit of the bigger picture.

Riley's YouTube channel was disgusting at first—

watching her play the victim, gaining sympathy and fame from my tragedy. But I have to admit, I've grudgingly come to appreciate her giving my grandfather the credit he deserves. *Riley Reclaims History* has introduced Henry Lawrence's work to millions of people who never would have heard his name otherwise. In a twisted way, she's accomplishing what I always wanted—proper public recognition for his genius, his discoveries, his theories.

Even if she is profiting from that genius herself.

I look down at the yellowed pages again, their edges soft from humidity and age. Six pages in total, but Marcus and I believed that twelve were missing. The ink has started to blur in places because of the moisture, making my grandfather's careful handwriting harder to decipher. Is it possible Corbin didn't have all of them with him? Surely he did. Surely he knew how close we were to the location where my grandfather was set to make another discovery.

I dismiss the thought and try to focus on what's in front of me. The machete blade glints in the dappled sunlight filtering through the dense canopy as one of my hired men clears another path. I've paid an entire crew to escort me through this jungle—men with weathered faces and suspicious eyes who ask no questions as long as the money keeps flowing. My security detail carries an arsenal that would make a small army jealous: machetes for the vegetation, assault rifles for whatever else we might encounter, and weapons I can't even identify but that look appropriately intimidating.

What matters is we're merely twenty meters away from the site marked on Grandfather's map. The GPS coordinates match perfectly with his notations, and the excitement building in my chest almost drowns out the constant fear that's been my companion since Guatemala.

Out here in the jungle, I finally feel free. Free to be myself without the constraints of polite society. Free to do what needs to be done, even when it gets messy. Back in Phoenix, I had to play the role of the concerned friend, the supportive companion, the normal person who followed rules and cared about consequences. But that was never really me, was it?

This is who I truly am—someone willing to push Meredith off that cliff when she became inconvenient, someone who could slice Corbin's throat without hesitation when the situation called for it. Society likes to pretend that everyone is basically good underneath, that we all have consciences that guide us toward moral behavior. But some of us are built differently.

Some of us are willing to do whatever it takes.

Hopefully this will pay off, because now that I'm a fugitive, I need that proverbial chest of gold. I've used what money I had stashed away in various accounts to ensure these men are well enough paid that they won't ask inconvenient questions about why an American woman on the run wants to dig up artifacts in the middle of nowhere. But still, I'm acutely aware of my vulnerability—a gringa alone in the dense forest with a group of mercenaries whose loyalty extends only as far as the dollars in my bank account.

The memory of Meredith still makes me smile. When I followed Corbin out to Mesa Verde and confronted him about the journal, I didn't expect to bump into his perfect little fiancée on that narrow trail. We had quite the chat, and I discovered that she was angry—angry that I existed, angry that she didn't know the journal belonged to me, angry that her perfect boyfriend had been lying to her.

But when she started defending him, when she looked at me with those self-righteous eyes and told me I was wrong ... well, I guess I got a little angry myself. Call it jealousy, call it what you want, but it doesn't take a genius to figure out what happened when I gave her that final shove. The sound she made as she fell echoes in my darkest dreams—not from guilt, but because it was the first time I truly understood my own power.

Now I need to focus on what's in front of me—using these last six pages to get where I need to be, to find my riches, and then get the hell out of this jungle before the authorities catch up with me. The only question still nagging at me is: if I have six pages and twelve in total are missing, where the hell is the missing half?

Only Corbin knew, and that means the only loose thread left is Riley. I thought I might let her go on in peace, let her grieve, let her whine on camera and move on with her life. But if she finds those missing pages ... if she starts putting pieces together ...

Well, in that case, I might have to pay her a little visit.

ABOUT THE AUTHOR

Leah Cupps is a Multiple-Award Winning Author and Entrepreneur. She writes Thriller, Mystery, and Suspense as well as Middle-Grade Mystery Adventure Books.

Leah's novels are fast-paced thrillers that will keep you up at night as you can't wait to see what happens in the next chapter.

Leah lives in Indiana with her husband and three children. When she isn't losing sleep writing her next novel or scaling her next business, she enjoys reading, riding horses, working out, and spending time with her family.

Did you enjoy *Forget Me Not*? Please consider leaving a review on Amazon to help other readers discover the book.

Visit Leah Cupps on her website: www.leahcupps.com

ALSO BY LEAH CUPPS

One Last Bite

You Are Not Alone

Sweet Little Lies

Now You See Me

Forget Me Not

Printed in Dunstable, United Kingdom

74889134R00184